NEW EROTICA 1

NEW EROTICA
1

An anthology of sensuous writing

Edited by
Esme Ombreux

First published in 1993 by
Nexus
338 Ladbroke Grove
London W10 5AH

Typeset by Phoenix Photosetting, Chatham, Kent
Printed and bound in Great Britain by
Cox & Wyman, Reading, Berks

ISBN 0 352 32843 6

CONTENTS

Introduction *by Esme Ombreux*   1
The Domino Tattoo *by Cyrian Amberlake*   5
Plaisir d'Amour *by Anne-Marie Villefranche*   31
Engine of Desire *by Alexis Arven*   53
Wicked *by Andrea Arven*   73
The Slave of Lidir *by Aran Ashe*   97
Blue Angel Nights *by Margarete von Falkensee*   121
Stephanie *by Susanna Hughes*   147
Pleasurehouse 13 *by Agnetha Anders*   169
Laure-Anne *by Laure-Anne D*   185
Diplomatic Pleasures *by Antoine Lelouche*   205
Cocktails *by Stanley Carten*   233
Ms Deedes at Home *by Carole Andrews*   255
One Week in the Private House *by Esme Ombreux*   279

INTRODUCTION

I've just spent a week shut in a dungeon.

No, it wasn't what you're thinking, but it was almost as much fun. The Nexus publisher gave me the key to the archives and said he wouldn't let me out until I'd read my way through all the books down there. He wanted a list of thirteen titles, he said, and if I was good he'd let me include *One Week in the Private House*.

There are almost a hundred and fifty Nexus books, and every single one of them is at the very least titillating. And most of them are downright arousing. It was just as well that the publisher had to come down every now and then to help me out.

I made several lists, but the publisher is a hard man to please. 'That's old stuff, Esme,' he'd say, 'Edwardian potboilers and imported Americana. I want a collection of extracts from up-to-date books. Now keep reading, keep your mind on the job, and I'll be back later to see how you're getting on. After all the other editors have gone home.'

Keep your mind on the job! When you're surrounded by all those shelves full of steamy novels it's impossible to do anything else.

Anyway, I managed to satisfy him in the end, if you

1

see what I mean. And the following pages are the result: extracts from the best of Nexus.

Most of the passages I have selected are from books published in recent years – many of them in 1991. However, whenever I came across a series of novels I took an extract from the first novel in the series, so a few of the featured books are from earlier years.

I've tried to choose books that convey something of the breadth of the Nexus range: from racy science fiction to medieval fantasy, from Weimar Germany to modern California, from closed-in worlds of perverse obsessions to rollicking romps in the tropics. Apparently Nexus is the biggest collection of erotic novels published in Britain – at least I assume that's what the publisher means when he says he's got the biggest list.

I hope you like my choices, anyway. The publisher says he'd like to have me downstairs again – I think this means he'd like me to do another collection like this next year.

Esme Ombreux
October 1992

THE
DOMINO
TATTOO

Cyrian Amberlake

I've always considered the Domino trilogy to be three of the brightest jewels in the Nexus treasury, so I was delighted to be able to select as the first item in this collection an extract from Cyrian Amberlake's first book, *The Domino Tattoo*.

Although the three books share the same leading lady, Josephine Morrow, and are all terrifically well written, each has its own style and subject. *The Domino Tattoo*, in which Josephine Morrow first appears as a dissatisfied, under-achieving office girl, starts the trilogy in a parochial setting and a reflective mood.

After several disconcerting incidents Josephine is led to Estwych, an isolated country house where she begins to comprehend the symbolism of the dominoes that recur throughout the story. For domino read dominance! And for Josephine, without the tattoo, that means submission to everyone else at Estwych – lots of sex and lots of lovely spankings.

In the following extract, which is made up of two short chapters from the middle of the book, Josephine has arrived at Estwych, and has been angered, confused and yet excited by the strange rules of the house. She has endured punishments of increasing severity, and has now met an ally in Jackie, who appears to be a nurse on the staff. Read on and enjoy . . .

The Domino Tattoo is followed by *The Domino Enigma*, in which Josephine, now self-possessed and successful, discovers that Estwych is child's play compared to other establishments run by the Domino organisation.

4

The trilogy is completed by *The Domino Queen*: now one of the leaders of the organisation, Josephine oversees the induction of new recruits.

'**W**ould you like a drink?'

Josephine lay on her stomach, her head turned sideways on the pillow. Rarely had she felt more relaxed, more alert. It was as if a new sense had opened up in her body.

'I'd like some gin,' said the nurse. 'How about you?'

'Yes,' said Josephine. 'Yes please.' She looked up at her in the dim light. 'Was all that true?' she said.

'Every word of it,' said Jackie. She sat back on her heels again, her knees spread, making a taut lap in her uniform dress. 'How do you feel now, Ms Morrow?' she asked, professionally.

'All right,' said Josephine.

There was a catch in her voice.

'Not in pain now?'

'No.'

She really wasn't. There was a quiet burning sensation where the whip had marked her, but she couldn't have called it pain. Jackie had taken all that away with her ointment, and her hands, and her story.

Jackie stepped down off the bed, smoothing her dress, lifting an automatic hand to check her cap was in place. Josephine felt a sudden pang of distress, not wanting her to leave. Jackie must have sensed it. 'Just a minute, dear,' she said.

She went into the bathroom again. Josephine heard water running, briefly. Then Jackie was approaching with something small and shiny in her hand. She was shaking it up and down.

'On your back now,' she said gently. 'I want to take your temperature.'

Obediently Josephine rolled over. The burn of the whip flared as her back came into contact with the sheets, then subsided again. She opened her mouth.

Jackie came to the bed. She shook her head slightly.

'Open your legs,' she said.

Josephine spread her legs.

Her crotch was hot, her vulva soft and moist.

Jackie nodded approval. With deft fingers she slipped the thermometer into Josephine's vagina.

She could feel it there, cold for an instant, then warm. A tiny shudder of pleasure ran through her loins.

Jackie looked down with a smile of amusement. She reached down and brushed Josephine's fringe from her damp forehead.

Josephine said, 'Are you really a nurse?'

'If you want me to be,' said Jackie.

She turned her hand and ran the back of her fingers down Josephine's cheek, down her neck, letting her knuckles stray down between her breasts. Helplessly Josephine felt her body respond, her pelvis rising up from the bed as if to thrust against the little thermometer.

Jackie left her lying there and went over to the table. She crouched down and reached underneath it. Josephine saw the white fabric of her skirt tighten along her thigh.

She stood up with two tumblers in her hand and a

bottle of gin in the crook of her arm. Coming back to the bed she sat down beside Josephine, stood the glasses on the bedside table and poured gin in them. 'I haven't any tonic,' she said gravely, 'or even any ice. I'm sorry.'

Her knees still spread, Josephine inched gingerly up the bed, trying not to disturb the thermometer. She reclined against the pillows and took her glass from Jackie. She drank. The raw spirit was a chemical on her tongue, a fire in her throat. It was like a new drug, a secret potion that would change her into something not human, a creature of quicksilver and chemical fire. She grimaced at the violent taste, drawing back her lips and sighing with fierce delight. She drained her glass.

The planes of the room, the face and form of Jackie sipping her gin and watching her tenderly, shifted subtly into new configurations. She felt the pores of her skin open, the hairs in her nostrils stir as Jackie bent over her again.

Jackie said, 'I think you're done.'

She slipped the thermometer from Josephine's richly oozing slit, drawing a string of silver mucus after it, and held it up to the light. Reading it, she raised her eyebrows and gave a small chuckle.

'What does it say?'

'It says you'll survive,' said Jackie. Then, catching Josephine's eye, she dipped the little glass tube into her glass like a swizzle stick, and stirred her drink with it.

'Antiseptic,' she said, 'gin.'

She took the thermometer from the glass and tapped it on the rim, shaking the last drops off. The clink of glass on glass rang distinctly in the silent bedroom.

Jackie lifted the glass to her lips and took a sip. She licked her lips, twitching her eyebrows suggestively.

The light of the lamp showed the soft down on her cheek, the glistening of her steady eyes.

9

Josephine pressed her greasy back against the pillows. Her heart was racing. Her breathing was fast and shallow. She was naked and fragile and defenceless. She took a large swallow of gin. Perhaps this was not happening. Perhaps it was a hallucination of alcohol on top of stress, disturbed sleep, pain and shock. Perhaps there was a drug in her glass again, or in the ointment. Fear fought with longing in her breast.

'Can I stay tonight?' she asked. 'Here, with you?'

Jackie looked down at her hands. She didn't want to reply. Josephine wondered what she'd said wrong.

'I don't want to be alone,' she said; and it was true.

Jackie looked up at her from under lowered brows. She smiled her mischievous smile.

'All right,' she whispered. 'But don't tell anyone.'

'No, no, of course . . .'

Jackie patted her hand: a reassuring, sexless gesture. She swung her legs to the floor and stood up, finishing the gin in her glass. She went into the bathroom and closed the door behind her.

Josephine put her glass down as gently as she could on the bedside table. She lay on the bed and listened to the quiet slither of cloth, the running of water. There was the rhythmic sound of Jackie brushing her teeth. Josephine switched out the bedside lamp. She climbed up and slid down in between the sheets.

The curtains were still open. While Jackie had been talking, the moon had come up above the trees and now it was shining directly in at the window, laying a lattice of shadow and cold silver light across the bed.

A woman, thought Josephine to herself. A woman's body.

She thought of Annabel and Dr Shepard, and then, at once, of Maria in the changing room at school. She frowned, pushing the memory away. Jackie's story was

10

a of a man, Dr McAllan. She had shared a room with another woman, not a bed.

The sheets were cotton crisp with starch, like Jackie's uniform. Josephine lay down flat and pulled the sheet up until it covered her breasts. She wondered if it would be safer to turn over and pretend to be asleep. She looked at the bathroom door, a black rectangle outlined in seeping yellow light.

At that moment, the light went out.

She heard rather than saw the door open. A shape came into the room, barefoot, silent as it came across the carpet to the bed. Josephine saw Jackie by moonlight, wearing a brief nightdress with a pattern of what she thought were little flowers. Her long hair was down now, sliding lightly across her shoulders as she put one foot up to climb into bed.

Josephine glimpsed a cave, a valley of black shadow between her thighs. Then Jackie was in bed, close beside her.

'Did you like my little story?' asked Jackie.

'Yes . . .' said Josephine.

Clumsily she put her arm across Jackie's body.

Jackie drew closer, snuggling up against her.

Josephine hugged her. An electric thrill of triumph sang through her bones.

'Did it excite you?' Jackie asked.

Josephine sniffed. There were tears in her eyes again. 'Yes,' she whispered. 'Yes!'

Hearing or sensing the tears, Jackie lifted her head. 'What's wrong?' she asked gently. 'Are you not happy?'

'I don't know,' Josephine said. Her voice sounded strange to her in the dark, feathery and high. 'I think I'm afraid.'

'I'll look after you,' said Jackie, patting Josephine's

11

stomach. 'You're safe now, tonight,' she promised.

Josephine sighed. Longing filled her.

She drew her hand across Jackie's back, caressing her.

She drew it across Jackie's arm, and laid it gently on her breast.

She felt Jackie catch her breath.

Then Jackie's voice in the dark asked: 'Will you tell me a story now?'

Josephine stirred, distracted. 'It wouldn't be true.'

'It doesn't matter.'

But Josephine said, 'It does. It does.'

She took her hand from Jackie's breast, levered herself up on one elbow and reached for her glass. She could see it beside the bed like a glass of liquid silver in the moonlight. She brought it carefully to her mouth and took a sip.

'I'm tired of fantasies,' she said. 'Tired of stories.'

She offered the glass to Jackie. She saw Jackie lift her head and open her mouth. Josephine thought, I shall spill it; but the gin had given her courage and she set the glass to Jackie's lips and tilted it so a little of the drink ran into her mouth. She felt Jackie swallow.

She took another sip herself and put the glass aside again. She leaned over Jackie. Her arms were like wings, carrying her across the crumpled moonlight landscape of the bed.

'I want you,' she said.

Jackie let herself be embraced. She did not respond.

'It was me took your clothes away this morning,' she whispered.

What on earth did that have to do with anything?

'I don't care,' said Josephine.

It seemed weeks ago, and worlds away.

Jackie said, 'My uncle Gil would have smacked my legs for a trick like that.'

Josephine held her close.

'I forgive you,' she said.

She brought her face close to Jackie's and kissed her on the mouth.

A shudder surged in her belly.

Growing bolder, Josephine fondled Jackie's breasts through the fabric of her nightdress. She brought her knees up and rubbed the inside of her thigh up along Jackie's thigh, feeling the cloth ride up between them, feeling the smoothness of Jackie's skin, the jutting corner of the hip under her thigh.

She kissed Jackie's face, her hair, her cheek. She was breathing hard now with relief and desire. She dipped her face between Jackie's head and shoulder, kissing Jackie's neck and rubbing her cheek against her shoulders. The nightdress was cool cotton, soft, not starched.

Josephine drew back her head, looking searchingly at Jackie in the moonlight. She seemed to have become completely passive, limp and unresisting in Josephine's arms. Josephine freed her right hand and stroked the hair back from Jackie's face.

'Are you all right?' she murmured.

Jackie made a small, soft sound, a wordless assent.

Josephine buried her face in Jackie's neck, nuzzling her throat, her hands roaming around her body. She reached down to caress her leg, ran her hand around the back of her thigh, pressing it between her bottom and the bed.

It was just like being with a man, and yet not like it at all. Larry was hairy; his body was all hard muscled shapes unprotected by fat; he had never been so inert, so sensitive. The gin percolated through Josephine's nerve ends and into her brain, and evaporated in a cool white flare. She was so tense now with sex and urgency she could not feel the drink at all. Her nerves were crystalline, her head was transparent. She was one with the moonlight, inside and out. Jackie's body smelt of soap and warm milk. Her pores breathed liquid joy.

Josephine slipped her hand between Jackie's legs.

Jackie gasped, bowing forward in the bed, hunching her shoulders as though something had pierced straight through her womb, pinning her to the bed.

Her crotch was dewy with the first trickle of desire.

Josephine kissed her, pressing her tongue between her teeth and into her mouth. She took her hand from her crotch and ran it up over her stomach, rubbing her pubic hair against the bone with the heel of her hand. She reached up under Jackie's nightdress for her breasts, and ran her fingers over her nipples.

The moonlight made Jackie's face the face of a strange creature, a child of the stars, of something other than flesh. But it was flesh under Josephine's hand, warm tender flesh.

She kissed Jackie's forehead. She plucked at the nightdress.

'Take if off,' she said.

Jackie sat up in bed. Josephine drew away to give her room as she worked the nightdress up and over her head, and flung it away into the dark, lost, unheeded.

Jackie lay down again. Josephine stroked her breasts. She rubbed her cheek against them. She thought of Sven, at the hotel, handling her breasts as if they were his to do with as he liked. Was it the truth?

She raised her head to look at Jackie's breasts in the mysterious light. When had she ever seen an adult woman's breasts, bare and free?

'What's that?' she asked.

'What?'

There was a mark between Jackie's breasts, a dark

14

design on her white skin. 'This,' said Josephine, touching the mark with one finger, slipping the other hand behind the small of Jackie's back.

Lying on her back, Jackie looked along her nose to see where Josephine was stroking her, as if she did not know what could be drawn there, in between her breasts. She put her finger where Josephine's was.

There was quite enough light to make it out. It was a tattoo, the same design as was on the key tag, and the handle of the spoon. The domino mask.

'What is it?'

'It means I belong here,' said Jackie.

Suddenly she ran the back of her fingers through Josephine's wet crotch, slicked them up through her pubic hair, making her gasp. She darted her head up and took Josephine's nipple into her mouth.

The room funnelled away to infinity. Josephine had never felt such a jolt of passion and power.

Josephine rolled over on her back, Jackie in her arms. Jackie wriggled. She straddled Josephine with her slim legs. Josephine let go of her wrist and slipped her left hand into Jackie's crotch again. She was hot now and dripping.

Josephine probed tentative fingers into the crack. Jackie squirmed, sighing. Josephine found the tight pucker of her anus, the elastic wet slit of her vagina. Jackie came up on top of her on her elbows and knees and Josephine slid her forefinger tentatively up between the open lips to the tense bump of her clitoris. Jackie moaned. She came alive in Josephine's hands. She collapsed and lay against her, one leg thrown up and over her, her mouth seeking Josephine's mouth, her hand pressing Josephine's hand harder against the bud of her desire, rubbing Josephine's wet fingers up and down, and up and down.

15

Josephine's silver wings unfurled again. Jackie's body was a strange land, a plane of being. Where skin met skin new nerves blossomed and fused. They drank each other, pressed their groins into each other's face. They gasped and crooned and flew. Jackie licked Josephine while a high wind rose and rose inside her. Jackie's hair was everywhere; Josephine held a fistful of it in her left hand and caressed Jackie's bottom with her right. The cleft between her buttocks was running with sweat and fluid. Then Jackie's thighs were clasped tight either side of her head, tighter, tighter, threatening to crush her head as she gasped and tongued at Jackie's quivering clitoris. Josephine could feel every stripe the whip had made cutting her back like a knife of steel. She was standing up from the bed on her shoulders and heels.

Everything blazed up in silver fire and melted.

They lay in each other's arms, breast to breast, their hearts thudding. The bed was a bed of fire. They panted into one another's hair.

Josephine drifted. She dreamed she was floating in a sea as warm as a bath, her feet on a level with her head. The seawater was deep turquoise, and the sun blazed from a turquoise sky, uninterrupted by the white ice-cream clouds that writhed and boiled in the blue.

She came back to herself. 'Dr McAllan,' she heard herself say.

'Who?'

'In your story. He was Dr Hazel, wasn't he?'

Jackie didn't reply. Josephine felt her take hold of her right hand and draw it down until it rested on her bottom.

'Go to sleep,' Jackie said. 'It's late.'

16

*　　*　　*

Josephine woke up from a dream of childhood. She had to go back to school, into a new dormitory. But she had all her adult belongings with her, her clothes and shoes, kitchen equipment and everything from the broom cupboard, and only a tiny locker beside her bed to keep it all in.

She woke and remembered that she wasn't at school; then that she wasn't at home; then that she was in Jackie's bed. She was lying on her side.

She opened her eyes. It was broad day. Jackie was curled up with her back to her, nude and warm.

Josephine slipped her hand between Jackie and the sheets, laying it gently on Jackie's stomach. It was warm and firm. It rose and fell softly with her breathing. Jackie didn't wake.

Josephine rolled on her back.

There was a woman standing at the foot of the bed, beside the TV and the floppy plant.

She was a Japanese woman. She was looking down at them. She looked displeased.

Josephine jumped, with a gasp that woke Jackie. Jackie turned on her back and gazed dazedly into the room.

When the woman saw Jackie was awake, she began to scold them.

'What do you think you are doing?'

Her voice was tight, her accent aristocratic English.

Jackie sat up in bed, the covers falling from her breasts.

Josephine, alarmed and at a disadvantage, sat up too, more slowly, holding the sheet up at her throat. Her back was sore. She remembered Sven, his whip.

Jackie was blinking, unable to speak.

The woman was short, her body angular. The planes

17

of her face were rigid with disdain. She stood with her legs apart, elbows out, the backs of her wrists resting on her hips. On one arm a cascade of bracelets and bangles rattled, clashing together.

She was wearing a short dress in deep metallic pink that left her arms and legs bare. When she moved, coming around Josephine's side of the bed, the stiff fabric of the dress rustled audibly.

She shot out a hand and snatched the sheet away, exposing Josephine's breasts. Josephine clutched an arm across herself.

The woman demanded: 'Where is her tattoo?'

Jackie, distressed, ran a hand through the tangle of her fine gold hair. 'Suriko –'

Josephine gathered the bedclothes up, covering herself again.

'You have broken the rule,' said Suriko implacably. Her voice was very loud. 'She is not ready. She has no tattoo.'

Jackie started to plead with her. 'Suriko, she's ready, she is, it's just . . .'

Suriko drew something from her pocket, something small and black. She threw it on the bed. It fell face up.

It was a domino: double one.

Jackie saw it and fell silent at once.

Josephine turned to Jackie. 'Jackie, who is she? What's that for?'

Suriko stared haughtily at her. 'Be silent,' she snapped. She told Jackie: 'Keep her quiet.'

To Josephine's dismay, Jackie complied, turning to her with a quick look and gesture that told her to obey. She seemed to have become completely docile. She reached out a slim hand and took the domino from the crumpled bedspread.

'Come to the attic at midday,' commanded Suriko, 'for your punishment.'

She turned on her heel and strode from the room.

Baffled, Josephine confronted Jackie as the door closed. 'She can't punish you for sleeping with me!'

'She can,' said Jackie quietly. 'She can. She's right, it's my fault, I shouldn't have led you on.'

She toyed with the domino, twirling it sadly between her fingers. Josephine looked at it. There had been a box of dominoes in the desk at Dr Hazel's London surgery. 'What does it mean?'

'Whoever gives you the domino,' said Jackie, 'they're your master or mistress for that day. They can call upon you at any time, to do anything. You must obey them unquestioningly.'

She set the tip of her finger between Josephine's breasts, on the place where her own tattoo was.

'If you haven't the tattoo, you're everybody's slave. And nobody's lover.'

She bent and kissed the place, a light, dry kiss.

'We broke the rule.'

Then she put her arms around Josephine and clasped her to her breasts. 'Will you come at twelve and watch my punishment? It'll be easier for me, having you there.'

Josephine's heart quickened. 'All right,' she said. Her voice was unsteady.

Kissing her on the lips, Jackie released her and got out of bed. Josephine pushed back the covers, looking down at herself.

'What can I wear?' she asked, unsure.

'Your clothes are in your wardrobe,' said Jackie, disappearing into the bathroom.

Josephine had forgotten.

Jackie had left the bathroom door open. Bemused,

Josephine followed her in. She was sitting on the toilet. Josephine could hear her stream splashing in the bowl.

Jackie smiled up at her. 'How's your back?' she asked.

'It's fine.'

'Well, that's something.'

Jackie tore off two sheets of paper. She spread her legs and wiped herself briskly.

'You must go,' she said.

'Like this?'

'Keep your eyes on the floor,' Jackie advised, 'and your hands behind your back. Remember, when they see you've no tattoo, you're fair game.'

She stood up and flushed the toilet, began to run water into the basin.

'Will you come at twelve?' she asked again.

'Yes,' said Josephine.

Preoccupied, she closed the door marked 9 behind her. She glanced along the corridor. It all looked quite different by daylight. Naked, she walked silently on the soft carpet, remembering to keep her eyes down. Turning the corner she found herself in her own corridor. No one was about.

Her door was unlocked. She went in. Her breakfast was sitting on a tray on the beside table, under a clean cloth of whitest linen.

She showered and dried herself, then sat on the bed wrapped in a towel. Breakfast was lavish, all perfectly cooked, and piping hot.

Absolute obedience, she thought. The Estwych law. And that was how they worked it, with the tattoo and the dominoes. Suriko said she wasn't ready, Jackie said she was. Because she hadn't got a tattoo, they could treat her like a slave, for their own pleasure. She wasn't even worth a domino.

20

When would she get her tattoo? Was there still another test she had to pass? Dr Hazel, she thought. It all depended on Dr Hazel. When would he come? Or was he here already, pretending to be someone else, secretly watching her?

She thought of Jackie: Jackie in her uniform, Jackie last night in bed, Jackie this morning in the bathroom. Suriko was going to punish Jackie. To her amazement she realised she was jealous of Jackie. She parted her legs, touched herself lightly, shuddered.

The day was already well advanced. The sun was high, and streaming in through the little panes of the windows. Josephine wanted to go out and laze naked in the sunshine. But she didn't want to meet anyone. Not Sven, not Suriko – no one.

She crossed to the mantelpiece and rang the bell.

A maid appeared, one she hadn't seen before. She wasn't at all disconcerted that Josephine was standing by the hearth carelessly draped in a towel.

'You can take the tray,' Josephine told her.

'Yes, ma'am. Will there be anything else, ma'am?'

'You can tell Dr Hazel I'm still waiting to see him,' she said.

The maid hesitated, then ducked her head. 'Yes, ma'am.'

When she'd gone, Josephine went to the wardrobe. She opened it.

Her clothes had disappeared again. Inside were the same things as before: the net stockings, the suspender belt, the collar, the spike-heeled boots. Josephine took a deep breath. She took them out. She held one of the stockings to her face, running its mesh up and down her cheek. She went and leaned on the windowsill, opened the window, looked out at the tree. The rich air of summer washed in, swept sensuously over her.

She lay and waited for Dr Hazel.

No one came.

At ten to twelve, she rose and put on her clothes. She left her room and found a staircase that led up to the top of the house. The steps were bare, old wood, unpolished. They creaked beneath her as she climbed.

At the top was a low door, hanging askew in its frame. Josephine pushed it open and went in.

She found herself in a dark attic full of cobwebs and old junk.

It was hot, the air stale and oppressive. Glancing around in the dusty light she saw a rocking horse, a big glass dome full of stuffed birds, an old wind-up gramophone with a horn, a golfing bag, a listing card table, a dressmaker's dummy.

They were all there, watching her.

Annabel was sitting in a big old armchair. She had a black wool suit on and a double row of pearls. She looked quite at her ease, less like a housekeeper, more like the lady of the manor. Her chair was covered in a dustsheet. Her hands were clasped in her lap.

Sven was sitting on the arm of her chair. He was wearing a long white coat and black trousers with a sharp crease. His fair hair had been smeared back over his scalp, dark with grease. He had a little pair of glasses on, the lenses round and tinted so his eyes could not be seen.

Suriko had changed her clothes. She was dressed to go riding. She had a red coat, black jodhpurs, thigh boots of shiny leather. She stood beside the rocking horse, swaying it gently back and forth with one gloved hand.

Josephine whirled round.

Behind her sat the cabby, straddling an old kitchen chair turned back to front. He took looked very different. He was wearing a flat black cap with a peak, black leather trousers and a black leather waistcoat, no shirt. He still had his sunglasses on, and his gold earring. There was a gold chain hanging in the hair on his chest. She supposed there was a tattoo there, overgrown with red hair. He had bound her hands and bandaged her eyes and spanked her. She did not know his name.

Two maids were in attendance: the one who had taken away her breakfast tray, and Dawn, who had sucked Sven's cock and let him spurt his seed deep in her mouth.

Jackie was not there.

Disoriented, Josephine stood looking around the group.

Nobody moved or spoke. The only sound was the squeak of the springs of the horse, rocking to and fro, to and fro.

Josephine noticed the dressmaker's dummy was wearing a black leather bra and panties, with heart-shaped holes where the nipples and the crotch would have been.

Seeing that, Josephine remembered. She lowered her eyes, looking at the sharp toes of her shiny boots. She clasped her hands behind her.

Sven spoke.

'Her presentation is commendable,' he said, drawling. He seemed to be congratulating Annabel, as if she were in charge.

'Doesn't she look fine, thought?' agreed the cabby softly.

His chair creaked as he shifted his weight.

Josephine felt the blood rising in her face. She willed herself not to look up. Her head was pounding, her breathing short and shallow. She felt as if any moment she might float off the floor.

23

She heard the rocking horse fall still. There was the sound of boot-heels on the bare wooden floor.

'She was disobedient,' observed Suriko.

'On the contrary,' said the cabby, not raising his voice. 'I'm sure she was very obedient indeed.'

He chuckled.

Sven laughed loudly and coarsely.

Suriko resumed her walk. She came close to Josephine.

Josephine could smell leather and wax and felt.

'Not ready,' Suriko declared.

Josephine heard the chink of metal, felt Suriko's fingers at her collar. She gazed at her boots. Cold metal links brushed her bare shoulders. A chain fell into her view. She felt the weight of it, hanging from the ring on her collar. Suriko was holding the other end.

Suriko led her, stumbling on her heels, into the angle of the roof. Josephine tried to keep her eyes turned down. She felt the chain being fastened to a rafter. She was standing hunched, the slope of the roof on the back of her neck, a foot of chain holding her to the rafter. Suriko was forcing her elbows together behind her back, pulling her shoulders back uncomfortably so that her breasts stood out. She felt the sweat break out, on her forehead and cheeks. Her jaw was damp where it rested on her chest.

They came to handle her. The red-haired hands of the cabby took hold of her breasts and squeezed them. Josephine gasped.

'She looks ready,' he said.

'Not until Dr Hazel says so.'

That was Annabel. Josephine noticed how much more commanding her tone had become, as if she was not the servant but the mistress of the house.

Sven grasped her by the shoulder, turning her about.

24

The chain tightened, pulling on her collar. He was examining her whipmarks. She could tell he was pleased.

'The slave knows me already,' he boasted.

He pulled on her hips suddenly, grabbed her by the buttocks and forced them apart, regardless how she writhed and squirmed. He pushed a finger painfully into her anus.

'Before the week is out her arse will know the length of my cock!'

Abruptly he let go of the struggling Josephine. She stumbled, trying to balance on the unfamiliar heels with her hands behind her. Unable to keep her eyes on the floor, she threw up her head. Sven and the cabby were kissing, demonstratively, roughly, lasciviously. Josephine caught a glimpse and dropped her eyes at once. She was hot. Her head was spinning. He heart was beating fit to burst.

She felt the cabby ruffle her hair, ungently, commenting on its beauty. Then he spoke in her ear, wetly, loud enough for them all to hear.

'I want to come in your hair,' he said, his voice deep with passion.

Suriko laughed and stamped her boot. She pinched Josephine painfully on the leg. 'Her thights are perfect for the crop,' she announced. 'I shall make her squeal. I shall hear her beg for my cunt against her mouth.'

The door opened and everyone fell silent.

Josephine risked a glance.

It was Jackie. She was in her uniform.

From the corner of her eye she saw them all make a concerted movement. They were all putting on domino masks; like the pierrot in the picture at the surgery.

Suriko pulled a pair of handcuffs from her jacket pocket and stepped forward to put them on Jackie.

Josephine wanted to look, to catch Jackie's eye. She dropped her gaze. She heard everyone resume their seats. It was a kind of tribunal, she realised.

'Jacqueline,' said Suriko sharply, 'you are charged with taking this slave, this novice, into your bed. You are charged with taking pleasure with her.' She laughed, lasciviously.

'Plead,' said Sven, brusquely.

'Plead,' said the cabby.

'Plead,' said Suriko.

Annabel did not speak.

Jackie's voice was intent and low.

'Guilty,' she said.

'Plead!' they all said, urgently.

In the moment of silence that followed, Josephine could hear the rustle of Jackie's starched uniform. She imagined Jackie raising her head, looking Suriko in the eye.

'I beg for punishment,' said Jackie.

She heard someone give a deep sigh of longing anticipation.

'Your sentence is the strap,' said Suriko. 'Fifty strokes.'

'Another fifty,' said Sven. His voice came taut and clear.

Josephine thought she heard Jackie gasp.

'Strip,' said Annabel. Josephine heard Suriko go to Jackie and release her from the cuffs.

She screwed her eyes up tight, swallowing, fighting herself.

The cabby's warm hand landed on the back of her head, ruffling her hair again.

'Does she want to watch?' he said, amused. 'Does she?'

Josephine gave a shuddering nod.

They laughed at her.

'Let her watch,' he said. 'Let her watch her girlfriend's punishment.'

Startled, she looked up into his face. He had taken off his glasses. Behind his mask his eyes were green and mysterious. He grinned and scratched his belly lazily. He cuffed her head, and went back to his old chair.

Josephine looked at Jackie. Their eyes met. Jackie's face was pale, her cheeks bright spots of pink. She ran her eyes down Josephine's pinioned body.

She stripped.

She stepped out of her shoes. She reached behind her neck, pulled the halter of her apron up and over her head, then reached behind again to untie the strings and unfastened her uniform. Apron and dress fell swishing forward into her arms, and she climbed out of them, letting them fall to the floor.

Everyone was motionless, watching, their arms folded, masks on their faces.

Jackie stood before them in her little white cap, bra and panties, suspenders and seamed black stockings. Her brassière was white, cut low. They fattened as she leaned forward to unfasten her suspenders. Balancing unaided, she lifted one knee and then the other, placing each foot on the other shin and deftly rolling down her stockings. One after the other, she wriggled them off her feet. She stood up straight, barefoot on the rough boards, reached behind her a third time and unhooked her brassière. She slipped the straps from her shoulders. It fell silently at her feet.

Josephine's lips arched for her long pink nipples.

Jackie threw away her suspender belt. She slid her thumbs inside the waistband of her panties and, bending slightly, pulled them down, down to her thighs, her knees, and lifting each foot in turn, stepped out of them.

She put her hands behind her back, and the cabby came forward and cuffed them together.

Josephine heard a rattle. It was Suriko at the golf bag.

Looking around, Josephine saw what she had not noticed before, that the bag was full not of golf clubs but of canes, riding crops, animal whips, a bundle of twigs she knew must be birch.

Suriko was drawing out a long strap of thick leather.

Suddenly Josephine heard herself crying out: 'It wasn't her fault! It wasn't!'

She shook her head vigorously.

They were all staring at her curiously.

'It was my fault!' she begged them. 'Punish me! Punish me! Oh, punish me, not her!'

They all exchanged a swift glance. Something relaxed in the room, though the air was as tense as ever.

The two naked women stared at each other's eyes.

Josephine's confession hung in the air.

Nothing had been said. They had come to an agreement. 'We shall punish both of you,' said Suriko, in a tone that sounded like a warning; as if there were still time for her to change her mind. 'It will be no less for Jackie if you share it.'

Josephine thought then of Jackie's story, of Nicola offering to take both punishments. The story had been a fantasy, not true. And yet it was.

She pulled forward on her chain, hollowing her back, thrusting her breasts out defiantly.

'Let me share it!' she cried.

Ceremoniously they released Josephine's chain and brought her face to face with Jackie, breast to breast. In the slave boots, Josephine was the taller.

With leather belts the maids bound them to one

another at waist and knee. Annabel chain their collars together, snicking a little padlock closed on one end of the chain. Josephine felt their sweat, mingling between their squeezed breasts. She smelt again the odour she had drunk so freely of last night. She stared longingly into Jackie's moist green eyes. When they kissed there was a warm murmur of approval. Sven was reaching up and slipping the free end of the chain over a hook in the roof.

Josephine bent her knees to press her crotch against Jackie's. She felt weak. They were all holding straps now, standing around them in a circle.

As the first blow fell, Josephine thought: The cabby is Dr Hazel.

PLAISIR D'AMOUR

Anne-Marie Villefranche

Plaisir D'Amour is the first in the six-book D'Amour series – the longest and longest-running series in the Nexus library.

The author, Anne-Marie Villefranche, seems to have lived between the two world wars in the Paris she captures with perfect clarity in the pages of her stories. Each of her books contains a wealth of anecdotes – mostly light-hearted, sometimes bitter-sweet – about the licentious activities of the Parisian *beau monde*. The D'Amour books are very chic and very cheeky – they're more French than I am!

Having been translated into English by Jane Purcell, Anne-Marie's stories have been re-exported to the world, and have appeared in Spanish, German and Portugese editions, among others.

Anne-Marie Villefranche's books can be read in any order, but for the record here are the rest in order of publication: *Joie d'Amour, Folies d'Amour, Mystere d'Amour, Souvenir d'Amour* and *Secrets d'Amour*.

The true pleasure of shopping is not to need anything. Setting out with an objective in mind, to buy a pair of shoes for example, that is to give oneself the bother of making comparisons, matching colours and styles, considering prices and reaching a decision. Such errands are more like work than pleasure. On the other hand, needing nothing, one looks into shop windows, goes inside to examine this and that, open to the delicious impulse to buy anything which attracts the eye and would be a delight to wear – that is the art of shopping at its most civilised.

By lunchtime Marie-Thérèse and her friend Adrienne Dumoutier had looked at a thousand things, stockings, underwear, scarves, hats, shoes, handbags, and bought nothing. Their outing was a complete success, to be crowned by a light lunch in a restaurant they both liked.

They were a striking pair, these two. They drew admiring glances from men wherever they went, instant attention from shop assistants and devoted service from waiters. They were the same age, in the full bloom of their late twenties. Adrienne wore that day a new-style knitted jumper-blouse to her hips over a pleated skirt that just covered her rounded knees when she walked and displayed them when she sat down. Her ensemble was in shades of woodland green, matched by a little cloche hat pulled down over her dark red hair. Marie-Thérèse was slightly more conservative in her taste, as evidenced by her cream silk frock under a matching three-quarter length coat trimmed at the neck with black fur.

After lunch they took a taxi to Adrienne's home. They sat together on the big sofa in the drawing-room, talking busily, until Adrienne put an arm round her friend to hug her.

'Do you know,' she said, 'when we met this morning and I saw how beautifully dressed you were, for some strange reason I thought of how awful we both looked when we met for the very first time. Do you remember?'

'That ghastly boarding-school at Vincennes! Blue serge uniforms and thick black stockings – what a way to make young girls dress! As much as I love my dear mother, I think I shall never completely forgive her for sending me there.'

Adrienne cuddled her affectionately.

'But if she hadn't, we might never have met.'

'True. At least the school did one thing for us, it made us friends. Though it did everything possible to discourage friendship. You haven't forgotten that we were forbidden to be in groups of less than four when we were allowed out in the grounds.'

'Instant punishment if two girls were caught talking together outside the classroom. That was one rule we discovered how to break without being found out.'

'Dear Adrienne! We learned so much, you and I, although the holy sisters tried hard not to let us. Those poor sad unfulfilled creatures! At the time I hated them but looking back now I have come to pity them.'

Adrienne's hand caressed Marie-Thérèse's slender neck.

'I don't feel in the least sorry for them,' she said, 'they were grisly old bags determined to make our lives miserable. They failed with you and me, but they made a lot of young girls very unhappy. You haven't forgotten Elise Moncourt, I hope.'

'Little Elsie . . . you are right. The regime crippled her emotions for life. She was so pretty then – but now! I told you about how I ran into her some time ago and discovered that she had been married off to a surly brute who treats her with open contempt. She has become thin and pale, her cheeks lined and her figure sagging and ruined from being forced to have five children. I almost wept for her.'

'What a tragedy! I intended to call on her, but thinking about what you told me, it seemed too depressing,' said Adrienne, her finger-tips sliding sensuously over the fine skin of Marie-Thérèse's décolletage.

'Ah, those busy fingers of yours! You know very well that I can never resist them.'

'I should hope not! After all the pleasure these fingers of mine have given you since we were at school together they have become dear friends of your beautiful body.'

'I could say the same,' Marie-Thérèse replied, kissing her friend's cheek warmly.

'Naturally. Remember our first time – in the dormitory after lights-out?'

'Of course I do. Our tender interludes were the only good part of our existence then. That horrid dormitory, as big as a warehouse, divided by curtains into cubicles, with a lay-sister sleeping in each corner.'

'They never slept, those gorgons. They lay awake in the dark right through the night, listening for a whisper or a rustle so that they could pounce.'

'They never caught us. You were the bold one, Adrienne – you slipped under the curtain between our cubicles and into my bed so silently that not even the biggest ears could detect anything.'

'The hours we lay kissing and caressing each other!'

'The first time or two, yes. When you thought I was ready for more than that, your caresses became insistent one night and you took me all the way. It was like entering paradise. I would have cried out in joy, except that you had a hand over my mouth.'

'And the other between your legs,' said Adrienne, smiling at the memory.

'Are the servants out?'

'Naturally.'

'Then I shall take my frock off.'

'Let me help you.'

Under her dress Marie-Thérèse was wearing cream-coloured cami-knickers edged with golden-brown lace. Adrienne stood close, her arms around her, hugging their bodies together.

'I expect you to return the compliment,' said Marie-Thérèse.

At once Adrienne pulled her long jumper-blouse over her head, dropped her skirt and stood revealed in a lime green georgette slip. This too she removed and took her place beside Marie-Thérèse on the sofa again wearing only loose silk knickers and a very tight brassiere. She tucked her knees under her and turned towards Marie-Thérèse.

'Let me kiss those delicious playthings of yours,' she said, easing the narrow straps off Marie-Thérèse's shoulders to expose her little breasts.

'Only if you let me stroke yours too. Turn round so that I can unhook your brassiere. It looks very uncomfortable.'

'I am not as fortunate as you are,' Adrienne complained, twisting her body to present the fastening to Marie-Thérèse. 'You've had two children and your breasts are still as pretty as when you were a girl. I've had one child and mine are big and obtrusive. Is it fair that I have to keep them swaddled up tight to be able to wear fashionable clothes?'

'Adrienne dear, yours were always big. When we first touched each other, mine were only the size of little apples and yours were already as full as a grown woman's. You know that's true.'

'Monstrous things,' said Adrienne, putting her hands beneath her breasts to lift them up, the gesture emphasising their fullness, 'it is not chic to have all this flesh sticking out in front.'

'I love them even if you don't,' Marie-Thérèse soothed her.

She put her lips to Adrienne's nipples, one after the other. When they stood firm, she devoted her entire attention to the one nearest her, flicking it with the tip of her tongue until Adrienne was sighing heavily.

'To think that it was I who taught you everything you know,' Adrienne murmured.

'Not everything. You awoke me to the delights of love, that I agree.'

'Who else has shown you anything you didn't learn from me at school or since?'

'My husband, of course,' Marie-Thérèse answered, both hands kneading Adrienne's breasts.

'I don't believe a word of it. I know that I've learned nothing from mine in the years we've been married. Men! The only experience a man can give you is the sensation of his penis inside you. We have given each other than many times with our fingers.'

'We have discussed this before and we never seem to

agree. However similar the physical sensations may be, lovemaking with a man is different emotionally.'

'For me sensations are more important than emotions,' said Adrienne.

She pushed Marie-Thérèse gently back against the sofa and put her hands on her small round breasts to roll the nipples under her thumbs.

'Little devils,' she said, 'all hard and greedy.'

When Marie-Thérèse was well-embarked on the magic voyage Adrienne undid the buttoms of the cami-knickers between her legs and pulled the thin silk up to uncover her. Her hand stroked between parted thighs, evoking little gasps of satisfaction from her friend.

'Do you know what I'm going to do to you, Marie-Thérèse?'

'Tell me!'

'Something which will amaze you. Close your eyes and enjoy it.'

'But I don't understand,' Marie-Thérèse mur-mured, pretending to be a child again, 'why are you touching me between the legs?'

'You'll find out in a minute.'

'But we have to keep our bodies covered up all the time, even when we're washing. It's a sin to let anyone see your body – Sister Hortense said so. It's a sin to look at your body, don't you know that?'

'What does Sister Hortense know about anything? Does it feel nice when I touch you there?'

'Very nice. Oh, Adrienne, what are you doing to me?'

'That's my finger going ever such a little way inside.'

'But you mustn't!'

'Don't you like it?'

'Adrienne!'

'I'm touching your little button. Does it give you a lovely sensation?'

40

'It makes me feel so strange . . .'

'Strange but lovely.'

'Don't stop – it really is lovely.'

Adrienne had one leg folded under her on the sofa and the other lay over Marie-Thérèse's thigh, pulling her legs wider apart while her dexterous fingers dealt out shudders of pleasure. Marie-Thérèse pressed her face between her friend's warm breasts.

'Now do you understand why I am doing it to you?' Adrienne asked.

'Yes, I understand . . . it feels so good.'

'And it gets better.'

'How?'

'Like this.'

Adrienne's hand turned under, two joined fingers slid into Marie-Thérèse's soft burrow and the ball of her thumb folled over the passionate bud.

'Adrienne . . . that's incredible! More!'

'As much as you like.'

Marie-Thérèse's small white teeth worried at Adrienne's breast, her exhalations now loud and exclamatory as she neared her zenith.

'Something is going to happen to me!'

'Of course it is, darling, you may rely on it.'

'I'm going to faint . . .'

Adrienne's thumb and fingers thrust with loving precision at their tender targets.

'Now,' she commanded, 'you are trembling like a leaf. It is now!'

Marie-Thérèse's back arched in spasms of delight. Adrienne's relentless manipulations prolonged the pleasure to its extreme and with a long moan Marie-Thérèse collapsed against her.

'I adore doing that to you,' said Adrienne, 'your response is so exciting. I watch your face change expression at the supreme moment and feel your body shaking against mine. There is no delight on earth to equal this.'

'Except,' said Marie-Thérèse, 'to experience those same delights in your own body. Bare yourself, my dear friend, for your time has come.'

'Has it then? Do you suppose for one moment that you can make me feel half of what I make you feel? Absurd!'

Marie-Thérèse's hand was up the wide leg of her friend's only garment, stroking her fur and belly.

'You intend to play your old game with me, do you?' she asked, 'you still think that because it was you who crept into my bed the first time and not I into yours – and you only dared do that because I'd hinted to you all day that a visit would be welcome – you think that you are the dominant partner in our love-making. That's what *I* call absurd.'

'I have always been the one to initiate our encounters,' Adrienne retorted. 'I am always the one to caress you first.'

'Only because I want it to happen that way. Accept the fact – it is I who initiate everything, not you. You make the first move only because I wish it so. How smooth your skin is to the touch!'

'You are distorting the truth,' Adrienne murmured as knowing fingers moved slowly in her soft groins.

'I am ready for my treat, Adrienne, and you are keeping me waiting with this ridiculous argument. Unless you remove these transparent frillies at once I shall lose all patience with you. I suppose you know that they are so thin that the dark shadow of your hair shows right through them? Is that how you attract your husband at night – standing before him in these?'

Without answering, Adrienne hooked her thumbs in the sides of her underwear and her legs waved briefly in the air as she slipped off her final flimsy garment.

'There – is that what you want?' she said at last, spreading her legs.

Marie-Thérèse, naked but for her stockings, knelt before the sofa, a hand on each of Adrienne's creamy-white thighs to push them further apart.

'At last!' she said, 'you always delay this moment because you know that I enjoy it. You deliberately keep me waiting for it.'

Year and years of the application of henna had made the hair on Adrienne's head dark-red. Between her legs the pelt was her natural ginger, vividly bright against her pale skin.

'The little fox is out of its hiding-place at last,' said Marie-Thérèse, combing the wiry hair with her fingers.

'Do you honestly and truthfully like it, Marie-Thérèse?'

'You should know by now. How many times have I told you that the colour is fascinating?'

'How can I be sure you mean it?'

'How often have I stroked it and told you that I admire it?'

'Hundreds of times.'

'Hundreds and hundreds of times,' Marie-Thérèse corrected her, her fingers probing delicately.

'I shall last about five seconds if you go on like that,' Adrienne sighed.

'We'll see about that,' and Marie-Thérèse nipped the soft flesh carefully with her nails, causing the other woman to utter a brief shriek.

'Five seconds indeed! I intend to annihilate you with sensation to punish you for daring to say that you are the leader of our games.'

'But I am. I always have been . . . oh my God, you're opening me up like a book!'

43

'A book I have read so many times that I know it off by heart. Who is the leader now?'

'I am.'

'Such arrogance. You will regret it.'

'I regret nothing.'

Marie-Thérèse lowered her dark head to touch her hot tongue to the pink surfaces she had revealed.

'You are kissing my little fox in homage. That proves it.'

Marie-Thérèse concentrated her efforts on the tiny swollen nub she had laid bare.

'What are you doing to me!'

'Teaching you a lesson,' said Marie-Thérèse, leaving off her caresses for a moment.

'Do it again, please, dear Marie-Thérèse . . .'

'Ah, now you being to suffer. I shall start and stop as I choose. We will settle once and for all which of us gives the other the greater pleasure. Beg me.'

'I implore you, don't leave me like this!'

Marie-Thérèse resumed her devotions and Adrienne's naked bottom squirmed about on the sofa. When there was another lull, she wrapped her legs about Marie-Thérèse slender body below the breasts to clamp her tight and urge her to continue her ministrations.

'You're killing me . . .' she groaned after a while, 'no one could endure this . . . don't stop . . .'

Marie-Thérèse had no intention of stopping again. The two women understood each other's reactions completely from their years of intimacy, each knew the other's body and its capabilities as well as her own.

'I'm dying!' Adrienne gulped abruptly.

A few more staccato flicks of the tongue within her ginger-furred lips and she moaned inarticulately in the throes of her rapturous crisis.

When it was over Marie-Thérèse got back onto the

sofa and they lay cuddled in each other's arms, enjoying the closeness of the embrace. Marie-Thérèse broke the silence by laughing.

'What is it? What is so funny?'

'I suddenly thought of Monsieur Huchette at school.'

'Why him?'

'Well, we were compelled to make our weekly confession to him. I wonder what he would have said if either of us had ever confessed what we did together.'

'Good thing we didn't. He was a nasty old pervert,' said Adrienne.

'We can't be sure about that.'

'Yes we can. That look in his eyes every time I knelt on the prie-dieu by him to recite my ridiculous confession. One word – the merest hint – of anything at all and his hand would have been up my skirt. And yours too, for that matter.'

'He was a strange man,' Marie-Thérèse agreed. 'He certainly did stare. Not that he could discern even the outline of my tiny bosom under the blue serge.'

'His eyes never left mine, blue serge or not.'

'Yours was far more prominent.'

'You surely haven't forgotten what Arlette Desormes told us about him – how he exposed himself to her during confession?'

'I think she made that up for the sake of effect.'

'No, it was too detailed and real. She was only thirteen – how could she have known about such things – it is not possible.'

'She was from the country. Children there have more opportunity to learn about matters than city children like us. They see the animals, I suppose – bulls with cows and stallions with mares.'

'Farm-hands with milkmaids?' Adrienne giggled.

'Anyway, you believed her at the time. We all did.'

'Perhaps we didn't know any better.'

'If you remember, Arlette told us that she was on her knees on the rickety old prie-dieu by his chair, confessing to the nonsense we used to make up to keep him quiet. She raised her eyes and there he sat with his apparatus out of his trousers, standing straight up in the air. She said that it was big and angry-looking and that he had a strange look on his face.'

'If he'd worn a cassock he could have played with it and no one would have been any the wiser,' said Marie-Thérèse. 'I never understood the need for the hypocrisy of the teacher-nuns pretending to be lay-sisters and Huchette wearing ordinary clothes.'

'Religion by stealth to circumvent the law,' said Adrienne, shrugging her naked shoulders and making her breasts wobble, 'Arlette was a pretty girl. I nearly went to her bed instead of yours.'

'What a monstrous lie! You had no choice in the matter. I drew you to me because I wanted you. Arlette looked like a doll with her blonde hair and pale face, but she was stupid. I wonder if she was telling the truth – she wasn't clever enough to make that story up by herself.'

'I'm certain it happened. He told her to lower her eyes and continue with her confession, but she watched him out of the corner of her eye and saw him stroking his penis up and down.'

'But seriously – would he have dared in front of her?' Marie-Thérèse asked.

'Who can say what a celibate will do when nature proves too powerful for him? You know what the old rhyme says.'

'What old rhyme??'

'Once is enough for a sick man to do,

46

A healthy man usually makes it two,
A hot-blooded lover will go up to three,
Four or five for a monk on a spree.'

'That's very good,' said Marie-Thérèse, giggling. 'Who told you that?'

'I can't even remember. But it proves my point, I think. Huchette was capable of anything, including ravishing little girls if he could have got away with it.'

'We must be grateful that his passions were confined to staring at us.'

'But they weren't. Evidently Arlette told her mother what had happened when she went home for the holidays.'

'Why?'

'Because she never came back to school and we didn't see her again.'

'But then her mother would have made a complaint against Huchette. But he was still there hearing our confessions right up to the day we left school. If Arlette's mother had complained they'd have got rid of him.'

'Not necessarily. The complaint would have gone to the headmistress. She was a friend of Huchette. She covered up for him,' Adrienne insisted.

Marie-Thérèse laughed.

'That awful woman in her full-length black! She was Mother Superior in all except name.'

'Five feet tall and with a body of a wrestler,' Adrienne said. 'Do you remember the stories we used to make-up about her and Monsieur Huchette?'

'The stories about how she and he did it together – we had a lot of fun inventing them, didn't we?'

'Monsieur taking the balance from the school-room and using it to weigh her enormous breasts one after the other and deciding that one was several kilos heavier than the other!' said Adrienne.

'And the one about how she jumped on him in the washroom and wrestled him to the floor and raped him.'

'If any of our tales were even approximately true, no wonder he fancied little girls as a change.'

'But in reality,' said Marie-Thérèse, 'she was far too religious to let a man catch a glimpse of her ankle even, let alone anything more interesting.'

'What was interesting about her ankles? She had legs like oak trees and wore thick black stockings. And as for *more* interesting – do you suppose that there was anything alluring about what she had between her thighs? Perhaps a blind man, if he were drunk enough, might have risked it, but no one else would.'

'She would have died before allowing a man to touch her, Adrienne, you know that.'

'That was what she wanted everyone to believe. But we all have the same desires.'

'That may be, but she was determined to save her body for God.'

'Poor God! I know that the priests tell us that he took the sins of the world upon himself, but surely he didn't deserve that body being thrust upon him.'

'Adrienne, you are being blasphemous, to say the least of it.'

'Am I? I've just thought of something – suppose it had been you and not Arlette who had the benefit of viewing Huchette's penis?'

'What should I suppose?'

'What would you have done? Obeyed him meekly, like her, and sneaked a look?'

'How can I possibly tell?'

'You were not as innocent as Arlette, of course,' said Adrienne.

'Thanks to you and your busy fingers.'

48

'You regret it?'

'Not for one moment. You and I will still be lovers long after our husbands have started to chase younger women.'

Adrienne kissed her friend's face warmly.

'Speaking of which,' she said, 'I'm certain that mine has already found a little friend. Not that it matters to me, of course. How about Maurice?'

'He is still very attentive to me. No doubt he is an opportunist like all men and takes advantage of any pretty woman who lets him see that she is willing. After all, he travels on business quite a lot and who can say what happens then? But there is no one of any lasting interest to him yet, I am sure. Who do you suppose that Edmond has found?'

'No one that matters – just some silly young creature to make him feel like a hot-blooded lover again.'

'Doing it three times – was it three?'

'You are evading my question, Marie-Thérèse. What would you have done if you had looked up from your confession and seen Monsieur Huchette's device sticking up in the air?'

'If only he had been a more sympathetic person,' she answered with a smile, 'I might even have held it for him. I'd never seen a grown man's penis then. And one standing up – it could have been more interesting.'

'You're only saying that to tease me! You would have done no such thing.'

'Are you so sure? You had taught me the pleasure in handling another between the legs.'

'What a sight that would have been,' and Adrienne laughed aloud. 'You on your knees in your serge uniform playing with that long-faced man! He'd have loved it, no doubt about that. He would have given you a double blessing that day.'

49

'Of course. He might even have sprinkled me with holy water if I'd held it long enough for him.'

'Holy *water*?'

'Some sort of holy fluid, to be sure.'

Adrienne's lips found one of Marie-Thérèse's nipples and sucked it gently.

'You were a wicked child,' she murmured.

'I learned it from you, my dear.'

'So you admit it at last?'

'You taught me all that you knew inside a week. Less than that, three or four days at the most. After that I surpassed you and since then you have been learning the delights of love-making from me. Oh, that feels very good.'

'And if you wish me to continue making you feel good you must confess that I am the leader of our games.'

'Never.'

'Dear Marie-Thérèse – very soon you will be so excited that you will say anything I want you to say. My hand is between your thighs. You are on the verge of surrendering yourself to me, body and soul. So admit that I am the leader.'

'You may touch me anywhere you choose – you are only doing what I wish you to do.'

'You wish me to do *this* to you?'

'Yes . . . that's exactly what I want you to do. How did you guess?'

'Little liar! That's three of my fingers in you now. How does that feel?'

'Divine – just what I wanted . . .'

'When you are lying here shaking with passion, as you will in a few moments, you will admit to the truth. You always have in the past and you will again. Ah, you are trembling deliciously – I am waiting to hear your confession of submission.'

50

'There is something you forget,' Marie-Thérèse sighed, stroking her own tight nipples as passion grew.

'What am I forgetting?'

'Afterwards – when you have pleasured me to the limit – I shall have your little red fox at my mercy.'

'And what of that?'

'I intend to tease it until you ask my forgiveness.'

'Is that what you think? For the moment I have you helpless and in my power, Marie-Thérèse. I too can be cruel in love-making if I wish. I shall not let you escape into quick release this time – no, I am going to make you endure quite unedurable sensations. You will laugh and weep at the same time. Your eyes will pop out of their sockets. Your nipples will swell like ripe grapes. Do you hear me?'

'Yes!'

'Good, because there is more. Already that flat belly of yours is beginning to swell as if there were a balloon inside it. Do you feel what I am doing to you? I shall make you become so wet that your thighs will glisten all the way down to your knees.'

'Adrienne!'

'Pleasure to the point of pain – that is what you are beginning to experience. Your legs are wide apart – soon you will stretch them so wide that your bones will creak and you will open yourself so wide that my whole hand will be inside you. Are you ready for that?'

'Do it!' Marie-Thérèse cried aloud. 'Do it!'

ENGINE
OF
DESIRE

Alexis Arven

The marvellous Arven sisters! These are two seriously raunchy women, believe me. You should have seen them at the Nexus authors' dinner party. In matters sexual I've always advocated a little restraint (I'm sure you understand), but Alexis and Andrea don't know the meaning of the word. Suffice it to say that when I met them they were displaying all of the joyous, messy naughtiness that shines through in their writing – and I'll never again be able to contemplate profiteroles without blushing.

Alexis writes novels with contemporary settings, complicated plots, and from the point of view of her wonderfully erotic creation, the gorgeous Lalla Gamboge. The following extract from *Engine of Desire* is a fairly typical example of her style – frothy and yet powerful, like champagne!

Dirty Work is the second Lalla novel, but both books can be read separately.

We were all girls together. We were supposed to be at some session to be told about the current trends in sensual enhancement but with a combined yawn several of us sloped off and bought half a crate of champagne. Now we were lounging round in Helen's room vying for who could tell of the dirtiest experience. All the learning I've ever done at conferences comes this way, behind closed doors, informally as it were, friends talking to friends.

Helen sprawled on the bed, entitled to maximum comfort as it was her room we were in, while the rest of us slummocked around the floor or lay across the couple of chairs provided. Most of us had loosened our clothing and the air was thick with cigarette smoke.

'Ever had a queer?' asked Janey. She was little, my height or less and very small and slim with it. Her bony face was surmounted with black spiky hair, elfin cut, and she had huge eyes.

'I've had bisexuals a few times,' said Helen.

'No, a real out and out gay, men only,' insisted Janey.

'Obviously not.'

'I was real mates with this guy. I still am, come to that, but he is bent all the way down the road. He was happy enough to have women as friends but could no more think of them as sexual partners than you would think of snuggling down with next door's Alsatian. But we got drunk one time together and I persuaded him to let me try. I laid him on his back after I got his trousers off –' Janey hesitated.

'Go on,' I said, intrigued.

'It was hell getting him erect,' laughed Janey. 'We both had a go before he finally got it up in the air and he had to keep his eyes shut so he wouldn't think of me being female. I sucked him a bit but even then I think he missed the size and force of a man's mouth.'

Helen wriggled her skirt up round her hips. 'All this talk of sucking,' she sighed. 'I could do with a man whose mouth was well up on the Beaufort Scale right now.'

We laughed. We were all feeling randy with the dirty talk.

Janey went on. 'I plastered his cock with Vaseline so the friction wouldn't put him off.'

'But your fanny would be looser than a male arse which he was used to,' I objected.

'You'd think so,' said Janey. 'But he said men loosen up with regular use and anyway, it was just different.'

'I like buggery,' said Zara, an Amazon of a woman, slow of speech but very simple and direct with it. 'You do loosen up, more's the pity. I give my bum a rest now and again so it will go back to being nice and tight.' Having effectively silenced the rest of us, she subsided.

Janey said, 'So as we got to business I peeled off my lower half but I made sure I kept on my jumper so that any glimpse of my breasts wouldn't put him off. I knelt across him and very slowly I lowered myself onto his greasy pole.'

'What happened?' I asked.

'He screamed.'

'What?'

'He screamed. He said it hurt him. He couldn't stand it. And as he lost his erection immediately, that was that. I wondered if anyone else had tried and whether they came up with a different result.'

But no. Several of us, like Helen, had had a guy who went both ways but none of us had tried to make it with a full-blooded gay.

Caroline, a slim dark girl with very full lips, took her turn. 'I went for a guy who was into birch twigs,' she said.

'Not whips?' I asked, thinking of my uncle and Deirdre.

'No, just lovely flexible birch twigs with a nice whistle and snap in them. We used to go for these really long walks every Saturday and collect a fresh supply and then we would use them at night and on the following day.'

'Did you like being beaten?' asked Helen. 'Or rather, do you?'

'No. I beat him and that suited us both.'

'Why did you bother?' I asked. 'Or did it turn you on to beat him?'

Caroline considered. We had all promised absolute honesty before the hen session began. 'I liked it all right,' she said, 'though I was getting bored by the end and I haven't had a boyfriend since who's into it. But he was such a fabulous fuck afterwards that it was always worth it.'

'You must describe exactly what you did,' said Zara solemnly.

'A typical session began with him getting undressed. He had this beating ring but he didn't use it right away. I would then very lightly feather him with twigs, all

57

over to begin with and then I would begin to tease the flesh of his upper thighs and round his bottom and over his prick and balls.'

'He let you beat him on his prick?' asked Helen.

'I had to do it or he found it hard to get an erection. It was the stinging that woke up his desire, you see.'

I remembered having my bottom smacked and squirmed. God, I wanted a man.

'I would build up the pace on his legs and backside whilst he hopped about the room pretending he wanted to get away from me. He would lie on the floor at my feet and crawl, holding my ankles, pleading for me to stop but I would just thrash harder until he was all flushed red across his rear. He would put his hands over his head and stick his backside right up with his legs apart and I would beat in between, flicking his balls and inner thighs. When the weal started to come and the skin began to break he'd tell me he'd do anything for me, anything at all. Then I'd make him put on the ring.'

'What on earth was the ring?' asked Janey.

'It was just a big sheet of balsa wood with a hole cut in the middle. He would stand up and then bend right over forwards and grip his own ankles. I tied his wrists to his ankles so he couldn't get free even if he wanted to. Then I jammed the ring onto him so that the cheeks of his arse stuck through, all rosy red and inviting. I took off my clothes then and got fresh twigs. They don't last long if the guy is really into it, you know. Now I really belaboured him, as hard as I could and he would shout and yell, urging me on but pretending to hate it. He was only satisfied when his arse started to bleed. I would whip off the ring and untie him and he would get his thingy up into me whilst the pain behind was still intense. He would drive away at me as though he had a motor going and he was superb.'

'But you liked beating him?' Helen was insistent.

'I suppose it was funny. The pleading and begging sort of turned me on. The more they submit, the more you want to abuse. That's what they love. It was very sexy. Yes, I liked it. It got me going, I have to admit.'

'So what finished it between you?' I asked.

Caroline looked arch. 'I like other things too and he was a one-style guy. It was always the same. I got to miss the mouthwork and other sorts of foreplay that didn't interest him. So we parted company. But it was fun whilst it lasted and I can still work myself up remembering his glowing backside. It was like stoking a fire. You load the boiler on a steam train and by God it charges down the line. I got a lot of benefit from the heat.'

We all contemplated hot bottoms and I think we all had wet fannies.

'Lalla,' drawled Helen. 'Any contributions?'

'Nothing special,' I said. 'Nothing very kinky. But I used to have a fella who really liked to look.'

'All men like to look,' observed Zara.

'Sure. He just carried it a little further. Before we made love he would get me on my back and then get me up into a shoulder stand, putting my legs over his shoulders so I could relax. Then he would very carefully shave me because he found that hair impeded his vision. I found that very sexy. He would clean me off after shaving me and then tease apart my lips till he could see deep inside me. He would push my legs as far apart as they would go to split my fanny open and then he would shine a torch into me and just look. Mind you, it was a pretty special torch, more of a periscope, really. It contained its own internal lighting so he could slip the whole thing up inside my fanny, which was a nice feeling, needless to say, and see everything, my entire internal works, my mystery revealed. It gave him a big visual turn-on.'

'Did he think you kept teeth in there?' giggled Janey.

'The hell he did. He loved it so much he couldn't bear not to see what he could feel. What a terrific hard-on he could get, just looking. That's all he wanted to do, look and stroke for a bit.'

'Sounds nice,' said Janey.

'It was. After we had fucked he would get me like that again whilst I was full of him, get me up on my shoulders, I mean, with my legs over his shoulders. Then he would squeeze and work my pussy so that the foam of our love-making bubbled up and sucked and slurped at him. He loved me full of juice, his juice, and he liked to see it.'

'Did he drink?' Zara, ever the direct one, asked.

'Oh yes,' I said. 'He drank.'

'I went with a market gardener,' said Zara. 'Every week he fucked me with a different vegetable.'

'What?' we shouted, more or less in chorus.

Zara was imperturbable. 'So I got courgette-fucked, and I got screwed with a cucumber, I had a leek up my backside once and I have made it with an aubergine, even. A slim one, though.'

'What?' I said again, helpless with laughter.

'An egg-plant.'

'I know what an aubergine is.'

'Throw in onions and tomatoes and you'd have a ratatouille,' squealed Janey hysterically.

'Italian plum tomatoes are very nice, very squashable, but onions, no,' said Zara. 'As far as feeling goes, the squashy fruits are of course the best. But to look and admire meant other vegetables were better.'

'What looked best?' asked Helen.

'A head of celery with the bright green frondy end sticking out between my legs was very pretty. And to feel it so hard and big inside me was most sexy. But it is really too hard and too unyielding to frig properly with. If you skin a tomato first you can actually fuck through it which is nice. I have a Gamboge Champagne Shingle,' Zara added to me. 'It cleaned me up real nice afterwards. Inside me, I mean.'

'It's meant to be more than a douche,' I said drily.

'It is,' said Zara. 'I'm a greedy girl.'

'What about the gardener?' asked Caroline. 'I mean, was it a one-way thing like me birching my Nigel?'

'He liked a carrot up his arse whilst he rode me,' said Zara blandly. 'I liked the green plumes too, waving about as he went up and down, up and down.'

When we had recovered from this I turned to Helen.

'Your turn now,' I said and we all looked at her expectantly.

'Fill your glasses, girls,' she said, and we did. 'The best I can come up with,' she said slowly, taking time to drink deeply herself, 'is the old three in a bed.'

'Two men and you?' asked Zara.

'No. Me and a man and another woman. Say, does anyone mind if I shed some clothing?'

None of us cared a damn. Helen had long slinky limbs and she shed shirt, skirt and briefs. The plump upper half of her breasts gleamed above the black lace and she laid her long legs wide apart, indifferent to our inspection.

'All this talk of pussies,' she murmured. 'Mine is so damned hot it wants some air.'

'I think we all have hot pussies,' said Zara and she stripped her lower half as we all watched. She was very big, not fat, but wide-hipped and with a generous bush

61

of lush hair about her lower stomach. She brushed it aside and opened her legs and I saw her wet interior. She fanned herself indolently. 'That's better.'

I followed suit and they watched my golden crown revealed. When Caroline, who was also a dark girl, showed her pussy she was actually dripping slightly with all our dirty talk. Any man coming in right then wouldn't have stood much chance, I thought. Then little Janey undressed completely, her small sharp body very attractive with the most kissable nipples. Her fanny was tiny but it looked deep.

Zara reached over and mediatatively stroked one of Janey's breasts.

'Go on, Helen,' said Caroline.

'It was this way,' said Helen. 'I had been going with this man, I'll call him James, for some time and we had a good thing going between us. One night I was expecting him and I had dressed with some care so as to be ready. I had bought these fantastic corsets, red satin striped with loads of black frothing lace at the bust and thighs, and I had laced myself into them really tight. I had my boobs bulging right up, like this.' She pressed herself and showed us. She made the soft flesh bulge upwards till just the nipples were caught under the material of her bra. 'You know, one deep breath and I'd pop a boob. I was wearing stockings but no panties so there was a clear way through to my fanny if James wanted to take me with my stays on. Anyway, I was good and ready, my hair and face all fixed and beginning to get a bit wet with anticipation because James was a very good screw, a first-class lover, when the doorbell to my flat rang. I was expecting James but I am not a complete lulu so I slipped a robe on and checked through my spy-hole. To my amazement it was a completely strange woman, but by hell she was gorgeous. She was very dark. I found out later she was half-Jamaican. But at that moment I didn't know anything about her, having never seen her before, and keeping in mind my state of undress, I opened the door on the chain.

'"Hi," she says. "You must be Helen." I still didn't recognise her and she wasn't one you'd miss in a crowd. She had a great profusion of tumbling black curly hair all down her back and her dark eyes were set slant-wise on broad cheek bones over a flattened nose and a full rich mouth. She was a real exotic and despite her fairly polite words I could see she was hopping mad. "What if I am?" I said cautiously. "Let me in," she says. "I won't bite. Not you, at any rate." "Who might you be?" I asked. "We have friends in common," she said bitterly. "Let me in and let's talk about it."

'I let her in and took her into the sitting room. She looked at my robe, her eyes glittering. "You don't know me but you do know James," she said, "and by the look of you you are expecting him." I was flabbergasted but the implication was obvious and to cut a long story short James was playing with both of us and Yvette, as she was called, had suspected and had him followed and so tracked me down.

'My God, I'm the jealous type,' said Helen, 'as you can guess by my red hair. But Yvette was as bad if not worse than me. We sat there slagging him off for a while and then I thought of a way of revenging us on him and I put it to Yvette. She agreed, and not a moment too soon as the doorbell rang again. This time it was James. Yvette went into my bedroom and I shed my robe and admitted him.

'I spent some time getting him thoroughly worked up and getting him out of his trousers before I took him into the bedroom. He was real man, made big and strong, worth getting aroused about and by the time we went through my stays were unlaced and though I still had them on, my boobs were swinging free and James had a clear look at me from nipple to navel and below. We got on the bed and I made him lie on his back whilst I knelt astride him, high up his chest, and I frotted my wet pussy up and down across his chest fur whilst he played with my boobs.'

Helen had her fingers at her pussy as she told us all this. Zara was still stroking Janey's boobs though she was mostly watching Helen, and Caroline had moved up and inserted her fingers in Janey's fanny. Janey seemed quite happy at these attentions and I found that between watching Janey being touched up and watching Helen gently frig herself, I was close to coming myself.

'I put my hands behind my back,' Helen went on, 'and James felt his tool being taken and played with. After a while I brought my hands back in front of me and I knelt up a little and began to frig myself with James watching me. It was a while before he realised I hadn't let go of his cock. I saw his face change as he began to think about it. But I moved up across his face and begged him to suck me a little. He forgot what was puzzling him and nosed and licked and sucked up into me, his hands still up at my bosom and meanwhile he felt himself being sucked at the same time. Realisation came slowly but in the end it came. He hesitated. He stopped sucking me. He thought a bit. He brought his hands down. I could hear a good deal of slurping going on behind me and James was looking red and breathless. Then two dark hands appeared on my breasts from behind me.'

Helen stopped and grinned reminiscently to herself.

'What happened?' asked Janey. We were all hanging on Helen's every word.

'He let out this most godalmighty yell and I fell off sideways. Then he saw Yvette and yelled again. Then he shut up. We came up either side of him. Yvette was stripped to a camisole, nothing else on, and James looked from one of us to the other and back again. He sort of gulped and swallowed but he kept quiet to see which way we were going to play it. Well, Yvette fetched him the most enormous swipe across the face and he caught her wrist and looked nervously at me. I gave him a sweet smile. "OK, big boy," I said. "You think you can manage us both. So do it, stud. We're both waiting."'

'And did he?' demanded Zara.

Helen grinned happily. 'Oh yes. I said he was a real man. He got Yvette down on her back and he got her legs up and he dropped his cock right into her with me just beside them both in the bed as well. I watched them for a while but that seemed tame so I stuck my finger in the Vaseline pot and making sure I didn't break his rhythm, I got my finger up his backside as he fucked away at Yvette. As he came up off her he went back on me so my finger dug deep into him and he was pitted, wriggling, but unable to escape except by ramming once more into Yvette. But after a while I stopped. I realised he was trying to make Yvette come and then he was going to service me without a break. So I let him go and came round beside Yvette and began to work her breasts. I'd never got right into a woman's breasts before and Yvette was superb, very beautiful. She began to moan and thresh but James was holding her wrists as he fucked so she couldn't escape us. I lay right beside her so I could feel the shudder of her body as he slammed into her and I sucked one of her nipples with James just above me, watching me.

'We all felt Yvette come. She gave a great shuddering

65

moan and her body shook and her pelvis jerked up in a spasm of pleasure. Then she flopped back, trembling, and after a moment James withdrew. He still had an erection; he hadn't yet come. He fixed his eyes on me and then he climbed off the bed and went and washed himself. I stroked Yvette who was gradually calming down and at the same time I took a peek at what Lalla was talking about earlier. I gently drew Yvette's knees apart and looked at her pussy, foaming with her spunk. I intended to see what it was like full of James' spunk later on in the night. But for now it was good to see such a juicy girl and what she could do of her own accord.

'James came back and watched my fiddling with Yvette. Then he lay down beside her on his back and put an arm under her neck, drawing her head onto his shoulder. "Fuck me, Helen," he said and I got across him. I was wet from his mouthwork earlier on and watching him and Yvette had driven me crazy so it was no problem. I slid his erection into me, lowering myself with greedy slowness till I had the whole of him fat and swollen inside me. He was loaded with promise and tight against my walls, a delicious fullness. I love a good cock. I began to move up and down. For a while he just lay there meeting me with his hips but doing nothing else except to watch me the whole time. After a while, though, he brought up his free hand and began to fondle one of my breasts. Then Yvette, who was gradually coming to, raised a hand and she fondled my other breast. That was fabulous. In return I slid a free hand between Yvette's legs and slipped a couple of fingers into her moist interior and for a while that was all we did. But it couldn't last. James was too worked up having already fucked Yvette to climax. I was too worked up having seen what I had seen and feeling James' shaft strong and hard inside me as I moved.

Yvette's cunt was delicious as well, richly moist, fecund, musky. Utterly attractive. I knew already I wanted to suck that lady though I'd never done such a thing to a woman before. I started to come. I felt that heat, felt the wetness inside me and my breasts were flushing in my passion. James knew my body well and he was bringing himself up to match me. He began to drive really hard into me and I was shouting, I think. Then I felt as though I would burst. Stars were radiating everywhere. I was freaking out. I didn't so much come as explode and at the same time James finally let go and drove his spunk right up into the heart of me, again and again till his balls were empty. And then we took a break.'

We were all gasping. We all took a break though I told Helen she was going to have to finish the story. She laughed and said that was fine with her. She was enjoying it all over again just remembering it in so much detail. We refilled our glasses and at Helen's invitation we climbed up onto the bed with her and made ourselves comfortable. Long limb tangled with short. Silky skin slid against silky skin. I had shed my top half and someone's hand drifted across to feel my boobs. I shut my eyes and lay back and quested gently with my fingers. When I found something warm and wet and inviting, I went in. Meanwhile someone else's fingers found my fanny and I lay relaxed, my head on someone's thigh and smelling their musk close at hand, very happy, very comfortable.

Helen's low voice went on. 'Yvette and I washed James' cock and then alternately, red hair mixing with black across his belly, we sucked him back to life. I got him to take Yvette from behind, doggy fashion, and for a while I watched his beautiful smooth glistening rod power into her dark purple vulva. I would see her fanny

67

lips moving each way as he went in and out, see them cling and suck at his balls as he rode her, letting my hand go backwards and forward with his action, feeling their soft swing and feeling them fill and enlarge and become more firm as he got nearer to delivering his spunk. I went round to Yvette's head and offered her my fanny but I could sense her reluctance. For all that, she sucked me as James fucked her but I could feel her heart wasn't in it. James brought her to climax and came himself and again I enjoyed feeling her body as she shook and trembled in the moment of coming. Then I really took a look at her fanny, James and me side by side, staring down at her, dribbling and bubbling with what he had put into her and what she had made herself. It ran down her thighs. Her pussy hair was wet with it. I can't tell you how exciting it looked. Her slit was dark purple and round it she had coffee-coloured skin and jet-black fanny fur. The spunk was pale and frothy. It reminded me of black sweet stout, love-foaming at the head and rich dark excitement beneath. I pretended to wash her but I barely wiped any of it away. I still wanted to taste her and taste James in her at the same time. And that was what I did. I got my face between her legs. She was half asleep and not bothering much. It was salty like a man always is and yet rich and musky because it was a woman I was sucking. It was great. At first Yvette dozed but after a while she began to writhe and moan. I don't think she really liked it, me being a woman, but she couldn't resist what I was doing to her. And James adored watching the two of us at each other. After a bit he got tired of being on the sidelines and he knelt across Yvette's face and let his cock go into her mouth. That certainly was to her taste and she worked away at him with a will. I invaded her pussy with my tongue and

sucked her clitoris into erection. Then James got me to
turn round so I had my back to him, my backside just in
front of him stuck up in the air as I bent my head to
work on Yvette. Like this.'

Helen stirred up the whole erotic soup of us by
turning round and burying her face into the pillow. Her
knees were straddled, pulling the cheeks of her backside apart, and we all saw the delicate line of fine dark
red hair leading to her brown crinkled rear entrance.
Below, superbly clear to see was a crimson gash like
split fruit, ripely inviting and framed by springing dark
red curly hair. Helen turned her head sideways on the
pillow so she could continue her story but she stayed
breathtakingly exposed for us to see. I ached to separate
her lips and feel the hot clinging velvet within. The ache
was real in my groin. I wanted filling so much that it
hurt me to be empty. Much more of this and only the
biggest cock in the world with the longest staying power
was ever going to satisfy me.

'James fingered my pussy. You can, girls, if you
fancy it. He massaged my clit until I was squirming
with pleasure though I didn't stop what I was doing to
Yvette. It was too good and I didn't know if I'd ever get
another chance. I could feel the sides of her fanny start
to tremble and though she had come already twice that
night, I was determined to bring her off a third time if it
was possible.

'Meanwhile James took his cock out of Yvette's
mouth and slid it into my pussy.' As Helen said this,
before our fascinated eyes she dripped slightly down
one leg. Janey leant forward and licked it off Helen's
thigh. Then very gently she brought up her fingers and
held open Helen's cunt. It was oozing, a complex of
ribbed engorged flesh demanding attention.

'It was red hot from her attentions and slick as silk.

69

Suddenly all my fanny was full of hot needles of pleasure stabbing through me, radiating out till my hips were trembling.'

Janey put her thumb on Helen's clitoris and we all saw it grow stiff, a tiny soldier rampant for duty. Helen's voice had become thick and slightly hoarse.

'And then James nearly undid me. He slid a finger up my arse. It was all too much. I had Yvette's dark rich musk at my mouth. I had James' superb weapon turning my fanny into a vortex of pleasure, great hot thrills reaching right through me. I damn nearly came but I wanted it to last so I fought the impulse with all the strength I had. I didn't know it then but Yvette was playing with James's balls as they brushed across her face with each stroke into me.

'Then it was all over. My insides exploded again and my fanny gripped James so hard in my convulsions that he came too, driving into me until he was completely drained. Yvette said afterwards that it was a fantastic moment. We were both on top of her, of course, and she could see exactly what was going on and feel every vibration of our bodies. She saw James's shaft creaming with spunk, thrusting into me at his climax. Spunk dribbled from my fanny down onto her face. She found that really beautiful. It finally brought her off too. My mouth added to what she could see and feel and smell finally did the trick.'

Helen fell silent, a dreamy expression on her face as she recalled the experience. I opened my eyes and looked at her fanny. It was dripping juice. Just remembering the occasion had brought her off. I envied her. Had I had a man right then I would have turned him inside out in my frenzy.

'Some punishment,' said Caroline wryly. 'He obviously adored it.'

'Only because he was man enough,' said Helen smugly. 'Had he been any kind of a wimp he would have crawled away from us. He knew better than anyone that we were both demanding women and we only stayed mad at him until he pleased us so much.'

'You saw him again, many times, after this?' demanded Zara. She had a faint and very attractive foreign inflection in her speech.

'No, I'm sorry to say. For all she enjoyed it, Yvette didn't really like the idea of me being there much. Once the novelty had worn off and she was less excited, she didn't want a repeat. I got over my jealousy in the fun of the thing but she didn't and James had had such a good time that he no longer wanted one of us without the other. The whole thing collapsed and now I never see him.'

'What a waste,' said Janey meaningfully.

'James was great,' said Helen. 'Don't get me wrong. But if you look hard enough good men abound, men willing to do all sorts of things if a girl will let them. I wouldn't have missed that evening and night for anything, even though in the end it cost me James. I'm a girl who likes to experiment, who likes to try things out.'

'Is that right?' asked Zara. Her eyes were glinting and she leaned forward across the bed and very slowly put her face to Helen's proffered sex. Helen sighed and stirred slightly, pushing her hips to offer herself more invitingly. I saw Zara's long tongue come out and delicately intrude in Helen's vulva. Helen gave a luxurious groan and we all stared breathless as Zara's tongue stiffened and she penetrated Helen, withdrawing her tongue and moving it back in, slowly at first to give herself time to taste and savour Helen, but gradually increasing in speed.

Then Janey wriggled round to Zara's rear end. The big girl made no sign and Janey sifted through Zara's

71

thatch till she could see the big girl exposed as Helen had been. A long pale creamy slit was revealed; Janey lifted her small peaky face and buried it deeply in it. Zara gave a muffled snort and broke off what she was doing to give Helen's clitoris a vigorous suck. After a few minutes Helen reached round and drew Janey's hips towards her face. Her own tongue extended and she ran its tip between Janey's lips, separating them and exciting them till they flushed darker and engorged as Janey's blood ran passionately through her.

Caroline and I looked at each other and then drew slightly away from the three on the bed. They were utterly wrapped up in pleasuring each other, a pretty ring, and Caroline and I stood and watched for a while. Janey's body, completely nude, was thin and pale with a dark thatch of hair at her crotch and a black cap of hair on her head. Helen's body was warmer tinted, a glowing peach colour much freckled, and her long auburn hair fanned softly against Janey's pale thighs. Big Zara was dark with a tanned skin, though her vulva had been the palest of the three. She had a big frame, well muscled, and I guessed she liked sport. She looked healthy and gloriously strong. Her dark hair hid Helen's red-framed charms from view but as Janey had stopped nuzzling and starting licking, I could still see much of Zara's intimate details.

Caroline grinned ruefully at me and nodded towards the door. I wasn't in principle against the idea of demanding a place on the bed and having seen such lovely girls, I certainly lusted to feel their delicious ripeness. But the pain between my legs demanded harder treatment than a woman could give me right now. I wanted a man, the more virile and demanding the better. So I agreed with Caroline and hastily we dressed and let ourselves into the corridor.

72

WICKED

Andrea Arven

Andrea is the (slightly) more serious-minded of the Arven sisters. Her novels are less bubbly than Alexis's, but more speculative and hard-hitting. *Wicked*, her first book, is a futuristic, science fiction tale of computer crime and political chicanery. That may not sound very sexy, but I'm sure the extract I've chosen will convince you that science fiction can be erotic.

You don't have to know the plot: all you have to know is that Fiona Cambridge, brilliant, beautiful and bored, is one of the privileged aristocrats in the City. Having discovered the wild pleasures of dangerous sex among the underclass, she is even more dissatisfied with her husband Rollo. And she enlists her innocent maid Janine to help her spice up her life . . .

You can met Fee Cambridge again in Andrea's second book, *Wild*, or read about a sexual role-playing game that's played for the highest stakes in *The Reality Game*.

Fiona stood up, moving with lazy grace, somehow insulting, going across the room to her maid. Her high heels made the muscles in the backs of her calves taut and her buttocks moved seductively up and down in relation to each other. Standing up, her nakedness was more apparent, her bare-breastedness, her naked dome and naked arse emphasised by her suspenders, stockings and her two clothed companions.

'Are you done yet?' she asked. One leg relaxed with the knee bent, she stood close to Janine seated over her task. Rollo watched them from the dressing table.

'Just finished,' said Janine, heatsealing the final seam. Her eyes, on a level with Fiona's belly, slid up her mistress. Fiona moved back slightly and Janine stood up. She held the dress up for inspection.

Carefully Fiona stepped into it and Janine fastened the short tight skirt and smoothed it over Fiona's hips. Then she eased each strap into position and carefully teased the nipples through each of the holes she had just made.

'Just rub them a little,' said Fiona huskily. 'They'll get stiffer and it'll make it easier for you.'

Across the room Rollo licked his lips and light

gleamed on the tight skin over his cheekbone. Janine frotted her mistress's plummy nipples and they stood proud, dark and firm, through the dress.

'That's great,' said Fiona. 'Fix my hair now, baby. And I need plum-coloured earrings to match.'

Janine's eyes flicked up to meet Rollo's and down again. 'They need ghost cream,' she said. 'Then they'll glow in the dark.'

Fiona came over by Rollo and sat down in front of the mirror.

'You do it,' she said to Janine.

Rollo had propped himself half-sitting on the dressing table to one side of the mirror. Janine now went to the other side and picked up the tube of luminescing cream that Fiona used for her lips at night. She leant round in front of Fiona so that her hair swung in a heavy curtain across Fiona's knees.

Fiona noticed two things. The first one was how far gone in her adoration of Rollo Janine was, and how much the girl was enjoying this by-play even if she didn't quite realise what was going on. The second thing she noticed was that the wheat-fair hair took on Titian lights under the artificial lighting of the dressing table.

Janine's tongue came very slightly out from between her lips and she gripped it with her teeth as she concentrated. Carefully and slowly she ran the tube of cream round the dark aureoles of Fiona's breasts. She applied it thickly. Then she put the tube down and with one finger she began to massage the transparent cream into the flesh and the projecting nipple.

'You do one, Rollo,' said Fiona.

His blue eyes were very bright as he leant close to his wife, his arm brushing Janine's hair. He rubbed Fiona's nipple till it was covered with a film of cream.

76

Fiona saw a pulse flutter in his temple.

As she sat there, her husband at one breast and her maid at the other, with nothing but a stifled silence between them, the plan Fee had been struggling to formulate fell into place with smooth precision. She almost laughed out loud.

Janine stopped and drew back. She was flushed a pale delicate rose, a faint wash of colour that Fiona thought had nothing to do with the intimate contact with her body. It was the nearness of Rollo, the lion man, her master. Fiona reached up a hand and took Janine by the shoulder, pulling her gently down.

She touched the young girl's lips with her own. 'Thank you,' she murmured. 'You are very precious. I wouldn't be without you.'

Rollo's eyes flickered. Fiona began to purr with contentment.

She gave Rollo one last chance. Late that night she stopped him before he took his sleeping pill.

'I want to go down on you,' she whispered. He lay on the satin sheet quite naked and breathtakingly beautiful. His body was mature and arrogantly firm, his muscle tone excellent. He was a shapely man, wide at the shoulders and narrow at the hips. His manhood lolled back across one thigh.

'I'm almost asleep, Fee.'

She ignored this, turning round in the bed and taking his member in her mouth. For a moment she tasted heaven as it thickened between her lips and she began gently to tantalise it to full erection with little sucks and kisses.

'Fee,' said Rollo. She felt him go soft within her mouth. 'Give me a few days, huh? When the pressure eases, maybe.' He put a pill in his mouth. In a few minutes he was deeply asleep.

Fiona sat there considering him for a while. Then she got off the bed and went along the corridor to the maid's suite. She tapped on the door.

A sleepy voice called out and Fiona went into the room and on and through to the bedroom.

Janine was reading in bed.

Fiona went over to her and took the girl's hand in her own.

'It's me, Janine. I'm sorry to interrupt you. I want to show you something.'

'Now?' Janine sounded puzzled and alarmed.

'Come along to my bedroom. I've something to show you.'

She stood and obediently Janine climbed out of bed. She was wearing something in artificial silk with a cluster of pink frills that came to midthigh. It was liberally adorned with little teddy bears wearing pink bows. Her heavy hair was plaited into a single thick rope.

Fiona took her hand again and led her back along the corridor to the master bedroom. She took Janine in and led her to the bed.

The girl gasped as she looked down on the sleeping man.

'You told me you were a virgin today.'

'That's right. That's the truth.' Janine's voice was squeaky and her eyes were round as saucers.

'Have you ever felt a man?'

She didn't pretend not to understand. 'No,' she whispered.

'Touch Rollo. Go on. He won't wake.'

Still holding Janine's hand she guided it down onto her husband's sex. She lifted the soft silky shaft from where it nestled in its warm bed of fur and pushed it into Janine's hand, closing her fingers over it so that it was cradled in their nervous grasp.

'I know you've got the hots for him,' she said gently. 'That's OK. I do myself. But Sleeping Beauty here needs waking up. I don't mean that literally. I mean sexually. The prince needs a princess. You help me to arouse this guy and bring him back to sexual life and I'll double your salary and let you bite on his apple, too. You get me?'

'I, I don't know.' Janine held Rollo's prick as if it was a venomous snake. Yet she could not let it go.

'Put it this way. You are a virgin.'

'Yes.'

'You don't want to be.'

'No.' Janine was vehement.

'You fancy Rollo.'

'I can't help it, Mrs Cambridge. He's so gorgeous.'

'Yes, isn't he?' said Fiona dryly. 'Now, tell me. If you want to become fully a woman you need an experienced man, yes?'

'Oh, yes,' said Janine fervently.

'Well, despite his present supine state, Rollo is an experienced man. And he is attracted to you.'

'He is?' Janine startled eyes flew to Fiona's. 'Oh no. He couldn't be.' She was as pink as her nightwear.

'I knew tonight. So did you.'

Janine hung her head. She kept her hold of Rollo's cock, though.

'What turned him on was you fiddling with my body. You didn't mind that, did you? Touching me, I mean.'

Janine fixed her eyes on Rollo's balls relaxed at the base of his shaft. 'Actually, I liked it,' she mumbled. 'I think your body is fantastic. I wish mine was like it. It makes me feel really funny to do things to you.'

'I thought so.' Fiona's voice remained calm and she

masked the flare of triumph within her. 'Would you mind if I touched you?'

'I don't know. I've never thought . . .'

'Take your nightshirt thing off.'

Stiffly, Janine released Rollo and removed her nightshirt. She did not meet Fiona's eyes. She stood, miserable with embarrassment, her arms hanging at her sides.

Her body was warmly peach and slightly chubby, her breasts endearing and her stomach a rounded perfection. Crisp fair curls hid her sex. She was indescribably sweet.

'Run your hands down Rollo,' said Fiona after a moment. 'He won't wake. Sit on the bed.'

As if in a daze Janine obeyed. Tremulously she began to caress the sleeping man, growing bolder as he did not wake. She felt his chest and shoulders, she ran her hands lightly down his arms, and then she returned to his sex. She was fascinated by his heavy soft limpness. She bent over him, trying to see him better in the dim light, and her rope of hair hung heavily to one side, the end brushing his thigh.

Fiona took the weight of the hair in her hands and then began methodically to unplait it, shaking it loose and then drawing it over one shoulder so it spilled down Janine's back and tumbled about her lower shoulder and caressed her breast on that side. Now she could see the girl fingering her husband's sex. She began to stroke her naked back.

'Kiss him, if you like,' she said softly.

Janine bent her head and touched dry lips to Rollo's chest.

'Kiss his manhood,' whispered Fiona. Her breath stirred the hair by Janine's ear.

She felt Janine shudder. Her head drooped, as if heavy, and with her pale gold hair spilling all around she brushed her lips against the silken sheath of Rollo's golden shaft.

He sighed and stirred very slightly.

Janine held herself stiff, bent over him, her bottom slightly lifted, trembling. Fiona ran her hands under the firm sweetness of her youthful buttocks.

'Kiss him,' she murmured.

Janine whimpered in her throat, opened her mouth and kissed Rollo, tasting him with her tongue. As she did so, Fiona inserted her fingers in the opened cleft between her bottom cheeks and ran her fingers lightly along it till she felt the dampness of sexual opening and the soft brush of intimate hair.

'Kiss him,' she said, her own hand trembling as one finger sought for and found Janine's tiny member. She caressed it with a mothlike touch.

Janine lifted Rollo's prick and put it into her mouth. She sucked lightly, her eyes shut, as Fiona probed delicately below her.

'There's a fire burning in you, sweetheart,' said Fiona. 'Let me help you with it.'

Janine released Rollo and laid her burning forehead gently on his cool chest. She gave a small stifled sob.

'Lie down beside him on the bed.'

Her head came up. 'May I?' she pleaded.

'Come on. On your back.'

Janine's face glowed as she moved carefully around the bed and lay beside Rollo, allowing her body to touch his in as many places as possible. Her expression was beatific.

'Relax now and open your legs.'

'Oh, please. I mean . . .'

'Don't be scared. I just have to check you really are a virgin and you aren't having me on before we get too deep into this thing.'

81

With a nervous eagerness Janine let her legs come up and fall apart. Very carefully Fiona inserted a finger into the extreme end of Janine's little pussy. The girl stiffened and became rigid, her eyes squeezed shut. Fiona went a short way into the tight small orifice, and then smiled and withdrew her finger. She had felt the obstruction. She bent over Janine and kissed her on the lips.

'You angel. Nothing but the truth. Your little fanny is divine. I envy Rollo his forthcoming pleasure.'

Janine blushed. 'What do you mean?'

'Why, what do you think I mean? Rollo is going to have your sweet body, if you want him to.'

'If I want him to? Oh, Mrs Cambridge, it's my dream. But he doesn't want anyone like me. He has you.'

'You undervalue yourself and what you have to offer, sweetie. You have something rare and precious. The first time you give yourself to a man matters. It needs to be good and it needs to be important to him. I think you will be, for Rollo. You are young, beautiful and untried, and you adore him. What man could ask for more?'

As she spoke, Fiona absently ran a hand over Janine's breast. She continued to stroke her whilst the tension went out of her young body.

'You want to touch him some more?'

'Please.'

'Go ahead. May I play with you a little while you do?'

'If you'd like to,' whispered Janine.

She turned to the sleeping man and for a long moment she worshipped him with her eyes. Then she ran her hands over him, coming back to his sex, lifting it and feeling it and finally cupping his balls and weighing them in her small palm.

Whilst she did so, Fiona aroused her own nipples and then brushed them against Janine's smooth skin, stroking Janine on her breast and back.

Then she thought she had maybe pushed things far enough for one evening. She kissed Janine on the shoulder.

'That's enough for tonight now. You run along and think things over. And take tomorrow off, so you can catch up on your sleep.'

Janine turned round, her young breasts swinging and brushing against Fiona's.

'Thank you,' she whispered, with shining eyes. 'It's been fantastic. I hope you don't change your mind.'

'You might change yours,' said Fiona, veiling her eyes.

'No.' Janine was suddenly fierce. She reached up her face and kissed Fiona hard on the lips. Fee was astonished and for a moment didn't react. Then her mouth opened and she felt Janine's tongue enter. Her hands came up and she clasped the girl's shoulders and for a moment the two women clung together, kissing with sensual abandon.

Janine picked up her nightshirt and fled.

For a long moment after Janine was gone Fiona stared down at her sleeping husband. She remembered the sight of those young eager hands and lips about his loins. She thought of Janine's freshness and simplicity and air of worship. Her mouth twisted wryly and she was visited by a powerful desire to slap Rollo hard and beat him with her fists.

The Valentine had arrived that day. Rollo had laughed, put it to one side and forgotten about it.

Fiona let three days and nights go by and then she asked

Janine if she might come to her room that night. Janine was agreeable. Indeed, she was eager.

During those three days Fiona had seen the eyes following Rollo about the apartment upon the occasions that they were in the same room, which was not very often. During the three nights, Rollo had continued to sleep the sleep of death.

When Fiona came along the corridor that night she hardly knew herself what she was doing. She was accustomed to being honest with herself and she knew that this played no part in the revitalisation of her husband. She was sure that had Rollo continued to satisfy her as he once had done, she would never have felt driven to explore the peculiar byways of sexual practice that now enticed her. She had begun by trying to find some sort of satisfaction for herself, some acknowledgement that she could arouse and satisfy men. That had led her out into the night where she had knelt before strange men and taken their essence into herself, herself anonymous and of the night. She had told herself that this was not adultery. Her body remained inviolate whilst she indulged her strange fierce passion to taste a man in his orgasm.

Yet it had not been enough.

She yearned for danger. A madness had come over her and her safe comfortable life had become a prison that she broke out of. The pirates were figures of great romance in her world, the subject of countless romantic adventures on the Screen, but the reality was quite different.

It was darker, dirtier, fiercer, more dangerous than she could ever have imagined. It pleased her that she knew the truth. It pleased her as she moved, beautiful, aloof and fasionable, through her elegant world that she knew the truth and they did not. As her fingers felt fine fabrics, as she ate luxurious food, as she enjoyed each and every refinement of her privileged life, part of her was on the ground rutting with Will, her cheek pressed in the dirt and his cock hard and arrogant shafting her from the rear in the hot public gaze.

She could remember the texture of his wiry chest, muscled under its leather straps. She could remember the sheen of firelight on his greasy breeks, how the bulges of his manhood were revealed. She could remember the fiery sweetness of his mouth and the rich musk of his groin. His skin was scarred and pitted. One eye was blind. Tattered elf-locks hung like Medusa's snakes from his head.

She longed to rake him with her nails and feel his calloused hands mastering her body. She felt none of the soft fawnlike devotion that made Janine melt and blush every time she saw Rollo. Instead she felt the fierce longing to abase herself, debase herself, and be purified by lust in the savage domination of her violent lover.

Even as these feelings washed through her, some kernel of good sense, a latent desire for self-protection, knew that she could play with fire and risk a little burning, but really she had too much to lose. Even as the danger attracted her, so she must plan to replace it with something new, something spicy, something not quite so frightening.

Diana, big, warm and womanly. Janine, sweet, girlish and infinitely appealing.

These were new fields to explore, new sensations to experience. Rollo's lack of interest had launched her on a strange journey and she would not shrink from what she discovered along the way.

She tapped on the door to Janine's suite and entered it.

Her welcome dispelled any qualms of conscience she might have regarding her interference in the girl's sexual development. Janine was a ripe fruit waiting to be plucked, crushed, split and sucked. Let Rollo sample her ruptured sweet moistness, if he would. Far better it was him that some other man not appreciating the prize he had, or too cold-hearted to reward Janine's warmth and eagerness with a like enthusiasm. As Janine's arms went round her in welcome, Fiona reflected that there was plenty for them all.

Janine kissed her mistress with saucy confidence. Their tongues met and mixed and for a while they did nothing except taste one another and explore mouth to mouth.

Fiona drew back at last and slipped off her robe. In her turn Janine took off her pastel slip with red love hearts all over it, and the two women were nude together.

There was something lovely in their bodies being essentially the same shape, yet such a variation on a theme. Janine took one of Fiona's breasts in her hands and began to examine it in frank detail, feeling its weight and shape, its undercurve and long, elastic nipple. In her turn Fiona took one of Janine's breasts in her hands. It was smaller and firmer than her own, the muscles more springy with youth. She touched her nipple with Janine's and the girl laughed and they were content to play like this for a while.

Then Fiona dropped her dark head and began to suck Janine's nipple.

'That's so good,' whispered Janine.

Fiona treated both breasts alike and submitted to the same caress from Janine.

'Suck harder,' she ordered gently.

'Doesn't it hurt when I do it that hard?'

'I like my baths stinging, my food spicy and my sucking firm. It's all a matter of taste. As you get older, you like your experience to be more intense. I'm twice your age, Janine.'

Then Fiona suggested they varied what they did a little. 'I want to play between your legs,' she said. Her eyes were slitted as she watched Janine, waiting for her response. Each time she was bolder, coarser with the girl, she watched to see if Janine recoiled.

Not yet.

'Won't it hurt me?' Janine was wide-eyed and curious but she certainly was not disgusted.

'I'll leave your fanny alone. The inside of it, I mean. That's for Rollo and I don't intend to spoil what you are going to offer to him.'

Janine blushed and her eyes dropped. Fiona could see that she loved to hear of her impending violation. Her breasts rose and fell in her delicious agitation.

'You have a lot more sensory equipment down there than what's inside you, sweetie.' Fiona's voice was low and husky. 'Why don't we find out about it?'

Janine lay back, her pupils dilated and her eyebrows somewhere up at the top of her forehead. There was no way Fee was going to admit that she herself was on new territory. Moreover, her longing to feel Janine's private and personal body was now so powerful that if she had been resisted, she might have boxed the girl's ears and told her not to be so stupid and bourgeois. Janine's malleability was useful, but not in itself a turn-on for her. Fiona wanted a female body to satiate her lust. She had no requirement for devotion.

She found she was trembling as Janine obligingly opened her legs. She tried not to let her mounting excitement show. She must remember to exercise restraint and not get carried away and frighten the girl.

Fleetingly, as the stunning moist sweetness of Janine's sex was revealed to her greedy eyes, she remembered Will, dark and powerful and lacking in all restraint. Ah – that was what it should be like between two lovers. It should be fierce and abandoned, an animal coupling with the added savour of human intelligence.

But for now, there was the sweet hors d'oeuvre of this little untried female organ laid out for her delectation, her secret pleasure. The girl was clay in her hands.

Fiona ran her hands up inside Janine's thighs and felt them quiver. They were faintly dusted with soft hairs, thickening to make the ripe curly mat that framed her pussy. Fiona felt and tickled the soft hair.

'Do you like that?' she murmured.

'I feel strange inside.'

Fiona caught her lower lip between her teeth. As gently as she might separate two leaves of gold foil, she picked apart the slightly sticky labia and for the first time caught the faint, sweet new mown hay smell of Janine's open sex. It quivered before her eyes and she did not know whether Janine moved or her own vision was blurring in her intense excitement. She felt a pulse between her own legs and she knew sharply how she would love to do what she was doing whilst a man shafted her and fucked her own urgent cunt. Her lips curled into a smile at the thought. She ran her fingers round the entrance to Janine's body and imagined how, if she had a penis, she would thrust the big hard thing in, riving the reluctant flesh and making it fit to be used, to be enjoyed and in its turn to enjoy.

She ran her fingers up and down the lovely place, wetting them with her mouth to make them slide more easily, and gently pressing them against the little entrance.

She licked them again, her pointed tongue dark against the bright rosy colour of Janine's sexual parts, and then she uncloaked Janine's clitoris and began to frot the tiny soldier.

'What's that?' gasped Janine.

'Like it?'

'It's incredible.'

'Have you never played with yourself down here?'

'No, never. Oh,' shrieked Janine. 'That's so good.'

Fiona suddenly bent her dark head and put her tongue where her fingers had been. Janine gasped and went rigid. Then her breath hissed as her back arched, Fiona's hair warm between her thighs.

Fee had never in her life tasted anything so wild and sweet and ambrosial as the virgin musk of Janine's untried fanny. She was a woman who adored the powerful thick taste of a man in climax, it feeding her imagination and her sexual drive in equal parts. But Janine was like the wild rose hip, tangy-sweet and good. Indeed, the girl was a briar-rose, simple and naive and natural, not yet bent to a man's hand.

She sucked the tiny clitoris and vibrated her tongue against it and then closed her mouth over Janine's entrance and began to suck hard. It was a moment before she realised she might break the fragile membrane in her greediness, and she tore her mouth away from the virgin wine lest she would spoil things for Rollo, coming after her to sample this place.

It was hard not to laugh out loud.

She released the girl and sat up. Janine was panting, her pretty little-girl breasts heaving.

'Did you like that?' asked Fiona. Her voice was low and mellow, her tones honied.

'It embarrasses me,' said Janine. 'Your mouth, down there.'

'Do you want to do it to me?'

'Yes.'

The slight note of reluctance in Janine's voice pleased Fiona. She worked her way on to the bed and lay back, her legs drifting apart.

She closed her eyes. 'Now, Janine, you must do just what you want to do. Don't be afraid of anything. Explore all you want. Know no boundary. Go inside me, if you want. You have the freedom to do anything. You can't hurt me or offend me or embarrass me. I long for you to know what you want to know, child. It is a privilege for me to help you overcome your ignorance and your fears.' Fiona's voice was like thick cream, richly inviting, caressing, warm and permissive.

First Janine laid a hesitant and slightly moist palm over Fiona's depilated mount, as Fee had known she would. Janine fingered it and palmed it and laid her cheek on its satin smoothness. She ran her tongue over it and dried it with her hair. Then she slid her fingers on down into the dark exciting wet crevice below the gleaming magnolia dome.

Fee kept her eyes shut. The shaking fingers were naive as they explored through her long weaving walls of erotic flesh, but they were fresh and delicious and she felt transported with pleasure. This business with women was wonderful, yet she was assured of her own heterosexuality at the same time, for even as Janine pried into her most intimate orifice, even as the girl's fingers slid within her hot, succulent, experienced cunt, she dreamed of having a man's cock at this very moment deep in her throat that she might suck it as her pussy was invaded.

Her fantasy was rudely broken by Janine withdrawing and beginning to cry.

'What is it?' asked Fiona, injecting concern into her

voice to overlay the impatience at the interruption.

'I knew there was something wrong with me. You are so large. I haven't played with myself, honestly Mrs Cambridge, but of course I have felt myself when I'm dealing with, you know . . .'

'Yes. But what's wrong?'

'I'm too small. I'm not normal. No wonder I am so afraid of men. Mr Cambridge will laugh at me if he ever tries to get inside me and he'll think I am just stupid and not properly made.'

She was really crying now. Fiona cast about in her mind for some way of convincing Janine of her normality.

'Listen to me,' she commanded sharply. Janine sniffed and her shoulders shook. Her eyes were already reddened and she looked pathetic as a lost puppy-dog.

'I'll prove you are perfect,' said Fee. 'Just give me a moment.'

Janine stared at her doggily, hope in her damp eyes as she cast round the room. Then she found what she was looking for and she came back to the bed. She held in one hand a slim penlight torch, maybe three-quarters of an inch in diameter.

She held it up before the puzzled girl. The tear-streaks down her face gave her a woeful appearance. Fee smiled reassuringly.

'You know what homosexual men get up to,' she said in a pleasant brisk voice.

Janine writhed. 'Yes. Sort of.'

'What orifices they use, not having a woman's fanny.'

'Well, as far as I know, their mouths and, er, their bottoms,' said Janine. She giggled uncomfortably.

'Right. Now trust me. I won't hurt you but you will be surprised and you might not like it. Turn round and

91

go on your hands and knees.'

Obedient to the last, Janine did so. Fiona found some cream and greased the penlight.

'Relax, now,' she said.

She nuzzled the thin greasy tube at Janine's trembling bottom. With the finger of one hand she tried to hold open the tight pucker of flesh as she attempted to slip the penlight inside. She pushed and Janine squeaked with horror. The very end, the narrowest part, had penetrated Janine and now the penlight projected from between her quivering buttocks.

Fiona resisted a surprising urge to thrust the thing brutally in.

'Do you want me to push it any further in?' she asked.

'No,' said a muffled voice. 'I don't like it.'

Fiona took one last regretful look at the instrument held in place by Janine's locked bottom, shaking slightly as the girl herself shook, and removed it.

Janine turned round, her face crimson.

'Look,' said Fee. 'That's how far it went in.' She showed Janine where the thickish cream was pushed back and wiped off by the restriction of the girl's tight valve.

Fee smiled. 'You see, when a man is homosexual, he likes to be penetrated this way. His rear gets softer and looser and he learns to admit even the gross inflamed penis of his male lover. An erect penis can be a very thick long thing, yet he takes it greedily up into himself because that's what turns him on. Even heterosexual men like a finger invading their backside. Well, many of them do. They find it sexy and stimulating if a woman puts a finger up their backside and moves it about a little. Women like it, too. I do. Feel me. Remember, I like it.'

She turned over and presented her rear to Janine. She knew her own puckered skin was dark like her nipples and that a wisp of hair still remained in the crevice between her cheeks.

She felt the hard penlight begin its violation of her rear. Janine pushed and Fiona relaxed her muscles and felt the lovely intrusion, the stretch of wall as it expanded to admit the invader.

She clamped her muscles tightly. Janine gasped and let go. Now it was Janine's turn to see the torch trembling, held by muscle power, projecting absurdly outwards.

Fee rolled on to her side with the penlight still sticking out of her arse. She rubbed it slightly on the bed so that it thrust a little further in. She tingled delightfully within.

'I'm tight,' she said. 'I'm not as tight as you, though. I like to be entered like this. I like a finger inside me. Rollo's finger,' she added slyly. 'He likes it, too. He likes doing it to me and me doing it to him. And because I occasionally do this, have this done to me, I am looser. I can accommodate the invasion. My backside has expanded and grown used to being entered. And that is exactly what will happen with that sweet little unused fanny of yours. It is made to receive an erect penis, full of lovely expanding flesh that will fit all sizes and lengths and give a man pleasure whether he is big or small. That little cunt of yours,' Fiona chose the word deliberately, 'will cling to his cock and he will love it. You begin small and tight but you get bigger and more elastic. Once your membrane is broken by Rollo, you will hunger for big sex. There is nothing abnormal about you, Janine. I promise.'

Janine sat for a while, considering. Fee felt she had been rather clever and was conscious of smugness. She slipped the penlight out of her rear.

Janine peeped up shyly from under her hair. 'I've been silly, haven't I?' she said.

'Go down on me, sweetheart,' said Fiona huskily. She couldn't wait any longer.

That first time a woman laid her mouth against her intimate flesh and kissed her and sucked her juices. Fiona would never forget. Janine knew little of what pleased, but she was aroused herself and going quite well on instinct. She had none of the knowledgeable skills of Rollo and nor had she the ferocious expertise of the pirate, but she had a quality that all Fiona's male lovers had lacked, something indefinable, something that could only have existed between two women.

It was strange, because Fiona was not adulterous by nature. She would have remained satisfied with Rollo had he continued their early vigorous and innovative sexual life. There had been men in her life before Rollo but they were pale and insignificant besides the fires of her passion for and with him.

The pirate had been her first infidelity. Janine was her second. She lay dazed with pleasure as Janine's tongue ran up and down the length of her fanny, thrusting carefully between the fleshy lobes and occasionally penetrating the outer reaches of her pussy.

Then the two of them came together and held each other sleepily in their arms. They kissed fondly. Fiona was surprised at the real affection she was beginning to feel.

'Have you been happy tonight?' she asked.

'Yes, I have, Mrs Cambridge.'

'Do you want to do this again?'

'Yes, I do.'

'I'll make sure you get Rollo, I promise.'

'Won't you be jealous?'

94

'That's not your problem. I don't mind if he synchs with you. You deserve it. I'm very fond of you.'

Janine sighed, blurry with sleep. Fiona kissed her one last time and slid from the bed.

The plan was going well.

The Chronicles of Lidir

THE
SLAVE
OF
LIDIR

A Saga of Erotic Domination

Aran Ashe

The four books known as The Chronicles of Lidir are, individually and together, among the most popular novels that Nexus has published.

Aran Ashe is a mysterious, reclusive author. But no-one else can capture in words the delightful humiliations, the outraged innocence, the lingering torments and slow-burning pleasures of enforced sexuality.

The heroine of the Lidir books is Anya, a copper-haired, voluptuous peasant girl in a medieval world whose Princes and nobles devote themselves to licker-ishness and perversity. Although brave and resource-ful, she escapes from one predicament only to fall into another. And her shame as she undergoes the ritual pleasurings and exquisite punishments is compounded by an even greater disgrace: she can't help loving every lingering minute of even the most uncomfortable situation.

I know just how she feels. The Lidir books are my favourite late-night reading!

The Chronicles of Lidir are: *The Slave of Lidir, The Dungeons of Lidir, The Forest of Bondage*, and *Pleasure Island*. The next Aran Ashe novel will be entitled *Choosing Lovers for Justine*.

From her vantage point, Anya looked out across the sunlit snow-clad countryside of Lidir – the black-latticed, blue-white forests and the pure white distant hills, the pale blue skyline and the weak November sun, which softly struck through Ildren's window and bathed Anya's skin in a gentle warmth and turned her flesh to gold. A golden woman, mounted on a horse, a wooden horse with a padded back – a solid horse that did not move.

The bondslave had found this view to be preferable to the one which would have confronted her if she had chosen to turn her head the other way and look again into the room, Ildren's sitting-room, which, although of quite innocent aspect in most respects – with that fur-strewn, comfortable-looking couch by the fire, for example – now had one or two additional features which were a cause for mild concern. There were a number of items on the table – a bowl and jug, some fruit, rope, pieces of material, lengths of polished wood of a type which had looked suspiciously familiar to the slave, and several other implements which Anya did not even recognise. But it was an object sitting over in the corner which had caused by far the greatest consternation in the slave. It had seemed to be a small square-based tapering tower built of wood, and it was about half as tall as Anya; it sat solidly on the floor; at the top, crowning this strange device, was a smooth and very thick vertical wooden cylinder with a rounded crest and a flared-out base. Worse yet, from one of the hooks in the sitting-room ceiling, a length of rope was dangling down towards the thing. Anya had found herself imagining too many frightening possibilities; her gaze had been drawn back, time after time, to this sinister device, as if its presence had cast a very evil spell, so she preferred instead to stare the other way, out of Ildren's window. Her plight was quite worrying enough, without her thinking about that thing.

Ildren had kept her slave in bed from early dawn till late into the morning, bestowing long and loving womanly pleasure upon this very special creature. And then at last she had allowed her slave to break her fast at Ildren's table, with bread, a mug of milk, dried apple and nuts, of which the slave had partaken under Ildren's constant, loving attentions, sampling morsels of sustenance which Ildren had fed to her in strange and intricate ways. And when at last the slave had suffered adequate refreshment, then Ildren had taken time to stem her unwarranted fears about the wooden beast, and now was taking more time yet to mount the slave in exactly the right position. She had taken care to position first the Horse, and then the slave, in such a way that the slave could admire the view, so Ildren would not be distracted during these protracted and precise – yet necessary – adjustments by constant fidgeting from a slave who might not fully appreciate the virtues of precision, and might perhaps be anxious now for action.

'My dearest, I am almost finished,' Ildren reassured the bondslave. 'Just one more tiny wee adjustment.'

Ildren pinched Anya's cheek in a very playful manner, and pouted. 'You see . . . this has not been so bad as you expected.'

Anya lay on her front, along the padded beam; her wrists were fastened underneath, but Ildren had carefully drawn them forwards along the underside of the bar before finally securing them, so that Anya's breasts, now unencumbered by proximity to her elbows, were pressed very firmly to the sides, and Anya's acorns pointed up and outwards; Ildren therefore merely had to squat beside her – at whichever side she happened to be – to take her suck, without, for example, first having to reach underneath to collect the nipple on her tongue in an unduly complex manoeuvre. Anya's legs at present dangled downwards from the end of the beam; her head was almost in the centre of the Horse, and her body formed a right-angle, as if, having walked up to the end of the beam, she had simply bent over and along it – except for the facts that her hands were tied, and her feet did not touch the floor. And this was where Ildren's little adjustment was required.

The Taskmistress produced a long band of pure green silk, about a handsbreadth wide, and laid it across Anya's back, above her golden chain, so the ends hung down to either side. Then she lifted each of Anya's legs in turn and bent it, feeding the band down the inside of the thigh and underneath the crook of the knee, then around the outside and up again across her back. Finally, Ildren fastened the ends by means of a slip knot. As she pulled it tight, Anya's knees were lifted till they nearly touched her breasts, and her thighs moved upwards towards the horizontal. Anya's bottom, with that black-lipped pouch slung so invitingly below it, projected out beyond the beam. And with each tightening of the knot, the pouch pushed out more prominently, like a large and succulent ripe black plum. Ildren could scarcely dare to look upon that sweet round juicy fruit – the sight of it sent licking shivers up her body.

Anya was apprehensive about the tightness of this trussing, which left her feeling very exposed indeed.

The Taskmistress held in front of Anya a wooden bowl of water; in her other hand she held a cloth. 'Your Taskmistress will wash you now . . . refresh you after your sweet exertions.' The water smelled of cloves. Ildren placed the bowl on Anya's back, immersed the cloth, then squeezed it. Any felt the weighted bowl of liquid sway against her; the tinkling droplets, falling back, sent a shiver down her spine. The freezing wetness of the cloth touched her in her armpit; the water felt like melted ice and made her jerk; the bowl heaved, the liquid swelled, and Anya knew – in that cruelly endless second before it finally happened – that the water would well over. She had to gasp for breath; it cut her like a freezing knife across her back, then trickled into the furrow of her spine.

'I see you find its coolness suitably uplifting. But my dear, you must keep still.' Anya had to grit her teeth.

The Taskmistress washed downwards and over the first of Anya's breasts, then moving round, she attended to the other, but this time only squeezed the cloth out lightly before moulding it around the breast, exactly to its swollen form, so the acorn pointed through it. The icy coldness there took Anya's breath away, but the Taskmistress held it still in place until the dripping had subsided. Ildren then removed the cloth and pressed the backs of her fingers against the frozen breast. 'Mmm . . .' she said. 'Your bosom is so tight and hard – like a marble sculpture.' Ildren moved around and stood at Anya's bottom. Anya closed her

eyes so very tight and tensed up every muscle, and then
the bowl was lifted from her back and placed above her
bottom, at the tail of Anya's spine. It balanced very
uncertainly.

'Do not jerk, my darling, for if it should tip, I fear it
might fully overturn.' Ildren's tone suggested that she
wanted this to happen, so Anya kept as still as she was
able, against her shaking and her shivers. She heard the
Taskmistress dip and squeeze the cloth again. She bit
her lip. 'Now, we will refresh you in that very special
place . . .' Anya waited for the icy touch; it did not
come. At last, she opened her eyes – and jumped. Ildren
was in front of her. And then she cried out with the
shock of coldness, as the bowl overflowed and the
splash of water dribbled down her groove. Ildren,
smiling very sweetly, merely shook her finger. 'Now,
don't say I didn't warn you. You must keep very still.'
And then she moved up very close to Anya's face. Anya
tried to pull away, for she had noticed, with anxiety,
that the pupils of Ildren's eyes had shrunk to tiny
points.

'Do you know, I think you moved deliberately . . .
you very naughty thing!' Ildren said, and tugged at
Anya's ear. Even though such a thing quite clearly was
not true, still Anya's neck and cheeks were burning
with embarrassment. This woman took delight in
trying to degrade her. 'If you like, I can pour it down
that sweet and tender parting – if that would bring you
pleasure. No? But my dear, you should never be
ashamed to take pleasure, if you wish it, in those perverse little ways,' she gloated, making Anya even more
ashamed than ever. Ildren pulled away, and held up the
cloth; she stretched it to a very tight straight edge. 'And
now,' she whispered, 'we will draw this cool delight up
and down your parting – but very lightly. Would you

105

like that – that tickling in that very special, very blackened place? Hmm?' Anya looked away. 'Does your blackness like such naughtiness and tickling?'

Anya's cheeks were burning bright; she hated this woman's words, but even more than that, she hated what those suggestive words were doing to her body, against her will, forcing that delicious sinking feeling deep within her belly. The Taskmistress tightened the silken knot across Anya's back, which lifted her thighs and concentrated the pressure there between her legs, and spread her buttocks even tighter, and then Ildren's fingertip seduced the slave, by stroking gently back and forth across the very tip of Anya's spine. 'There . . . does that feel nice? Now push that bottom out . . . pout that tiny mouth . . . Mmmm, that looks so delicious.'

Now Ildren was back again at Anya's head, kissing her fully on the lips, and teasing at her acorns. The Taskmistress was shaking. 'You sweet and luscious thing,' she said. 'Now place your head like this – lie upon your cheeck, and turn a little, like this – good – so I may look upon your face whilst I tickle you there . . .'

From the corner of her eye, Anya could see the Taskmistress standing behind her – she could see her place the cloth into the bowl to cool it once again, then wring it very deliberately, then hold it up and draw it out very tightly, and then Anya had to watch it disappear from view. 'Now you shall pout for me – turn your face and pout your lips and . . .' Ildren's very deep and husky voice had momentarily failed her, 'and pout that bottom . . . now.' And then a sweetly rasping line of ice was drawn across Anya's tender rim of pushed-out flesh; it vibrated up inside her; it made her suck her breath in sharply. The gentle rasping stopped. 'Your lips must remain at all times pouted – I wish to look upon your lewdness, as I brush you in your puck-

106

ering. Now, wet your lips and do it very nicely. Good
. . . and push that other little mouth out very rudely.'
The bowstring pulled across again, and Anya's hips and
belly quaked with pure sweet delecation; it felt as if a
silken thread of pleasure, rolled up inside her body, was
being drawn very slowly out of Anya's bottom. 'My
dear – you naughty thing – your bottom is pulsating. I
shall smack it. No, keep still, or you shall spill the bowl.
I shall smack it – for its rudeness – with my finger.'

Ildren was well aware that this style of discipline was
so important for a slave, for it served, not as a punishment – though certainly it could constitute an
embarrassment for any slave to have to suffer such
chastisement. No, it was designed by Ildren specifically
to excite a slave to the ways of lustful sensuality and, in
this respect, Ildren had never known this peculiarly
intimate lash to fail.

Ildren dipped her middle finger in the bowl of water,
saying, 'Pout that secret mouth for me . . . Do not be so
shy. Your secret mouth will love it.' Anya was so
ashamed at what the Taskmistress was forcing her to
do, but she was also frightened that Ildren would want
to hurt her there, in that very tender place. Now Ildren
sounded very much more firm. 'I expect to be obeyed,'
she growled. 'Do it now!' Anya hated and despised this
woman for making her do these things with such
abasement. 'That is better. Push out further. And now,
for your stubbornness, you shall count for me the
measure of your chastisement.' The Taskmistress forced Anya to count out loud her smacks. Anya had to
fight back the tears of shame. The cold wet pad of
Ildren's finger struck her with a sudden snap, precisely
in that spot; it made her jerk; her bottom mouth contracted. Ildren waited patiently, but Anya could not
bring herself to collude in this, her degradation. At

length, the Taskmistress gave up waiting for her slave to speak, and simply took the tender rim of flesh between her finger and her thumb. She pinched it hard, until Anya wailed for her to stop. 'Do I take it that you wish to co-operate, my dear?' Anya bit her lip and nodded. That tender flesh within her groove was throbbing very gently.

This time, as Ildren's moistened finger smacked, and she watched that mouth pulsate, she was pleased to hear the slave count, 'One,' and to do so very promptly.

'Good,' Ildren said, and reaching underneath to cup that ripe black fruit within her palm, she smacked her once again. Ildren loved that resilient slap of finger-end against that knot of black-brown flesh, that signalled – regardless of the sobs and murmured protestations – the first uncertain stirrings of pleasure in her slave. Ildren's fingers split that fruit and delivered within its moist warm flesh, amid the little gasps – those more definite pleasurable assertions – and searched out and closed around that hard little pip of lust. So now, each time she smacked that bottom mouth, and the slave called out the count, she gave that pip a gentle squeeze, until Anya's hips were shaking, her sex had liquified inside, and the oily, pushed-out pip kept slipping back each time that Ildren pulled it downwards, and the count was twenty-three. Ildren then had Anya open her mouth very wide indeed, while she soaked her middle finger in the water till it went quite numb with coldness, and then she pushed it very slowly into Anya's bottom, which, Ildren insisted, must remain throughout in that pushed-out pouted state, and must not contract, even though the bondslave found this posture so very difficult to maintain.

Anya gasped and could not help but tighten against the shocking coldness slipping up against her delicate inner warmth, and the simultaneous pleasure of that other finger circling round her nubbin.

'Open, my sweet; let your body reach to take this pleasure.' Anya felt as if an icicle had been pushed into her person. Ildren released the pip and pressed Anya's leaves together, then gently drew the finger out and dipped it back into the water. 'No . . . no, my darling,' she instructed Anya, whilst she waited for her finger to go sufficiently cold, 'keep your mouth wide open. We have not finished yet. Now this time, push your tongue out very slowly, as I enter you . . . hold still . . . pout out that little mouth . . . Good . . . Mmm . . . Does that feel very nice? Keep pushing out that delicious tongue until my finger is right in . . . Good!' Anya's tongue was pushed out very far indeed, and Ildren was regretful that with the slave in this position she could not reach that tongue to close her lips around it. She made a mental note that she should think about some readjustment to the slave's position before she tried this game in future. For the present, she contented herself by spreading Anya's flesh leaves, and exposing Anya's pearly bud, then pressing the tip of her little finger against it and rotating very lightly, whilst she continued slowly pulling her finger out of Anya's body, and pushing in again. She watched the slave's tongue mirror that penetration and retraction, more lewdly still with each occurrence, until her head arched back as if her tongue were reaching out to touch someone, and her breathing seemed to snag on something hard. Ildren understood that signal very well; straight away, she stopped moving her little finger, and gently, she removed it, and – very lightly – pressed those leaves together, which evoked a murmur of delicious protest. Then more carefully still, she removed the finger from that gently pulsating bottom, and patted it softly on the cheeks.

'There – was that so very bad?' she asked her coyly, then lifted the bowl from Anya's bottom and placed it on the floor. 'And tell me,' she insisted, 'did you like that slapping of your person?' Ildren had moved round to the side; her fingers brushed upwards across Anya's breast, and lifted up the teat to stroke it. 'Answer – did it bring you pleasure?' Anya had no choice; she nodded weakly. 'Good. Your Taskmistress next has a very interesting style of pleasure to which she will subject your body.'

Anya now became apprehensive about what the Taskmistress was doing – she was unfastening the chain of gold about Anya's waist. Ildren had to work the chain around in order to reach the fastening; Anya's heart was beating wildly at this treatment. It was as if in some way, she felt the chain to be a part of herself which Ildren, by breaking that symbolic loop, was trying to take away. This fingering at the fastening made her very much afraid; it seemed to her an assault upon her person, as if Ildren wished to strip her of her last shred of dignity, and to render her as nothing.

'No – please ma'am,' she tried to beg her, but to no avail. The Taskmistress had released the fastening, and now unfolded the chain so it dangled down from each side of her body and across her bunched-up thighs.

'I wish you to be totally nude,' the Taskmistress said quite coldly, though with a tremble in her voice. She removed the chains from Anya's wrist and ankle.

Anya's tears welled up inside her. She did not understand it, but she could not help herself; the shame was overpowering as the Taskmistress slowly pulled the large chain through from underneath her belly. However, Ildren did not take the chain away entirely from her slave. Anya felt her pin it with a finger or thumb to the small of Anya's back, and then drape it down the groove of her bottom; its weighted presence clung to Anya's parting, but it barely touched her sex before dangling straight down towards the floor. Anya's sobs had ebbed away under that pressured weight which seemed to fit so precisely to the split between her buttocks. She was reminded of that chain that Ildren wore and the way it had been lowered against her in that very place, while she lay on Ildren's bed, as a prelude to that pleasurable release which Anya had found to be so sweet and so delicious. Therefore, she was anxious to know what might happen next. Ildren's fingers parted Anya's leaves, which had gone so soft and so compliant that they remained open where Ildren pressed them back against her mound. 'Mmm . . . just the way I like those love lips,' Ildren murmured, then gently lifted the end of the chain from Anya's parting, until it was held horizontally, level with her back, and then she let it fall. The heavy, swinging line of pressured contact travelled down Anya's groove, making her gasp in mounting pleasure, and then emit a tiny grunt, as the lick of pressure curled between her open leaves and pressed against her nubbin. Ildren caught the chain on the backward swing and sent it down again, repeatedly and at a constant rate, until that squeezing line of luscious pleasure, that pendulum of delight, made Anya want to squirm and close her legs around it and beg for Ildren to finish her, to press those links against her nub until she burst her pleasure. Ildren caught the chain again, and reaching underneath pressed the end to Anya's belly, so the links pulled tight along the divide of Anya's separated flesh. That pressure was exquisite, yet cruel; not rolling against her in the way she needed, not firm enough to bring release.

The Taskmistress sounded distant, as if she found it difficult to speak. 'Now I shall feed this chain of love

111

'. . .' she trailed away, then finally managed, 'into your body . . .' Anya opened her mouth to cry out, but no sound at all came out. The icy fear and horror had sucked her breath away.

Ildren began by tightening the silken band, so Anya's sex felt pushed out and downwards from between her thighs, impossibly far. Anya shuddered as the Taskmistress touched her there, and those precise and probing fingers opened out her proffered sex, and then she shivered as each cold, heavy metal loop touched against the smoothness of her tender inner self as the Taskmistress worked it, link by link, into that living pouch. Anya felt herself distending under the moving weight of metal pushed inside her. That sinking kind of weight which she had suffered many times in imagination, at the stirrings of her pleasure, was now transformed into reality. Her sex felt like a swollen, over-ripe fruit, which was weighted down with liquid; the pulling pressure concentrated here, the heaviness behind her nub was sublime; her fruit was more than ripe for picking. Ildren gathered it up and closed her fingers round it, and traced its line of split. She sealed its leaves around the dangling end of chain, then tickled Anya's spine whilst Anya basked in the weighted plesure slung beneath her belly. Ildren gently shook the chain and swung it to and fro, and then from side to side, and carefully pulled it; each movement was transmitted up into Anya's body; the pulling felt so deep and so delicious.

'Your honeydew is dripping from the chain,' Ildren murmured very softly. 'Now tell me, sweetest – does this give you pleasure, as I promised that it would? A deeper pleasure than the cockstem? Tell me.' Ildren softly squeezed her sex. Anya's sight was deep and heartfelt.

112

'Good. Your pleasure shall be sweeter yet.' Ildren jumped up and moved over to the table. She collected up a jar, then dipped her finger in and tasted. She closed her eyes and threw back her head. 'Mmm . . .' she said. She dipped her finger once again and offered it to Anya, who was apprehensive as Ildren forced it through lips and smeared it on her tongue. It tasted very sweet and musky, like nectar overlain with female heat; it was the distinctive taste of honey. Anya knew it very well for she had tasted it before, on quite a few occasions. Now Ildren held up the chain which she had removed from Anya's ankle; she took a sidelong look at Anya, then she dipped it in the pot. The slave was now a little worried. A stream of honey ran down the chain and back into the jar. 'Now, this is a little messy,' Ildren smiled. 'But quite pleasant, I assure you. Open your mouth and push your tongue out very far.'

Anya felt the sticky chain, coaxed by Ildren's carefully probing fingers, being fed into her bottom. She closed her eyes against the shame of it. Ildren carefully wiped off the excess, and after she had licked her fingers, she dipped them in the bowl of water sitting on the floor. Taking hold of the end of the chain which dangled down from Anya's bottom, she said, 'Open your eyes and look at me.' With a cold, wet finger, she tickled very lightly down Anya's spine, from the level of her silken waistband, to the very tip. Anya shivered with that icy tickle, and that pulling deep inside her. It made her close her eyes in delectation. 'No . . . keep those delicious eyes open, that I may look upon their beauty whilst I pleasure you.' Ildren wet her fingers once again. 'Now, that delightful little tongue . . . push it out again, and make it as pointed as you can . . .' Anya felt that wave of pulling, drawing down and making her contract. 'Now move that tongue round

113

and round, in a circle.' And as she did so, Ildren stroked her moistened fingertip round and round that tender, pouted, pulled-out rim of bottom flesh that gripped the tautened chain. 'There, isn't that nice? No, keep that tongue moving. There . . .' Anya was almost passing out with pleasure at this treatment. 'Your little mouth is pulsing its delight. Good. Now, we shall try another very naughty kind of pleasure. Take a breath – a very deep one – and hold it . . .'

Ildren now had hold of each of Anya's chains and pulled them, alternately, very slowly but very fully, so Anya felt that pulling pleasure shift inside her, as it rocked from back to front. 'Breathe out . . . and in . . .' Ildren kept doing this to Anya until her sex could take no more and went into a deep and pulsating spasm. 'My darling . . . you really must contain that recklessness of spirit. I want you to promise me that you will stay quite relaxed for this next procedure. I do not want to witness so brazen a display of rudeness again. Is this quite clear?' Ildren forced the slave to give her word, but Anya knew that Ildren would just as surely make her break it.

'Mmm . . . your love lips are so soft and warm.' They felt so sensitized that the slightest touch was making Anya want to squirm with delight. 'Let me spread them very fully . . . Oh! What is this hard little knot in there? It feels so firm and so deliciously naughty. Let Ildren stroke this little wet tongue of pleasure.' She used one hand to hold back Anya's hood and to hold her leaves apart. Ildren's middle finger slowly and systematically tickled Anya's poked-out nubbin, whilst her thumb wrapped around the chain in Anya's sex and kept pulling at it, then releasing, at a carefully timed rate. The Ildren's free hand took that other chain and very firmly pulled, increasing the strain

114

until it began to move, whereupon she ordered her slave to begin to pant, whilst she very slowly, so deliciously, and with so very cruel a pleasuring, drew that chain out of Anya's person. Anya tried so hard against that drawing pleasure, and pulling in her sex, and that finger pressure round her nubbin, which Ildren was tickling so exquisitely, and she very nearly succeeded – until that thread of dripping honey trailed upwards in her groove, and Ildren deposited that sticky weight of drawn-out chain along the base of Anya's spine, and the line of liquid pressure there was just too much to bear. Ildren was already kneeling down beside her, not touching her at all, but looking deeply and very lovingly into Anya's eyes – those deep black pools of defenceless pleasure – as Anya's trembles swelled and waned and swelled once more, against those wrenching gasps, and the honey welling slowly down her groove, and then her belly shook in wave upon wave of delicious liquefaction.

Ildren shook her finger. 'You are very naughty girl, and after you had promised me so sweetly.' But even so, Ildren's voice had faltered, for she was filled with so much love for this very special slave that she was almost moved to tears. She washed her slave, so very lovingly, deep within her groove, and dabbed her dry, and then she washed her ankle chain. She closed Anya's love lips round the chain that still lay nestled within her sex, and left the end dangling. She stroked her back, while she waited patiently.

A sudden noise – a thumping sound – made Anya jump with fright.

'Oh,' cried Ildren, in obvious dismay. The banging came again. 'Oh no! – Who could it be? Who is at my door?' Ildren sounded quite surprised at this un-announced intrusion. Anya was distressed. 'Just one

115

minute!' Ilden cried, then whispered, 'Let me get my robe . . . and here, my darling, let me cover you up.' She threw a blanket over Anya's body, leaving only her head exposed. 'There – you never know who it might be,' she said, in a kindly, protective way.

The thumping came more loudly. 'Open in the Prince's name!' a voice boomed from behind the door. Anya's heart stood still; the blood drained from her face.

Ildren then admitted the Prince, and all his retinue, who arranged themselves in a half circle near the door. Anya froze, her eyelids almost closed; she held her breath and wished that she were invisible. Why hadn't Ildren placed the blanket over her head, so she could hide completely from her shame? She could not bear the thought of him, of all people, seeing the depth of her depravity.

'We thank you, Sire,' the Taskmistress began, with unction on her tonuge. 'Your noble presence brings honour to our humble quarters.' Now Anya's lungs were bursting, and she had to breathe; her heart was thumping in her throat.

'Yes, yes. The slave – ?' The Prince was speaking now, referring to her. 'Is she not here, Taskmistress – as your message has advised us?'

The force of meaning in these last few words pierced Anya's heart like a knife blow. It cut her to the quick, for at that point she realised just what this evil woman had done. Now she understood the wicked inner purpose behind these cruel seductive games. Ildren had contrived that Anya's presentation to the Prince would be crowned with degradation.

'The slave is here.' Ildren stood aside and Anya could feel the weight of the Prince's gaze upon her, even though her eyes were now so very tightly shut.

For a second, he did not speak; then his voice sounded tense.

'But Taskmistress, I do not understand . . . Why is she being punished? And have I not made my own feelings very clear to you on the use of that contraption?'

'Sire – the slave is not being punished.' Ildren now could barely contain her delight. 'This is the manner in which the slave prefers to take her pleasure.'

'Taskmistress,' the Prince's voice was stern, 'do not try my credulity, and do not try my patience. Release her now.'

Now Ildren sounded hurt. 'As Your Highness requires . . .'

Anya was powerless to prevent the blanket from sliding down her body, and then she heard the Prince's gasp. She wished she could have closed her ears against the shadow of that gasp. The pit of Anya's shame was bottomless. She kept sinking down and down, and wishing with her heart and soul that this was not really happening, that the Prince was not witnessing her humiliation in this way. If Anya had been allowed a knife, she would gladly have cut out Ildren's poisoned heart and burned it, and then cut out her own, and watched it shudder and then lie still, in a mirror of that mortal blow to her hopes and her desire.

'Open your eyes, in the Prince's presence,' the venomous creature said.

'No! No. Do not oblige her so to do.' The Prince sounded shaken.

Ildren was quite undaunted. 'Shall I untie her now, or – ? Her blackness is set out for your noble self to examine, at your pleasure.'

The Prince cleared his throat, but did not speak.

'Your Highness will observe, within the cleft, that

117

knot of flesh. That is not normally so prominent as it now appears. It has been accentuated by the spanking – in which the slave took pleasure. She will confirm this if you care to ask her.' Anya died a thousand deaths. 'Oh, and the chain – that is there because the slave insisted she prefers it to a cockstem. It seems to give her fuller pleasure that a man's part ever could. Perhaps your noble self would wish to touch and test the . . .'

'No, I – No.' The Prince sounded very upset, and very uncertain and embarrassed. But Ildren did not seem to notice this.

'You will find the slave has worked herself, in preparation for this moment. The chain is moistened with her juices . . .'

'No, I must – No. Thank you, Taskmistress, I . . .' Daylight was a tiny point above Anya's pit of black despair.

And now the Prince was gone; the Taskmistress was left alone with Anya, whose leaden body slowly heaved and dropped, and heaved again, in shudders of misery. Uncontrollable thick salt drops of fire stung her eyes and wet her cheeks and dribbled in her mouth.

'My darling dearest,' Ildren put her arm about her slave and gently comforted her. 'Do not upset yourself. These men are all the same. They are quite indifferent to a woman's feelings.' Ildren stroked her brow. 'After everything the Prince had said about you, and promised for you too. And now, when you have prepared yourself, displayed your body for his pleasure, His Highness does not want to know, and – who can tell? even now is probably in another's arms . . . some other slave who has chanced to take his fickle fancy.'

But Anya's tears would not stem, not even when the Taskmistress, with a swelling, nervous bosom, filled

118

with love and sadness for her charge, very softly cupped Anya's weighted flesh within her palm and squeezed it, sealing those lips of love about the chain, then wrapped the suspended end of it around her fist and pulled it, link by link, from Anya's body, saying, 'There, there, my precious pet, never fear, for your Taskmistress loves you very deeply.' Anya's sobs came louder now, and Ildren's heart swelled as if to burst through her breast. Those sobs were music to her ears.

The Taskmistress wiped the tears from Anya's cheeks and smeared the tear juice round her nipples, then sucked upon these salted, blackened, fleshy droplets one by one. She untied the slave and stretched her limbs and tenderly massaged them, until Anya's tears had slowly ebbed away. Ildren pressed her soft cool lips upon those swollen burning cheeks and, lifting Anya down, she replaced the chains about her wrist, her ankle, and her wrist and led her to the window.

Slave and mistress looked out, across the grey stone turrets, to the rollowing snow-white scene that merged to distant blue, and each, in her own way, was uplifted by the vision of that vastness of Lidir.

Anya's heart and soul could gladly have soared, out above this place, out into the air, out into the sunlight, through that cold blue air above that endless snow, and let its icy crispness wash away her fears and deliver her to freedom.

'Together, we could rule this land,' Ildren's voice had broken Anya's reverie. 'The legend could come true . . .' Anya did not understand. The voice became seductive. 'Who needs a prince – when we have a princess?' Ildren kissed Anya very fully on the lips. But Anya pulled away when she realised exactly what this evil woman was saying, and she backed against the wall.

'No, no!' Anya was horrified at such visciousness and

119

calculating malice – and treason – at the suggestion that the Prince should somehow be set aside, or done away with. She raised her arm against the thought; it had made her very angry. 'No! How could you dare to plot against his noble person?' Anya's heart was beating wildly; she was shaking – cold sweat beaded on her forehead – but somehow she had found that strength to speak out now for truth, and honesty of purpose. 'How could you be so cruel?'

'Cruel? *Cruel?*' The Taskmistress drew herself up until she seemed a tower of terror; her face was roaring thunder. She struck that slave down to the floor, for her honesty of purpose, and then she kicked her, for her forthright stance. Such candour was unwelcome, as far as Ildren was concerned.

'You thankless bitch! You jumped-up little harlot! I'll show you cruelty, if that is what you wish to taste.' And with that, Ildren stormed over to the door. 'Let us see how your Prince protects you now,' she said, and flung the door wide enough for it to crash against the wall. 'Guard! Guard!' she cried. 'This silly slut desires to entertain you in the guardroom.' Anya began to wail. 'You may do with her precisely as you wish.'

Then later, in the quiet calm, when Ildren tried to work out what had gone so wrong, she wondered whether things would have turned out differently if, after Ildren had untied the girl, she had taken that exquisitely – and yes, Ildren now quite genuinely admitted it – beautiful body, that sweetly sobbing tear-stained body, which was dripping with desire, and moulded it to the Rod, *before* she had attempted to divulge her plan? What might have happened then? Ildren was unsure. As it was, she could only hope that the grey guards could, by way of contrast, perhaps underline the virtues of a woman's touch, and thereby help this silly little bitch to see the error of her ways.

120

BLUE ANGEL NIGHTS

Margarete von Falkensee

Translated from the German by Egon Haas

The Weimar Republic: a brief interlude in German history, between the First and Second World Wars, between the Second and Third Reichs. An interlude of democracy and depression – but also of decadence and delirium. Or so it says in my dictionary of world history, anyway.

Margarete von Falkensee's first volume of stories, *Blue Angel Nights*, captures the brittle sensuality of Weimar Germany. The mood is erotic rather than salacious, with the characters acting our their scenes against a darkening backdrop. The pleasures of life have to be grasped quickly and enjoyed to the full.

Isn't it a pity that some people don't discover that philosophy until someone like Hitler is breathing down their necks?

Margaret von Falkensee's subsequent books, *Blue Angel Days* and *Blue Angel Secrets*, lighten in tone as the amorous characters from her first book try to make their fortunes in Hollywood.

Hildegard Buschendorf was a pleasant enough woman, cheerful, talkative, fair-haired and overweight, with the prominent bosom and backside which Manfred associated with women of his mother's generation. That was a little unfair, for Frau Buschendorf could hardly be forty yet, but her plain way of dressing and her overblown figure placed her quite clearly for him.

He met her at a lunch given by his Aunt Dorothea in her house on Bellevue-strasse. The purpose of the lunch, as he quickly made out, was so that he should make the acquaintance of Fraulein von Ettlinger and her mother. Aunt Dorothea never lost an opportunity to try to marry Manfred off to suitable young ladies and she had invited some of her other friends in order to disguise her motives. Fraulein von Ettlinger was a pretty enough young lady of eighteen, though too subdued for Manfred's taste. He was polite and charming, made a note of her telephone number without committing himself to calling her, and thought no more about her.

It was raining hard that afternoon and Manfred's aunt, aware of his lack of interest in the young lady she was promoting, saddled him with the task of driving

123

Frau Buschendorf home, she living right across the other side of Berlin. On the journey she admired his Mercedes volubly, praised his driving skill and told him a little about herself. She was a widow, her husband being of a military family, and he had met his end in the service of the Fatherland in 1916. All very sad – and very familiar.

As they passed through Alexander Platz they saw a fight in the road – about a dozen men brawling, spilling over the pavement and dangerously near the traffic. Some of them were in the brown uniforms of the Nazi Party, some of them in ordinary workmen's clothes. They were all shouting as they punched and kicked at each other. One man was lying in the gutter in the rain, face-down and evidently unconscious.

'My God, what are they doing!' Frau Buschendorf exclaimed, clutching Manfred's arm in terror. 'Why don't the police stop them?'

'They are settling a political disagreement,' said Manfred thoughtfully.

'They'll kill each other! Look – there's another one on the ground and they're kicking him!'

'Perhaps it would be for the best if they did kill each other, dear lady.'

He drove away as fast as he could. When they arrived at Frau Buschendorf's apartment, she invited him in to meet her children and he, with nothing else to do that afternoon, accepted. The children proved to be two daughters, one about eighteen and other two years younger. Manfred wondered wryly whether this was the second try that day at getting him interested in a suitable young lady. The two girls were dressed alike, in white blouses, grey pleated skirts and white knee-socks, which he took to be their school uniform. They were both extremely well-mannered and sat quietly with their mother and her guest in the old-fashioned drawing-room, while Frau Buschendorf told Manfred how clever they both were, as mothers do.

He paid little attention as she rambled on, his interest caught by the older girl, Monika. She was cast in the same mould as her mother – the same solid bone-structure and breadth of hip. At her age she presented a slightly heavy attractiveness, but no doubt she would look much like her mother in another twenty years. The younger girl, Angelika, resembled her mother in facial features and would develop in the same way as her sister in time, though as yet there was little indication of a bosom under her blouse.

His attention was dragged back to Frau Buschendorf's monologue by the unexpected word *discipline*.

'. . . so important for growing girls,' she was saying. 'Otherwise they run wild these days. I've seen it happen with my friends' girls and it leads to the most dreadful scandal and disgrace. I'm sure you know what I mean.'

Manfred nodded solemnly, without the least idea what she meant.

'My late and dear husband's brother Gunther has been a great help to me. He deals with the girls firmly and they respect him for it.'

'Is he too a military man, Madame?'

'In his youth, just as his brother was. He left the Army after the War and went into business. I never understood the details, of course, but he has done extremely well for himself. He has always been too busy to marry and so, in a sense, we became his family. He has been a great comfort and support to me. He understands what duty means, you see – something which the young people today seem not to care about. We miss him sadly.'

125

'May I ask what has happened to him?'

'Nothing has happened to him, thank God. His business has taken him to Spain. He imports and exports, you understand. He has been away for nearly three months now and I hope he will be back soon. He is a good influence on my girls.'

'By his example, you mean?' Manfred asked, not at all impressed by this absent paragon of virtue.

'That, of course, and also his method of disciplining them.'

Manfred glanced at Monikia and Angelika, sitting demurely side by side on the heavy old sofa. They were looking attentively at their mother and there was nothing to be gleaned from their expressions.

'This method, Madame – what is it?'

'The only method that works with young girls – a strong hand.'

He was almost sure that he caught a flicker of amusement on Monika's pretty face.

'I see that you understand me,' said Frau Buschendorf, 'Gunther's method is a strong hand across their bottoms.'

'He beats these charming children?' Manfred asked, aghast.

'Certainly not! Do you think we are barbarians to beat our children? He has a regular routine of smacking them once a week.'

Manfred could hardly believe what he was hearing. He addressed himself to the older girl.

'What do you think of these weekly smackings, Fraulein Monika?'

'It is for our own good, Herr von Klausenberg. It doesn't hurt much and it is soon over.'

'You are fond of your uncle?'

Both girls nodded at once.

126

'You see,' said their mother, beaming, 'they miss their Uncle Gunther now he is away. Perhaps I should have remarried years ago to give them a father, but so many fine young men never came back from the War! And with Gunther to stand by me, I felt no need.'

Frau Buschendorf's recital of the problems of a woman alone with children to bring up became dreary and Manfred decided to take his leave. He was not listening to what she was saying, his thoughts set on the idea of eighteen-year-old Monika having her bottom smacked by Uncle Gunther. He nodded and smiled from time to time when Frau Buschendorf looked at him for a response and was surprised when she fell silent and she and her daughters stared at him expectantly.

'I beg your pardon – my thoughts were wandering.'

'So you agree?'

'Oh yes,' he answered vaguely, having no idea of what he had agreed to and thinking it of no consequence anyway, now that he was about to go.

'Then we will proceed at once.'

'I fear I may have misunderstood you, dear lady. What are we to proceed with?'

'To administer the discipline my daughters have missed for three months. I shall be most grateful to you.'

Manfred stared at her in amazement.

'You ask me, a stranger to your home, to punish your daughters? Have they behaved so badly? The idea is unthinkable.'

'I have explained myself badly – there is no question of behaving badly. My girls are very well-behaved. The discipline is a reminder to continue to behave well in future. Isn't that right, children?'

'Yes, Mama,' they said in unison.

Manfred was perplexed as how to escape from this

ridiculous situation – and as to how he had got into it. Finally his sense of humour asserted itself and he decided to oblige Frau Buschendorf by giving the girls a quick slap on the backside and make his departure quickly.

'I am at your service, Madame. Please explain what I am to do.'

'Thank you – we are truly grateful, aren't we, girls?'

'Yes, Mama.'

'There is a necessary routine,' Frau Buschendorf explained, 'Monika receives ten smacks because she is nearly grown up. Angelika receives six smacks because she is still only a child.'

'Could you not carry out this domestic routine yourself?' Manfred asked.

'That would be to miss the point. They must be disciplined by a man, not by their mother.'

'Why is that?'

'To remind them of their place.'

Manfred gave up trying to make sense of the proposition.

'I have no experience of domestic routines, but I shall do my best.'

'There, girls! I knew that Herr von Klausenburg was a kind-hearted gentleman as soon as I met him.'

She rose from the chair, Manfred stood up and the girls vacated the sofa.

'It is better if you remove your jacket,' Frau Buschendorf advised. 'Your actions must not be hindered. A strong and steady hand is the main thing.'

Manfred took off his jacket and watched Monika fold it neatly and lay it on the chair.

'We always start with Monika,' said Frau Buschendorf. 'As the eldest it is her right. And it is her duty to show her sister how to conduct herself properly.

Correctness is essential.'

'I'm sure it is,' said Manfred, wondering if she were slightly deranged.

'Monika, prepare yourself,' her mother ordered.

What Manfred expected to happen was that the girl would bend over and touch her toes while she was spanked. His expectations proved to be wrong. Monika hoisted her pleated skirt to show her thighs and white knickers, lay on her back on the sofa and raised her knees to her chest. The position exposed her bottom, drawn taut by the raising of her legs. Before he had recovered from this first surprise, another followed. Monika hooked her thumbs in the sides of her knickers and wriggled them down over her bottom and on to her thighs. Manfred stared at the smooth cheeks she had bared.

'The discipline is carried out on the bare flesh,' Frau Buschendorf explained. 'It is more effective like that because it humbles the recipient.'

'Just so,' said Manfred, now convinced that he was dealing with someone not quite sane, 'but the position is awkward. Why must it be so?'

'Surely that is obvious. If she bent over she would not be able to see your face. It is of the utmost importance that the girls see the face of the man and know that he is not angry with them but carrying out his task in a proper spirit of duty. Now, if you are ready, please deliver ten smacks.'

He looked at Monika's face to see how she was taking all this. Her eyes were wide open and she was gazing steadily at him, her expression giving no hint of her feelings. He stepped up to the sofa and smacked one cheek of her bottom, not at all hard.

'One!' Frau Buschendorf counted aloud.

He smacked the other cheek and heard 'Two!' From

129

his vantage point above Monika he had a perfect view, not only of her smooth-skinned bottom but, more interesting, of the pouting split between her thighs and its light fleece of brown hair. He thought it was very pretty and continued the smacking, stopping when Frau Buschendorf said loudly 'Ten!'

The younger girl had been standing throughout at the end of the sofa, leaning against it and staring at her sister's bottom, now blushing faintly pink from the smacks.

'Excellently done,' said Frau Buschendorf. 'What do you say now, Monika?'

'Thank you very much, Herr von Klausenberg, for teaching me what I have to learn, I promise that I shall remember this lesson and profit by it,' said Monika, her words evidently a formula used on these occasions.

'Give her your hand,' said Frau Buschendorf.

Manfred held out his hand, thinking to help the girl to rise, and found instead that she kissed it. Altogether, he thought, a very strange family.

Monika got off the sofa, pulled up her knickers and smoothed her grey skirt down.

'Angelika, your turn, my little angel,' said Frau Buschendorf fondly.

The smaller girl placed herself in the same position, knees up and knickers down, to present a taut little bottom. Manfred smacked it very lightly. Angelika went through the same formula of thanking him, word-perfect, and of kissing his hand, before she scrambled off the sofa and stood, skirt held up while she rubbed her bottom as if he had really hurt her.

'I am pleased with the way you have behaved,' Fraud Buschendorf told her daughters. 'Off to your room now and read your school-books until dinner-time.'

Manfred smiled and bowed as both girls gave him a

little curtsy before leaving the drawing-room.

'My dear brother-in-law says it is necessary for women to be reminded of their place. You see the truth of this in the good manners of my girls.'

'He must be a remarkable man,' said Manfred cautiously.

'He is, in every way. And you have been so understanding and so very helpful that I feel I can confide in you further.'

Manfred inclined his head, not knowing what to say.

'Every week, after the girls have been dealt with and sent to their room, Gunther treats me in exactly the same way.'

'But you are a grown woman – don't you resent being treated like a child?'

'I welcome it,' she answered, pink-cheeked and vehement.

A mental picture of plump Frau Buschendorf on the sofa with her knees up and her bottom being smacked almost made Manfred laugh. He contained himself with an effort, wondering if he could prolong the joke.

'If I can assist in any way . . .' he said.

It was no joke – she seized upon his words instantly.

'You would be doing me a very great favour!'

Before his startled eyes, she was on the sofa, skirt up round her waist and knees on her bosom, displaying a large round bottom encased in dove-grey knickers. She pulled them down and let Manfred see her white cheeks and the prominent fleshy lips between her heavy thighs.

'Ten?' he asked.

'Twenty – it's always twenty for me.'

Manfred took his position by her side and swung his hand hard at the target offered to him.

'One!' she gasped.

He continued, landing his smacks on each cheek in

turn, trying to make it sting. The massive cheeks wobbled as he struck and their pale skin flushed red after the third or fourth blow. By the time he reached ten Frau Buschendorf was sighing loudly between her counting and her legs were trembling wildly.

Manfred too was breathing faster. Without being aware of it, he had become aroused. What had started as a joke on his part had ceased to be only that and was taking on a very different aspect. By the count of twenty his stem was standing upright in his trousers. Immediately after the final smack, which rang out resoundingly, Frau Buschendorf seized the hand that had disciplined her and pressed her mouth to it.

'Thank you, thank you,' she exclaimed, her face as glowing red as her bare bottom. 'You have a strong hand and a willing heart.'

Manfred wondered whether he had laid it on too hard – the red marks on her bottom were very bright. He laid his hand gently on one of the afflicted spots to see if it felt hot to the touch.

'Is that painful?' he asked, breathing quickly.

'Discipline must hurt, or it has no meaning,' she murmured, her eyes half-closed.

Manfred's finger-tips had somehow found their way between her raised legs. While he was lightly stroking one reddened cheek to ease its pain, his finger-tips were tickling the thinly-haired and pouting lips exposed to him.

'After your brother-in-law has spanked you, what does he do next?'

'He completes the lesson,' she said softly.

'And how is that done?'

'He reminds me in the most forceful way possible that I am a woman and that I must at all times remember my duty. Do you understand what I am saying?'

132

'I believe that I do. Shall I proceed?'

'If you would be so kind.'

He knelt on the sofa, unbuttoned his trousers and tucked his bent knees under her bottom to raise it. Frau Buschendorf strained her thighs as far apart as the knickers round them would permit and sighed when he used his fingers to open the thick lips presented to him. His stem slid in easily, the smacking having prepared her for what was to come. He looked at her face and saw so greedy an expression on it that he leaned forward and plunged deeply before going at her with a will. Nothing about this strange woman surprised him any more, not even when she began to count quickly to his jabbing: 'One, two, three, four, five, six, seven, eight, nine . . .'

He was soon so engrossed in what he was doing that he no longer heard her voice. He had been aroused more than he knew by the variety of female charms that had been displayed for him and smacking Frau Buschendorf's bottom while staring at her split peach had wound him up like a spring. He went off like an alarm-clock, rocking the heavy old sofa under them with his impetus. When his spring finally ran down and Frau Buschendorf stopped squirming, he sat back on his heels and grinned. She reached for his hand and kissed it.

'It's months since I was disciplined by a man,' she said. 'Thank you, dear Manfred, if I may call you that.'

To cut short what seemed an excessive show of gratitude for so easy a favour, Manfred asked her how high her counting had gone.

'I lost count at four hundred and something.'

'I suppose you always lose count at some point.'

'Not exactly. With Gunther I always reach six hundred and something before he reaches the culmination of his discipline. After that I relax and experience the

133

deep pleasure that comes from accepting my destiny. But you are younger and stronger than he is and you drove everything out of my head before you were finished. I am sorry, but I cannot tell you the final count. It's wrong of me, I know.'

'Why on earth should I want to know?'

'Gunther insists that it is part of the discipline to make me count for him. He always asks afterwards.'

'He is an unusual man. Personally I am more interested in pleasure for its own sake.'

'That is the failing of many young people nowadays. It was otherwise once.'

'Maybe it was. But you are educating your daughters in the old ways of submission and duty and the world no longer sets the same value on these things.'

'The old ways are best,' she said firmly.

'We must move with the times or we shall be left behind as relics,' said Manfred, as he climbed off the sofa and buttoned his trousers.

'We are passing through a time of moral laxity and rebellion by young people, that's what Gunther says, but they will exhaust themselves by their excesses and the old ways will come back,' she said stubbornly.

She stretched out her legs along the sofa, her frock still up round her waist, showing off the plump article Manfred had just made good use of.

'The pendulum may swing,' he answered, 'but nothing is ever the same again.'

'Only wait. You will see.'

'Suppose that I prove to you that pleasure for its own sake is far to be preferred to the shadowy pleasures of duty and obedience – will that make you change your mind?'

'How can you prove that?'

She got off the sofa to pull up her silk knickers and

smooth out the creases in her frock.

Manfred thought for a moment or two.

'Come to my apartment on Thursday afternoon,' he said. 'About three in the afternoon. One of us will be proved right and one wrong.'

Thursday was when Manfred's servants were free after lunch for the rest of the day. Not that he had any qualms about them seeing his visitors, married or unmarried. Many was the time that Geiger had brought his his morning coffee and found a young lady cuddled up beside him in bed. His instructions on such occasions were to bring a second cup. There was one memorable morning when he had brought in the coffee just as Nina was perched above Manfred, giving him a special morning greeting, though that was in the days before she married Gottfried.

In the matter of Frau Buschendorf it was different, Manfred considered. She was, after all, twenty years older than himself and much more bound by convention. Delicacy suggested that it would be needlessly embarrassing to her to subject her to the scrutiny of the servants. When she arrived he could not fail to note her smile of approval at his thoughtfulness. He helped her out of her coat and took her straight to his bedroom, there being no reason he could see for elaborate courtesies first. She knew what she had come for – matters might as well proceed without delay.

She was wearing a woollen frock in shades of dark blue and cream and, by the look of her, had come straight from the hair-dresser. Her only make-up was a little powder on her cheeks, but even that was more than she had worn when he met her at Aunt Dorothea's lunch party. As soon as Manfred tried to get her out of her clothes, she blushed and asked him to turn away

135

while she undressed herself. This coquettishness was in such marked contrast to the way in which she had exposed herself to him to be *disciplined* in her own home that it was clear that she felt herself to be on unsure terms with him. He stared out of the window for a few minutes until she said that she was ready, then turned to find her in bed, with only her head showing. He shed his jacket and shoes but, before he could continue, she brought her naked arms out of the bed and asked him to hold her.

This unnatural modesty on the part of a woman who had already allowed him the most intimate access to herself made Manfred slightly impatient. Moreover, this encounter was to be on his terms, not hers – that was the whole point of it. He flicked back the covers and saw her fully naked for the first time. It semed to him then that Hildegard Buschendorf was the most naked-looking woman he had ever set eyes on and he sought to explain this to himself as he lay beside her and fondled her big soft breasts. After all, he told himself, a naked woman is a naked woman, a head, a body, two arms, two legs, two of these and one of those. Why should Hildegard create this impression of being more naked than a naked woman generally looks? In his mind's eye he compared her with other recent guests in this same bed.

Partly it was to do with her physical size, he decided. Hildegard had so much more flesh to expose than, for example, Vicki Schwabe, who was slender, or even Jutta von Loschingen, who was small-breasted and firm all over. Hildegard was heavy-boned and solidly built, with wonderfully plump thighs, a belly that curved roundly and, of course, her over-sized breasts, each a double handful in itself. But in addition to sheer size, Hildegard's colouring had something to do with the impression of ultra-nakedness. Her hair was chestnut-brown and her skin was extremely pale, a creamy-white with the merest touch of flesh-tone in it. Against this alabaster appearance the pinkness of her nipples was in high contrast. And there was something else – she had little hair between her legs, as he had noticed before when she took up her extraordinary posture on the sofa to be smacked. There was only a sparse covering of brown over the fleshy lips down there and the effect was to make her seem more exposed than, one might say, Helga, who had a fine curly tuft.

All in all, to make love to Hildegard was like gorging oneself on a huge Black Forest gateau – there was so much to enjoy and it was all so rich and creamy! Manfred stroked and felt her all over, thinking as he did that her brother-in-law Gunther must be mad to confine himself to his uncomfortable in-and-out and deny himself the pleasure of all this warm flesh.

For a woman unused to so much handling – or perhaps because of that – Hildegard enjoyed it enormously. She sighed and squirmed, her legs trembled and, when his hand was between them, her belly quivered and heaved. Manfred sat up to get his clothes off and multiply her pleasures by pressing her body to his, but at once she took hold of his arm and pulled him back down beside her.

'Please . . . keep your clothes on.'

'But why? It is so much nicer to be naked together.'

'It couldn't be nicer than it is now. It is right for me to be undressed to submit to you, but you must be strong and demanding.'

'Damnation! That's not the idea at all! Forget this strong man and weak woman nonsense for once. We are two human beings, giving each other pleasure.'

'My way is better. Touch me again and remember

137

how you disciplined me. It was because I was submissive that you were so forceful.'

'What makes you think that?'

'Because you did it so hard and fast! It was wonderful.'

Manfred stroked her belly and then down between her thighs.

'It can be better than that,' he told her.

'What could possibly be better than lying on a submissive woman and exerting your strength? And what could be better for a woman than to feel the weight of a man crushing her as he thrusts into her body and tries to split her open?'

Manfred began to feel baffled by this extraordinary woman – extraordinary to him, that is. He was excited enough from handling her to follow her suggestion, to climb on top of her and do what she wanted. But that would be to admit defeat. He approached the point in another way.

'I understand what you mean, Hildegard. I shall be strong and force you to submit to me. That is what discipline is about, yes?'

'Oh, yes!'

'After I smacked your bottom the other day you thanked me and kissed my hand. Why did you do that?'

'It is correct to kiss the hand that punishes you.'

'But after I had, in your words, split you open, you did not kiss the instrument of punishment. That seems to me to be most incorrect.'

As the import of his words sank in, her eyes opened wide and she stared at him unbelievingly.

'I never thought . . . but Gunther has never suggested . . .'

'Search your conscience,' said Manfred firmly. 'Perhaps he is so shocked by your dereliction of duty that he

138

cannot bring himself to speak of it. Have you considered that?'

'I don't know what to say,' she muttered uneasily.

'I suggest that you begin with an apology.'

That was something she had been taught to understand.

'I ask you most sincerely to forgive me. Believe me, there was no slight intended. It never entered my mind.'

She looked as if she was about to burst into tears. Manfred spoke sharply.

'Your apology is unacceptable until you have put matters right.'

'You mean that you want me to . . .' but she was unable to say the words.

'It is not what I want that is important here, it is what is correct. Your sincerity can only be demonstrated by your actions.'

She looked so confused that Manfred found it hard not to smile. He rolled on to his back beside her and put his hands behind his head.

'I am waiting.'

Hildegard sat up slowly and unbuttoned his trousers with awkward fingers.

'Never in my life . . .' she began, then trailed off.

There was a pause while she gathered her courage to pull up his shirt. She gasped and almost drew away when his hard stem jerked out through the slit in his underwear.

'You flinch from your duty,' Manfred reproached her.

She took a deep breath, bent her neck and leaned down to kiss his twitching stem. Once committed, she did not skimp her duty and he felt her kisses from the head to the root of his stiffness.

She raised her head to look at him.

'Is my apology accepted?' she asked timidly.

'I believe that you are sincere. It would make matters better between us if you proved your submission to this instrument of discipline beyond the mere formality of what you have done so far.'

Hildegard took his meaning. She turned round on the bed to face him, took his stem in her hand and kissed it repeatedly. After a while she said breathlessly:

'This is so strange that you will not believe me. I was married for six years and I have two children. And for the past six or seven years Gunther has been disciplining me weekly. Yet this is the first time I have ever touched this part of a man, or even seen it properly.'

'How is that possible?'

'My husband always came to bed in a long night-shirt and embraced me in the dark. I never once saw him naked.'

'But your brother-in-law – with him you are in your drawing-room and it is not dark – how could you not observe what he uses?'

'When he makes me lie with my knees up to be smacked, I can see little more than his head and shoulders. And afterwards he puts it away before letting me move. At times I catch a glimpse of pink flesh, but no more than that.'

'There is much for you to learn. Now that you see how a man is made, what is your opinion?' Manfred said, amused by her confession and yet sorry for her.

Hildegard stroked her new discovery thoughtfully.

'I've often been to look at the old Greek statues in museums, but they have little things hanging down, not in the least like the big hard things I have felt inside my body. You will laugh at me, but last year I bought a book in one of those dreadful little shops that sell books

and pictures about sexual matters. It was so embarrassing to go in – I nearly died of shame.'

'What did you buy?'

'A book of pictures of young men, all aroused. It was
a tremendous shock for me to see the different sizes and
shapes. But it was very educational.'

'My poor Hildegard, the men you have known have
treated you very oddly. They seem to have given you
little and asked for little.'

'How can you say that? They gave me all they had
and I did the same. What more can any woman give
than admittance to her body?'

'I shall try to enlighten you before you leave.'

'But it all comes to the same thing in the end,' she
said. 'Whether we are dressed or undressed, in the light
or in the dark, whether we touch each other or not, it
leads to the same joining together of the man and the
woman for a minute or two.'

'That is like saying that all meals are the same
because they consist of putting food into your mouth.'

Her hand still held his stem but she had no idea of
how to handle it. He showed her how to clasp it and
move her hand up and down.

'I do not understand,' she said, 'this must be a poor
substitute for putting it where it should really be.
Would you not rather have it there than in my hand?'

'This is not a substitute at all,' Manfred sighted, 'the
two pleasures are only slightly related. No one has ever
told you that in love-making only part of the pleasure is
between the legs. The rest is in the mind. The touch of
your hand produces another sort of pleasure in the
mind from the pleasure I would feel if I were inside
you.'

'Surely not,' she said.

Before Manfred could attempt any further explanation, the inevitable happened. His loins jerked upwards from the bed and he poured his stream of passion through Hildegard's busy hand on to his white shirt-front.

'My God!' she exclaimed, her hand moving faster, 'I never guessed!'

He took her wrist to halt her movements.

'What didn't you guess, dear Hildegard?'

'I had no idea of how tremendous a destiny it is to be a man! To see how this wonderful part reared itself up and flung outs its torrent! It was awe-inspiring! I never knew!'

Manfred almost despaired. Perhaps she had been too well-trained in her role of submissive female to be rescued now. His well-intentioned attempt to remove the mystery from what a man's stem did when it was inside her had produced the very opposite result. She sat staring as it as it softened as if she had received a divine revelation.

He got off the bed, stripped completely and stood to let her look at him.

'See, Hildegard – I am no marble statue in a museum. I am a living man made of flesh and bones. Now you know what a naked man looks like. Forget your picture book and fix the real thing in your mind.'

She lay propped on one elbow, staring at him.

'You are more like the statutes than the picture book, Manfred.'

'Why do you say that?'

'In the pictures the young men are all hard and strong. You are small now like the statutes. It was better before, when I held you.'

'A temporary condition,' he said, laughing. 'Soon I shall be like your pictures again.'

She rolled on to her back and smiled. Manfred got

back on to the bed, parted her fleshy legs widely and lay between them. He stroked the protruding lips between her thighs.

'There is something I am trying to explain to you, but you have not yet understood me.'

'I know I'm not clever,' she sighed. 'Tell me again and I'll try to understand.'

'I doubt whether words will convey it. What I am trying to get you to grasp is that this warm slot between your legs is every bit as important as anything a man has.'

'That can't possibly be true,' she objected. 'You have a proud and arrogant thing – now that you've let me stroke yours I know how wonderful it is.'

Mandred stopped listening to her nonsense. He opened her widely with his fingers and tickled her exposed pink button. After a while while her legs began to shake and she gasped loudly.

'Ah, no! Not with your fingers – do it the correct way!'

'There is no such thing as a correct way, Hildegard. You must have been played with like this before when your husband took off his night-shirt.'

'Never!'

Manfred worked slowly, determined to make her experience more than she was used to. She moaned softly and rolled her head from side to side on the pillow.

'What did he do to you – at least he took off your night-gown?'

'No,' she moaned, 'no . . . he stroked my breasts through it . . . he never put his hands on my body . . .'

'And then?'

'He had me pull my night-gown up to my waist and he lay on top of me and did what men do . . . this is not possible . . . you must stop!'

Her plump body was shaking all over and Manfred was certain that she had never before felt such wild sensations of pleasure and she was half afraid of them. Her curved belly rose and fell to her panting. Manfred put his hands on her thighs to force them further apart, bent his neck and touched the tip of his tongue to her slippery bud.

'No!' she screamed. 'It's too much!'

She tried to slighter away from him. Manfred used his strength to pin her thighs flat to the bed while his tongue flicked over the sensitive button. The conclusion was spectacular – her thighs overcame the pressure of his hands in a spasmodic upwards jerk and clamped round his head. Her body convulsed as if in a seizure and, though his ears were muffled by her legs, he could still hear her staccato screaming. The outburst grew louder and with a final window-rattling 'Uh!' she collapsed as completely as if she had been shot dead.

Manfred sat up and looked at her. For a moment he thought that her climactic release had been so extreme that she had fainted, as Magda had done when she nearly knocked his brains out with her spiked helmet. But Hildegard's pink-tipped breasts were rising and falling regularly to her breathing and her eyes were open. He moved up the bed to cradle her head in his arm.

'What have you done to me?' she asked softly.

'I hope I've shown you what the plump little delight between your legs is capable of.'

'But it can't always be like that . . . it would be too much.'

'The women I know expect pleasure like that two or three times a day and sometimes more. You will soon come to expect the same.'

144

'I feel so content . . . and so sleepy. Is that dreadful of me? I know you must want your pleasure, but would you mind waiting a little?'

Manfred saw that as real progress. Half an hour ago she would have parted her legs and let him do as he pleased, however she felt. Some of her submissiveness seemed to have evaporated.

'Sleep for a while,' he said, 'I'll wake you later.'

STEPHANIE

Susanna Hughes

The sexual adventures of Stephanie will eventually run across four novels, I'm told. I've chosen an extract from the first book, entitled *Stephanie* (no suprises there), which describes our heroine's transformation from a hesitant career woman into a jet-setting furnace of libidinousness.

On the next few pages you'll read about Stephanie's initition into pleasurable practices that she had once thought depraved and bizarre. Her mentor is her lover Martin; however in subsequent novels it is the remarkable Devlin, mentioned only briefly here, who provides Stephanie with the means to explore even wilder byways of debauchery – and in luxurious style.

The second book in the series, *Stephanie's Castle*, is already available. *Stephanie's Revenge* will be published very soon. The fourth book will be called *Stephanie's Domain*.

It was one of the best meals she had ever had. Delicate, fresh and beautifully presented food; elaborate but cooked in such a way as to bring out the true flavour of the sauce and sauced. Scallops and crab, a round of puff pastry, the lightest butter sauce. Nuggets of lamb stripped of anything but meat grilled and served with carrot puree and crips haricot beans. A meringue made with hazelnuts, stuffed with raspberries and a rose of fresh cream.

His performance was very different over this meal. Definitely not the egomaniac or, to reserve judgement, the egomaniac making a hearty attempt to find someone else at least as fascinating as himself. He asked questions. Listened to the answers. Asked supplementary questions as a result of the answers – to prove he'd listened? From the cradle to the grave, well, at least to her present employment. Parents, place of birth, star sign (a mistake perhaps, he seemed to know nothing about star signs), schooling, university, first job.

A virtuoso performance, she thought. It was not until the dessert that her hunger was truly satisfied. It was not until the coffee that she found that the story of her life was more or less complete (a sad commentary, life measured if not in a coffeespoon then only three courses

and a half a cup of coffee) and she could ask a question
of him.

'Why didn't you want to come?' She was obsessed
with sex.

He smiled more broadly than she had ever seen him.
A smile that transformed his face, made it older,
avuncular, slightly unpleasant. 'I was hungry.'

'Not for me?'

'It's not necessary.'

'What?'

'My pleasure doesn't have to be orgasmic. That's
such an old sexual cliché. I can have pleasure without.'

'And were you hungry?'

'Do you think the sole aim of sex is orgasm?'

She thought about it. It had never occurred to her to
think about it before. 'Yes.'

'I don't. Especially when you're hungry,' he smiled.
He laid his hand on top of hers. 'We're very good in
bed.'

'Yes.'

'You said I make you feel something. It's the same
for me, what you make me feel.'

'You're more in control.'

'Only of the situation.'

She wanted to go on, ask him if that was really true,
ask him if he had ever experienced sex as good before,
ask him if he'd done to another woman what he'd done
to her. But she stopped herself. Not because she
thought it would matter to him but because actually she
didn't want to know nor did she want to talk about it
any more. What happened in bed between them happened. It was its own explanation, for the moment at
least. More coffee please, but not another brandy.

They talked about other things. He touched her as
they talked, laying his hand on her shoulder, her arm,

her hand. His hands felt cold. It made her want to
shiver but she managed not to. Earlier, over the food,
she had forgotten the effect his physical presence had
on her, but now as one need was satiated another arose,
and the feeling was there again; a breathlessness, the
inability to think about anything other than his nearness. It was like feeling a drug beginning to work; like
taking an aspirin for a headache, feeling the blood carrying the drug up to the brain, feeling the ache dissolve
and wash away. Except that this drug washed away no
aches; it created them, enlarged them, placed them in
positions where they pushed aside other things, other
concerns, other priorities, until it sat massive and
alone. The ache for Martin.

She would have liked to say that she wanted to go up
to the bedroom but she felt she had been so demanding
before dinner that to repeat the performance now might
be avaricious. She accepted another cup of coffee from
the offering waiter.

'You don't seem to care that I'm married.'

That was completely out of the blue. She had not
wanted his wife to sit at the table with them. 'I don't.'

'Why not?'

'Does it matter?'

'No. Just curious.'

'If you weren't married I don't think I'd have ever
seen you again after that night at my flat.'

'It makes you feel safe.'

'Exactly.'

If he was satisfied with such a glib response she saw
no reason why she shouldn't be. It might even be the
truth.

In the lift she felt her heart beat increase. They were not
alone so he made no attempt to kiss her but his still cold

hand reached out for hers. He did not lace his fingers into hers but instead made a circle by touching his middle finger to his thumb and holding two of her fingers there. The ring and the stone. She looked at him and he stared back into her eyes. Joke.

Outside the bedroom door, as he found the key and fitted it into the lock, she realised that her mouth was slightly dry; some psychological reaction to her increased heart rate, she supposed. She swallowed hard. The body's reaction to excitement was so prosaic. In fact, of course, it was anticipation of excitement. Behind the green baize door. Behind closed doors. Her secret. He opened the door and stood aside for her to go in. As far as she could judge his face was expressionless.

Stephanie sat on the corner of the bed, her hands in her lap. He said nothing. Picking up the small black case he put it on the table but did not open it. He sat down on the bed beside her and unzipped her dress. She made no attempt to help him as he pulled it down from her arms until it lay around her waist. He stood, taking her by the arm to make her stand too. The dress would not fall to the floor; it had to be pulled over her head. He gathered it in his hands and stretched it up over her head. He held her just above both elbows and with downward pressure indicated that she should sit again. She felt unable to move.

He hung the dress up neatly and went into the bathroom. She sat unmoving, her hands in her lap.

Her hands felt light, numb, unmuscled. She knew she was giving a performance but it was not a performance for his sake. She was doing it for herself and for what it made her feel, and for that reason she wanted the performance to be perfect. She heard him undress but did not turn her head towards the bathroom when he came out. She waited until he came into the line of vision she had from where she sat on the bed.

He was wearing a towel knotted around his waist. From the outline of the towel she could see that he was not yet erect. He stood in front of her, flicking her hair out from the back of her neck until he could touch the bare flesh. He rested his cold hand there. By the slightest pressure he made her look up at his face. He did not smile.

'Take your bra off.'

She obeyed, quickly replacing her hands in her lap once the task was completed. She felt the sides of her breasts pressed against the flesh of her upper arms. Her breasts felt heavy, the nipples light.

He licked a finger and immediately transferred the saliva to her left nipple. The sudden contact made her catch her breath. The tip of the finger made little circles on her hardened nipple but the touch was not hard, not even firm. It was the lightest touch, the softest touch like being brushed with the petal of a rose. He licked his finger again and wet the other nipple again using the lubricant to ease the circling movements he made with his fingertip.

He held both nipples between thumb and forefinger and simultaneously pinched both; not hard but not gently either. He ran his hand down the valley between her breasts pushing them outward against her upper arms. He ran his hand under each breast finding the crease that they made under their own weight. He lifted them as though weighing them in his hands. And all this time he stood in front of her looking down at her, looking down at his hands working on her breasts. And all this time she sat with hands in her lap, not looking at his face.

He moved behind her. She heard the black case being opened but did not look to see what he was taking from it.

153

She wanted to know, she wanted to see; she wanted to know everything that was in the case but she knew that was against the rules. Her rules. His rules. The rules. She remained passive, feeling the remnants of sensation his hands had left in her breasts.

Martin sat behind her on the bed. She could feel the side of his towel against her naked back. He kissed her between her shoulder blades and up to the nape of her neck, holding her hair out of the way with his hands. Then he knelt on the bed behind her and reached around with both hands to cup her breasts and pull her back towards him. Now she could feel his erection stabbing out from the towel into the small of her back just above the clasp of her suspender belt. He kissed her back again.

She felt him move back slightly. No contact now, not even his penis in her back. He smoothed her hair down with his hand where he had lifted it to kiss her neck and then pulled a black velvet blindfold over her head. It was sculptured at the front to nose and cheeks and fitted perfectly. She sat open-eyed and could see nothing. After a moment, as her eyes adjusted, the faintest light seeped in through the edges of the material but not enough to allow any sort of vision.

'Have you done this before?'

'Who have you done this with?'

'How long have you been doing this?'

'Does this excite you?

'Does this excite you more than anything?'

'What if I did it to you?'

'Who taught you?'

'Who did you do this to first? Who was she? What was she to you?'

'Shall I spoil the game and move?'

'Where did you get this blindfold? Did your wife

make it? Does she make all your equipment? Do you do this with your wife? Do you do this with every woman? Why are you making me do this? Or am I making you do this? Am I making you do this? Is this your response to me or my response to you? I never told you how much this excites me? Did I? Did I?'

'What are you going to do next?'

Stephanie wanted to ask all these questions but remained silent. She sat, hands in her lap, knees together, the black velvet covering her eyes.

Now there was no temptation to look round to see what he was doing. She felt him get off the bed. She discovered she could not hear footsteps on the carpeted floors; perhaps he wasn't moving. Then she felt his hands on her arms pulling her into a standing position. She stood and he moved her away from the bed slightly so she did not have the comfort of feeling the bed against the back of her knees. She supposed he was kneeling now because his hands were moving up one of her legs, one at the back, one at the front, from ankle to upper thigh, caressing the stocking, smoothing it, gliding over the suspender up over the white exposed flesh, just brushing the lace of the french knickers, then down again. Very slowly. Very lightly. The same with the other leg. Then higher, both hands moving over her buttocks up to her waist. The same soft gentle movement. Over her navel, over her hips. Up to the waist again.

His hands took hold of the knickers at the waist and pulled them down to her ankles. Not gently as he had done before, but suddenly, as if he was losing patience. He guided her feet out of them by holding her ankle, indicating with an upward pressure that she should raise her foot. The same with the other ankle. He flipped the knickers clear then pulled her ankle over to one side so she stood with her legs apart, the perfect marionette, her legs opened enough to expose her labia and her pubic hair still matted together from the frantic sex of earlier.

'Put your hands together in front of you.'

The perfect peformance. She obeyed immediately. A soft material fell across her wrists. In a moment her hands were bound together. She could not resist the temptation to test the efficacy of his work and she wriggled her wrists against the bonds. The scout had tied his knots. There was no escape. And she had to admit to herself she was glad she had tried to get free because the knowledge that she couldn't, that the bonds were not a thin charade, thrilled her instantly.

'Lie down in the middle of the bed.'

She wasn't sure she knew where the bed was any more but she inched back until she felt it against the back of her knees and sat down. It was difficult to sit down with your hands tied: no balancing controls. She edged to her left but felt the edge of the bed so moved to the right until she was far enough over to be more or less in the middle of what she imagined was the foot of the bed. Then she lay back, difficult again, and putting her feet up used her legs to lever herself back until she felt the pillow.

'Good.'

The awkwardness of movement excited her: the foreignness of not being able to reach out with a hand. Her breath was coming in short pants. My God. He seemed to know exactly what to make her do to get her feeling . . . Just feeling. Feeling everything. Feeling sexually awake. Feeling everything, every part of her alive, every part of her sexually alive. What he had just made her do, crawling across the bed on her back, made her feel her thighs, her knees, her elbows. Made her feel exposed. Open. Made her feel wanton and wild. It had occurred to her, the first time he had tied her in his house, that he was trading in on the male belief that all women have a fantasy about being raped. It was true in part of course, provided, and provided very strictly, that the rapist was incredible attractive, that the scene of the crime was exotic and glamorous, that actually the rape itself had as much violence, as much real violence, as an over-enthusiastic embrace, and that the difference between saying 'stop' and meaning 'stop' were always clearly understood. But what she felt now, what he was doing now, was quite different. Not the stuff of clichéd fantasy.

He was pulling her hands above her head. He tied them to the headboard. She immediately tried to pull them down again without success. She felt his hands on her ankle. Felt him tie it presumably to the leg of the bed. And then the other ankle, spreading her legs open as he had done before, spreading her open across the bed as he tied the other leg. She tried to pull her legs away. The bonds were firm. Tight and firm. Just as before. Open and spread as before. His. The wave of pleasure rolled over her then ebbed away, sucking her down with the sand and the pebbles.

He was not on the bed. She imagined he was standing at the foot of the bed, immediately in front of her open cunt looking at it, looking at her. Staring at her. She hoped so. She could not hear him move. She could not hear a sound other than her own breathing, her own excited breathing. She wanted him to do a thousand things to her. Pinch her nipples. Rub her breasts. Stroke her clitoris. Kiss her clitoris. Suck her. Suck her nipples. Bite her nipples. Fill her with his fingers, with his penis. Lie on her. His full weight on her. His full penis in her. Pull her up off the bed against the bonds, pull her out of her bonds. Kiss her mouth. Tongue her mouth. Kiss her thighs. Tease her. Tease. Touch and tease. Touch her arms, her inner arms, her lips, her navel, her knees. She writhed against her bonds trying to move towards him, to push her cunt up at him wherever he was, make herself more open, more desirable. To provoke him. He did nothing. She stopped moving and listened turning her head from side to side to catch any sound.

She heard him pick up the telephone. She heard him dial. Seven numbers. Waiting. She could not hear a ringing tone.

'Hello. She's ready. As I promised.'

She heard him kneel between her open legs. The bed gave under his weight. He leant forward and licked her cunt, long wet licks like a child exaggeratedly licking an ice lolly, the tip of his tongue starting at the opening of her vagina and licking up to her clitoris. Long wet licks, covering her already wet labia with his own saliva. His hands held her on either side of her lips, steadying himself. Long wet licks. At the clitoris his tongue seemed to pause, flicking at the little bud, intensifying the sensation.

She moaned quietly. She could not help herself. It was not a cumulative pleasure, like the pleasure that would bring her to orgasm, but each stoke was its own pleasure, a little monument of pleasure complete in itself.

Martin stopped. His hands moved from her hips to her breasts. He began to knead at her breasts, squeeze and knead them. Taking great handfuls of flesh in each hand he pulled them upwards, sideways, down towards her navel, made circles of her flesh, made intricate patterns, figures of eight, Greek letters. Kneading and squeezing. Stopping to release them momentarily while

158

he took one nipple or both nipples, pinched them, pulled them out from her breast, pushed them down into her breast, tweaked them lightly or strongly.

He got up from the bed. He had built a fire in her breasts, a lake in her cunt. She lay, unable to move, unable to do anything but feel the pleasure he was giving her. She was glad he had stopped. Or rather she was glad he had stopped playing with her; without his coming inside her she could not take much more.

The silence was broken by a knock at the door. The phone call. She had forgotten the phone call. She knew, of course, that he hadn't made a call. It was part of the game. What was extraordinary to her was that he knew this had been her fantasy. He knew she had fantasised a stranger last time he had tied her to his bed, fantasised a grizzled hoary stranger thrusting into her. How had he known, how could he have known? And now he was performing for her.

It was a performance. Perhaps she said that to herself a little too emphatically. It was a performance. The knock on the door again. It was him knocking on the door from the inside. It was him. It *was*. She heard him open the door. She listened intently trying to keep her body perfectly still, trying to keep her breathing under control so she could hear less of herself and more of what went on in the room. She was certain she could only hear him breathing.

'Don't make a sound.' She heard him walk over to the bed. She couldn't hear another set of footsteps but she could barely hear footsteps at all. Almost instinctively she tried to close her legs, pull her thighs together. The bonds allowed a little movement, but too little to make any difference. And it didn't make any difference because there was no stranger.

'As I promised, you see. Just as I promised.'

There was silence. She listened. No movement. Then a hand, the back of a hand against her cheek. She realised she had almost stopped breathing. She tried to relax.

He sprung on her like a tiger. Leapt on her, his full weight landing on her body, his penis pounding into her navel and then in a second embedded deep in her cunt, so suddenly she had no sensation of thrusting, just the immediate hardness of him deep inside her. Hardness like iron. Coldness like iron. He felt cold in her. He was pumping in and out of her now, breathing heavily. It was him. She had never heard him breathe like this before. It was him. The stranger tore at her, gripping her breasts, slipping his hands under her buttocks to pull her up to him as he thrust, pushing a hand down between their bodies so his finger could rub at her clitoris, rub at it, prod it, pull it. Breathing faster and faster. It was Martin. She told herself it was Martin. The she told herself it was not. It was the stranger. The gnarled stranger, the knotted craggy cock, the blue veins, the black hair, the ugly knotted cock; foul breath, dirty stranger, inside her delicate flower of a cunt. Inside her. Taking her. His enormous cock filling her. His sperm ready to spout into her. His dirty sperm, his stained yellowing sperm, in her.

She had no control of her orgasm. It was not in her cunt but in her mind. Her mind was sending the pleasure down to her cunt, her breasts, the clitoris he was pushing at. It was only a matter of seconds before the orgasm in her mind was overtaken, bettered, covered by the orgasm in her cunt. She thought she heard a scream, her scream. Forgetting the bonds she tried to bring her arms around him. The sudden jerk from wrists and ankles, she was bound, unable to move, that feeling pushed her down into her orgasm even deeper down into the dark of it, the darkness in her eyes, the moving throbbing darkness in her mind. And then she felt his penis swelling and throbbing, felt his back arch out and his penis withdraw to plunge into her for the last time, felt its plunge and then his hot shooting sperm. And that took her deeper still. Like three orgasms, three seamless orgasms, so much part of each other, that each made the other deeper, bigger, more full of raw endless sensation that she knew would have to end.

He lay on her breathing more evenly. She could feel his penis begin to shrink inside her. She could feel his sperm begin to trickle down her cunt. Not for a moment did it occur to her that it was a stranger lying on top of her. The fantasy was over. *That fantasy*.

It was strange not being able to hug him. She wanted to wrap her arms around him. The fact that she couldn't still, to her surprise, provided the faintest thrill, a *frisson* of realisation that her position was still vulnerable and exposed. She was still open. Still wild. She stopped herself. Better not pursue that thought. Too much excitement. It'll end in tears as her mother would say. And she banished that line of thought quickly too, her mother didn't belong in this bedroom, near this bed.

Martin untied her ankles and then her wrists. He massaged them as he did so but there was very little discomfort.

'Close your eyes against the light.' He rolled the blindfold off her eyes. It took a moment before she could see properly again. She realised he had not kissed her on the mouth while she had been tied to the bed and she wanted to be kissed now. She sat up on the bed.

'Kiss me.'

He took her in his arms and kissed her on the mouth his tongue vying with hers for territory. She hugged him to her, relishing the sensation that a few minutes earlier had been denied. It felt good to be able to hug him, pull him into her, squeeze him. His mouth felt good too. Warm, welcoming. Normal. Comfortingly normal. (Reassurance after depravity? Is that what she thought it had been – depravity?)

There was a moment when the kiss could have ended, when they could have broken free from each other's arms and sat on the bed to talk, perhaps, to have a drink and be polite. But that moment had passed, was passing. Far from feeling sated and sexually exhausted she found the kiss was making her heart beat faster again, pulling her mind back to thoughts of sexual excitement, making her hands caress him more specifically, more urgently, more rhythmically.

They lay back on the bed. Stephanie couldn't tell whether he'd pulled her over or she'd pushed him, but they ended with her on top. She started to kiss his neck, his chest moving her hands over his chest as though to blaze the trail for her mouth. He was still flaccid. She could feel his slack wet cold penis just below her breasts and she moved down his body. She took him in her hand and squeezed gently. Then she slid further down the bed and took him in her mouth. He tasted different. He tasted of her, of course, her saltiness, her juices. It did not bother her. She circled the tip of his penis with her tongue, nudging it, sucking it gently, then more strongly. She wanted to feel him stir, feel the blood begin to pump back into him, feel him grow inside her mouth until he filled it and she could sit on him, push her cunt down on him, have him in her again and again and again.

It was a little while before she realised her efforts

162

were having no effect. He was not swelling in her mouth, he was not growing. Instinctively – she had no reason for thinking it would excite him – she pivoted round until her thighs were level with his head, so he could see her pubic hair opposite his head. He took the hint and pulled her up over him, adjusting himself until his head lay down under her cunt as her mouth continued to suck at his penis. Looping his arms around her waist for leverage he pulled himself up to the lips of her cunt and started to kiss her. Her instinct had been right. She had felt the effect that just moving into this position had had on his penis; now what he was doing to her increased his own excitement. His penis began to uncurl. She pulled her mouth away for a moment to watch as the flaccid flesh began to blossom like some strange tropical fruit. Then she covered him with her mouth again using her tongue to coat him with saliva and tease and stroke his now almost full length. Trying, for a moment, to ignore what he was doing to her, and concentrate on him.

Straight sex. What she'd done before a million times. Well many times. Good clean fun. It was good, it felt good and perhaps if this had happened earlier and nothing else was going to happen other than straight intercourse it would never have occurred to her that this was less than exciting. But that was not the case now. He had changed her perspective. The light came from a different direction; different shadows and different highlights. Other things had happened. And she wanted them to continue to happen. She was not here to have a George, or even a Devlin.

Martin may have felt her enthusiasm wane, her concentration lapse. He may have felt that she was not applying herself to the job in hand with much verve. He may have sensed that she was not responding to the

163

contact of his mouth on her cunt. His sexual sensitivity to her was acute, she knew that. And obviously it was a mutual sensitivity, because she was aware of a change in mood in him before he started to move.

This time she was sure who it was applying the pressure. He was. He was pushing her over and getting out from under her. His penis popped out of her mouth. It glistened with her saliva. It looked angry. One angry eye. She sensed he was angry and knew she was innocent. That was the performance. Her renowned innocence.

He was pushing her again moving her on to her stomach. In her mind she wanted to make a round 'O' of her mouth and ask him what he was doing. He got up off the bed but almost before she could look round he was back again. He kissed her between the shoulder blades, a hard kiss pushing his head down on to her so she was pressed into the bed covers. He moved his mouth so he could kiss the nape of her neck, clearing her hair away with his hand. He was kneeling now, knees either side of her thighs, and she could feel his hard penis resting against her buttocks.

She opened her legs so he could kneel between them, then raised her buttocks so his penis slipped down between her legs. In this position her breasts hung down from her chest and his hands immediately reached round her to clasp and fondle them. He pinched her nipples hard then pulled them down until they were almost touching the bedclothes. His penis was between the lips of her cunt but it would need a hand to press it into the right position for penetration. As it was, he was rocking it back and forward along the narrow wet slit, nudging her clitoris at each movement.

Stephanie felt him reach out and a moment later was aware of a cold wet sensation around the puckered hole of her arse. My god he was going to bugger her. Bugger her! His fingers were working the lubricant around the hole and up into it. His finger was inside her arse. Then she felt him greasing his penis.

She had never been buggered and couldn't even remember an attempt. Now she appeared to be seconds away from it. Unless she acted now, unless she pulled herself up off the bed or did something. Of course she had no intention of doing anything, anything other than feeling the extraordinary sensations that were racing through her. Her most immediate reaction had been panic and shock. Now those feelings were mixed, interlaced with total excitement. It was like being a virgin again. She couldn't help feeling a sense of fear too; everyone had said it would be painful. But God it was exciting. He was exciting.

He leant forward again and was gently pushing his penis up against her hole. She could feel its heat and hardness so clearly, more clearly than with her cunt because there were no hot wet flushy lips to confuse the sensation. Then he pushed into her. She felt her arse give, felt it try to accommodate his width and fail. She was too tense. The muscles were contracted and hard. She must relax. (Why must she? Why didn't she tell him to go to hell?) She made a effort to relax the muscles and he responded immediately pushing his penis home. It was in. She couldn't tell how far. The whole thing was so different, the feelings, the wetness, the heat, the geometry of their bodies. A whole world of newness. But he was inside her arse. She felt him push again and this time she could feel, or thought she could feel, him move deeper. He was still not fully home. She could tell because she couldn't feel his navel against her buttocks or his balls down between her labia.

For that moment the concentration had swamped her

excitement. Now as he began to move inside her, move back and forth as though fucking her, and each stroke upward taking him deeper and nearer to being all the way home, she could feel her excitement reassert itself. It hurt, but it was not painful. Or it might have been painful but for the other things converting the pain into pleasure. She was moaning. She could hear herself moaning. She was breathing in short gasps. There was something so different about having this sword of flesh inside her here, in her arse, and that alone was swelling all her sexual awareness.

Her mind told her what was being done to her. The words repeated in her mind over and over again. 'I'm being buggered,' 'He's buggering me,' 'Buggering me.' The words were an incitement to her other senses.

It was so like intercourse. The rhythm. The feeling of a penis buried deep inside her body. And yet her cunt was free. Her clitoris untouched. Her vagina empty. Penetrated and full of his penis; a penis deep inside her and yet her cunt unused. That was the strangest sensastion.

He was all the way home now. On his upward strokes she could feel his balls bounce into her labia and his navel push into her buttocks. She seemed to be so wet down there. She wasn't sure where all the lubrication was coming from but now he had no trouble moving freely in and out of her. He was breathing heavily and started to moan. He was near orgasm. She was nowhere near.

He moaned in rhythm to his action. His hands held her hips to pull her back on to him until he stopped and leant forward on to her arched back. His hand went under her and found her clitoris. It was actually cold. He pushed at it hard. He rubbed at it in a way which could only be described as vicious. He was angry again.

166

Angry that she was not excited. He had to make her excited. He was rough. He plunged his fingers into her cunt. Suddenly she could feel herself penetrated in two places, could feel his fingers up alongside his penis inside her, separated only by some thin membrane of her own.

Then he was up again and holding her hips to steady him as he ploughed into her with complete abandon. He was not being careful, he was not making sure he hurt her as little as possible, he was only concerned with himself, with coming hard and hot in her arse, right up in her arse where he wanted to be.

And she was concerned with the very same thing. She pushed her buttocks out at him, ignoring any pain, relishing the pain, turning the pain to intense pleasure, wanting him there, wanting to know she'd been buggered by him. She pushed her buttocks back into his navel, feeling his balls, feeling her breasts bouncing under the effort, her nipples grazing the bedclothes. She listened as his rhythmic moans became one long moan and realised that she was moaning too for exactly the same reason. Somehow this man was bringing her off; his action, motion, was making her shake into orgasm. He came first but as she felt him relax slightly and pull back she came too, an orgasm like none she had ever had, an orgasm seated in her clitoris and caused by lack of touch, caused by absence in the presence of total excitement. An orgasm of the head pulsing through her body. An orgasm so unlike anything she had felt before she wondered whether it was an orgasm at all.

A delicious feeling of relaxation overtook her suddenly. She curled up slightly and decided she would just close her eyes and rest, just for a moment. He lay beside her unmoving. In darkness behind her closed eyes she felt a rush towards sleep, felt consciousness pulling away from her like a boat accelerating away and leaving the shore far behind, so that in a matter of minutes it was impossible to see the barest suggestion of land.

From somewhere in sleep some part of her registered that he had turned off the light. It did nothing to deter her from sleep.

PLEASUREHOUSE 13

Agnetha Anders

Pleasurehouse 13 is an unusual novel. It's very difficult to categorize, and it wasn't easy to find an extract that would be readily understood by someone who didn't know the story.

It's science fiction, but set only a little in the future. It's full of humour, but some of it is dark and savage. It has a lot of sex in it, but it's too closely linked to the story to make it easy to find scenes of sheer unbridled lust.

In the end, I decided to feature the book's opening chapter. It introduces the characters and the setting that predominate in the book, it shows the style of the writing, and it consists of nothing but a detailed description of a young man and a woman having a wonderful screw. What could be better than that?

The events of *Pleasurehouse 13* are brought to a conclusion in *Last Days of the Pleasurehouse*.

Everyone else might be fucking themselves silly as per normal on a Tuesday, but there was a nasty flashing spot of trouble on Twozec Salkeld's screen.

For normal instance – there was normal pigging, poking and contentment among the Threes in City MK (as Milton Keynes was now called). The MK Threes were, as normal, so bombed out and shagged out that they couldn't be bothered to make the kind of waves which caused trouble on Salkeld's screen.

City HH was also calm. The last spot of bother in what used to be Hemel Hempstead had been a year or two ago, when the Regional Centre computer sent in double food but no alcohol. Everything went unstable for a day and a half, until the computer system was fixed and the Threes of HH, whatever their turn-on, could wallow continuously in it once again.

Tuesday's reports to Salkeld from the Pleasurehouses continued to indicate the required percentage of full satisfaction with all the ad-lib sex, sport, entertainment etc., etc., which it was Salkeld's business to provide.

Except, of course, this morning, 26 September 2030, there was that irritating problem for Class Two Executive Salkeld.

A possible answer to his problem, even if he didn't yet know it, was currently sitting naked in her kitchen about fifteen kilometres from Salkeld's office. She was very beautiful, not tall but with the sort of body which often illustrated downmarket reading matter. She was in a state of eager anticipation. Today was her own private treat day. Her eyes glittered as she speculated gleefully on how she would spend the next hour or two, and positively gleamed as she compared that in her mind with the pallid, mechanical, missionary instant her husband provided as a weekly passion allowance.

Up in the Berkshire Downs she sat, in the large, picturesque, period farmhouse so typically favoured as a residence by Class One.

There she was, Ann, Salkeld's potential answer, splendid and solo, sitting on an old oak chair worn glassy smooth by centuries, wearing it still more glassy smooth with eager little squirms of her bottom. Her eyes were fixed on the kitchen window, chin cupped in hands, elbows and glorious tits resting on the kitchen table top at White Horse Farm. She was Ann Richmond, 36, not to mention 40, 29, 38. She wanted her heart's desire and got something like it when Lancelot Brough, 17, arrived at the window and very nearly broke the glass with his eyeballs.

Ann swung up and moved to the door with that certain special walk that female dancers have, a sort of flat-footed duck walk yet a light and bouncy movement with the lower leg thrown out from the knee joint.

Ann, the lovely Ann, got to the door and opened it standing behind, hidden from view although there would be no-one to see. Having non-marital sex outside the Pleasurehouse, even having a regular relationship with a student under full privilege age, was not a desta-bilising offence. But probably it was against the wishes

172

of the Social Committee, so there would still be trouble if it came out. Oh well. So bloody fucking shitting bloody what. The bored Ann took the risk. Being a wife in these days meant being strictly non-working. You were supposed to be a mother and homemaker only, when all the homemaking was done for you anyway by the robot and the computer. It was not exciting.

In walked the boy with a fragile bearing of self-assuredness. Back at college he was like a king, among other boys envious of the number of his conquests and the size of his weapon, and among those girls who were keen to surrender their sovereignty. But here he was a mere apprentice to a great sorceress and he always felt a peculiar mix of sensations when he saw Ann – powerful desire, wonderment at his good luck, and anxiety about what she might do.

'Don't speak, boy,' whispered Ann. 'Just pick me up and carry me.'

This superb woman had grey-green eyes, deep red hair just short of shoulder length, and a mature, slightly aquiline, subtle and remote beauty that reminded the boy somehow of days long gone by, of those actresses they used to call 'film stars', or the legendary symbols of animal femininity like the Roman Empress Messalina who outperformed the city's top prostitute. He carried her upstairs to the attic bedroom she reserved for adventures.

He lifted her with her legs over his left arm and his right arm round her back. Her left arm was round his neck while her right swung free, her fingertips brushing ever so lightly against his thighs as he mounted the stairs.

He breathed more heavily than normal with the effort of carrying Ann, and he inhaled her perfume deeply. Its reverberations filled his head. She wore something quite unlike the sort of stuff the girls at college had. Their perfumes' messages were unmistakable, as matter-of-fact and open as their attitudes. With them the scent was either 'Miss Permafrost Discusses Thermodynamics in the Refectory', or 'Fuck Me Sideways and Bring All Your Friends'.

Ann's perfume, however, was from another world. It had all sorts of complicated messages in the background, all kinds of depths and dark corners – and he could smell her through it. Her smell was of hair, and skin, and excitement, and it all mingled deliciously with those few drops of distilled essence which, if he only knew it, came out of a little bottle, which came out of a fancy box, which came out of a pack of six given to Ann in return for certain favours in Paris, as long ago as 2012.

By the time he turned along the landing her palm was on his vital part. She idly wondered if she could, from her current position, undo his zip, get his cock, fit it between her cheeks and let it find its own way home.

She had the zip down anyway by the time he placed her on the blue duvet, so she ordered him to stand still while she sat on the bed edge and lovingly extracted the warm, soft as silk, hard as iron glory which, with the vigour of its youth, could give her hours of delight. There was another side to youth, however, and that was the initial overexcitement of, as it used to be called, the bull at the gate.

Ann felt that surge of emotion within her as she held the boy up to her lips. She wanted the first bed-shivering, sense-quivering moment, the first of maybe four or five that she knew that thing in her hand could give her. She wanted him pushing and shoving on top of her, in her, all over her, but she couldn't have it yet.

Sure enough, the closeness of her face to his cock, the soft sensation of brushing breath on it, the thought that any moment her tongue would run its roughness along it . . . all this proved too much for the lad. As she stroked the sturdy scimitar she felt it begin to pulse inside her fist. Like lightning she loosed the waistband fastenings of his trousers and whipped them and the tiny briefs he always wore, down to below his knees. Her lips opened just enough as she fed the boy's personal vibrator into her mouth.

Back and forth she went, pursing and sucking as he let got with the first of the day. Fellatio was routine for her. She got no great pleasure from it, but she knew it was a supreme feeling for him and so, like the artist she was, she made certain she gave her best performance. She knew (from great experience) just how to suck in rhythm with his spurts, just how to squeeze the most ecstatic feelings for him so that he was soon looking down on her with an even more devoted, ever-grateful and adoring expression on his young face.

He had quite a nice face, actually, thought Ann as she looked up, swallowing. Sort of craggy, with scrubby blond hair, just a few freckles and a little snubby nose. Little and snubby was soon a description equally apt for the item she held in her hand.

'Come on boy,' she said. 'Shoes and socks . . . off!'

This was their private cue, dating from the first time he'd had her, which had been after a dinner at the college where Ann's husband Arthur Richmond was on the Technical Committee and the senior boy Brough had been seated on her left.

She'd had her stockings round her ankles and her shoes on as she leant over the back of the Founder's Chair on the stage of the school hall, and she had wondered what on earth would be the reaction if the curtains opened onto the port and cheese below. Now, whenever she said shoes-and-socks . . . off, each had to strip as fast as they could, and the last one to be naked was underling and the winner was overlord.

The boy had got shoes, socks and trousers off before he twigged. The luxurious wife Richmond lay, already without a vestige of clothing, as she had been since before he arrived, a half-smile on her reflective red lips as she watched the boy's frantic Pavlovian reaction.

'Caught you,' she said, as he completed his strip at a more leisurely pace. 'Now, I'm the big boss for the day.'

The boy Lancelot was hesitant, wondering where this all-knowing, never-fazed woman would take him if he let her put him in too weak a position. So, he hoped she would keep it to a little light trick or two, a token, just enough to add a hint of spice.

Just a hint, thought Ann, as she rummaged through a drawer for a roll of sticking plaster. Binding thumbs with plaster is hardly the real thing, but still, can't have everything.

'Hands behind head, boy,' she commanded, 'and sit up.'

She quickly taped his thumbs together behind his neck, making sure to include plenty of blond hair just in case he should think of bringing his hands forward over the top.

'Lie back.' My, she loved this. Power gave her good sensations. It always had, and issuing orders was fun, whether it was to a troupe of chorus girls when she'd been captain and choreographer all those years ago, or to a muscular, hard, youthful man who delighted her eyes and her most secret wishes right now.

In both cases, the chorus girls and the boy, she was in command because she knew the most. Knowledge is power, she thought, and power is an aphrodisiac.

He lay back as ordered and, swinging her leg over him like mounting a bicycle, she presented her divine red muff to his lips. At full stretch she could rub her considerable saddlebags against his stomach, give his crossbar a little lick and, while he was busy exploring her seat with his tongue, tape his big toes together.

He tried to protest at this double securing, but he was really in no position. The protest went unheeded and was largely unintelligible. Muffled, as it were, thought Ann.

She gave herself two or three minutes of pivoting on his tongue but was careful not to let herself slip too far. She had plans for young Brough.

Suddenly, lifting away and kneeling beside him, she kissed him on the lips. She pushed her tongue into his mouth, tasking her own fluids and snorting her own pheromones like a line of coke. Then –

'Back to that college next week, is it, Lancelot?' she whispered. 'Back to that dreadful concentration camp of sadists and woofters?'

Colleges for future members of Class One were highpowered educational establishments which naturally concentrated their academic efforts on computer systems, programming languages, robotics and the like, but they retained much of the philosophy and lifestyle of the old public schools.

'But,' continued Ann, 'you'll be a senior prefect now, won't you, Lancelot? You'll be able to beat those naughty little boys and girls with your cane, won't you, Lancelot?'

Since she was saying all this while fondling his assembly into a more riotous state, Lancelot was a bit slow catching on, and was too relaxed to stop her as she moved sharply, flipped him over like a nurse giving a bed-bath, and sat on his calves. The small riding crop was behind her, hidden under the bottom of the duvet, and the grin of complete amusement was on her mouth, and the glint of purified lust was in her eyes.

Lancelot tried to lift her off with a kind of swimming butterfly kick as she tickled his darkest little corner with the leather tab on the whip end, but a quick and hard flicker of the whip across both buttocks stopped him dead.

'Now, Lancelot. What is it we're going to do to those little boys and girls? What do you call them? Faggots?'

'Fags, Ann, fags. For goodness' sake, look, you know I'm not terribly keen on . . .'

He stopped dead again, as she flicked that evil little tab across his white buttocks, one-two, then thrust it into the crack at the top of his legs and pressed it up hard against his balls. Go on, you big bastard, she thought as he raised his hips from the bed and she raised herself slightly to allow his legs to slide. You great big fucking machine, you with the strength and the biceps, you do what I tell you – she almost spoke aloud as she pressed the whip up harder to lift him further and further until he was kneeling, hands behind head, forehead on the pillow, arse in the air, feet tied by toes, and Ann dismounting as she slipped the whip from its position of ultimate power.

'Don't move.' She spoke matter of factly, as if the instruction were unnecessary, to be taken as read, assumed. 'Now Lancelot, remember when you were a fag thingy, and how you used to get a hard-on when the big boys beat you?'

Oh why did I ever let that out, thought the increasingly worried Lancelot.

'Well Lancelot, I'm now going to take you back in time, and I want you to pretend that I'm just another big, big boy.' By all the gods above and stuff me gently but I love this bit, she continued – to herself.

'Ow! Fucking hell!' cried Lancelot, as she thwacked him smartly right across both cheeks.

'Language, Brough, language. I won't have such language in my class.'

Lancelot confined himself to sharp intakes of breath for the next three strokes, while Ann paused after each to see if she was having the desired effect on his member. She wagged it this way and that with the end of the whip, like an old farmer she remembered seeing as a girl, moving a lamb's tail with his walking stick to see if it had been castrated properly. No farmers now, she thought, just Food Production Facilities and robots. But this little lambikins certainly is no gelding . . .

'Dear oh dear, Lancie baby. Dear dear dear. We shall have to beat you harder. I can see that being nice to you isn't appreciated.'

And she gave him two real crackers, two full strength ones that had him arching and yelping.

'Fucking bitch! Aargg!' he shouted as he brought hands, arms and a large tuft of hair over his head then turned and grabbed the whip. 'I'll show you being nice!'

The two thumbs went together for her throat, and the fingers spread round and forced her back on the bed. His knees moved up between her legs in short jumps and he spread her apart as far as he could. His cock was bouncing hard now, nodding its eagerness and swaying in its search for the spot. He collapsed into her, they met like an armour-piercing shell going up the spout, he flipped his hands behind her head and kissed her fiercely.

Ann Richmond moaned and sighed. Lancelot

Brough bounded and rebounded, hard and regular, plain and deep. Ann Richmond (36), ex-professional dancer, mature and plentiful, let herself go. Lancelot Brough (17), boy stallion, vigorous and dedicated, went for the big fences.

They came together in a huge, panting, floorboard-squeaking, window-rattling climax and when their breating became regular and their heartbeats had slowed to near normal, the pink plaster was snipped, their eyes closed and they slept.

Ten minutes or so later, Ann was awake. The boy slept on, his head in the crook of her arm, resting on the universe's most comfortable pillow.

Young Lancelot Brough had been quietly awake for a minute or two. While Ann was contemplating her fate, he contemplated at the closest of quarters the pillow on which he had slept.

It was a large, firm, generously curved breast with a nipple which, he now saw, must be all of a centimetre high. Around the base of it was a pinky brown circle, also raised but only slightly and with a higher rim around it as a border with the white china surface of the lovely globe. The rimmed disc had numerous minuscule hairs and tiny little hills and pits in it. Under a microscope that must look like a wild terrain where only giant reeds can survive. He sniffed in its odour. Like her neck, the same smells, perfume, skin, body fluids, were there but in different proportions. More body, less perfume. He blew gently on it to get the reeds waving in the wind.

It was a beautiful breast, he thought. His heart went out to that breast. It induced in him a wish to write a poem while simultaneously licking it.

The young girls he knew might have boobies which

were more pert, more nearly perfect like those you see on sculptures. But this lady, this bountiful garden of delights, had so much more to interest a chap. And even though her tits were big, they did hold their shape and they were firm and bouncy. What sumptuousness, yes, that was the word, sumptuous.

His hand went to this glorious object of desire and his rod began to stiffen. Ann rolled over to see the time on the bedside clock. Lancelot thus had a hand trapped under her on her right breast. The other went to her left. Her left hand reached behind, found his fast-rising cock and swiftly drew it to its full height.

She thrust out her bottom a little, raised her left thigh slightly, diddled her little pleasure peg with the big round end of his knob, then guided him right in. The sheer satisfaction of it almost sent her straight back to sleep. It was like a really good massage, a sunlamp and a jacuzzi all at once. It was just wonderful, totally, utterly, wonderful.

He pumped her gently at first, giving most of his attention to those luscious breasts and those centimetre-long nipples which he could feel hardening and growing as he tickled their tips with the centres of his palms. Round and round the garden, like a teddy bear . . . she gave the groan he knew, the groan which was the signal for all systems go.

She rolled flat on her stomach and he began the big pushes from behind. Almost immediately she groaned again, louder this time and meaning her first climax of the bout. He felt the extra lubrication make his journeys in and out that much more slippery.

With the energy of youth he speeded up and thrust even harder. She came again, really copiously this time, and the boy felt as if her juices had given him a second skin over his tool which was also now operating in what

181

seemed to be a much bigger space. Sensation diminished as the steel-hard member went back and forth no less effectively for Ann but automatically for Lancelot.

He felt himself becoming detached. I could do this all day, he thought. This is what they call 'giving her one'. I'm nothing more than a reciprocating pump, an engine for engendering, in, out, in, out, there she goes again, that's three.

He raised himself up on his hands and looked down at her back, her beautiful back, those curves, the big, ample, lovely, *sumptuous*, bottom, with the shaft of his prick slurping in and out, in and out. And a wicked idea occurred to him.

On the count of seventeen, he thought, since that's my age. One! Two! Three! Four! In went his most powerful thrusts, with every millimetre of length and circumference and every kilojoule of energy he had, slap, slap he went, eleven, twelve, thirteen. She came yet again, a fourth flow which gave him even more love-oil for what he wanted, fourteen, fifteen, sixteen, SEVENTEEN!

In a quick movement he pulled out, grabbed himself for extra firm direction, presented the head of his cock to her little back gathering and drove it in with one stroke.

'WaagoooooOOWFF!' she cried in a combined gasp of outrage and trill of ecstasy. Lancelot had never felt anything like it, a magic mixture of close-fitting tightness but with all that extract of delight acquired from the other entrance giving him easy sliding.

He didn't carry on counting. If he had he wouldn't have got through another seventeen. Just two or three pushes in this new haven and he was into the final phase, jerking and bucking as he came with a gush into (for him) unknown territory.

182

Ann had been making curious half-whispered wails, a high sound that meant wonderful moments, but which also expressed total surrender, the complete absence of the last vestige of self control. Then, they lay exhausted and splayed out, silent except for their breathing which took a long, long time to grow quieter. His prick stayed up, not allowed by the grasp of her muscles to slacken and drop out as it would have done had he been at a more orthodox destination. Eventually, Ann spoke.

'What made you do that, boy wonder?'

'I don't know. It just came to me to do it. I hope I . . .'

'Don't you worry none, honey chile. You ain't de first to go in by de trademan's entrance. Why, when we poor dancin' folks was lookin' fo' a job, we got front line chorus if de Great White Chief could stuff our ass, yeah boy.'

'It was the first time for me, anyway,' said Lancelot, all prim and proper, not liking her frankness about her past, not understanding her theatrical argot, and feeling threads of jealousy for those older men, the men with the power, who had enjoyed the younger Ann when, he knew from her photographs, she had been a quite spectacular beauty.

'Don't be such a pompous little fart, Lancelot. Everybody has to use what resources they've got in this world. And don't think this arse-banditry is something you'll be having every day, young Lochinvar. Conditions have to be right. I'm not having you dry-drilling whenever you fancy it. Conservation is very important in these matters. There's such a thing as overexploitation, you know, and leaving the landscape exhausted. Think buggery, think green.'

She pulled herself away from him and turned to kiss

183

his mouth. He looked into her eyes, her green eyes, such a powerful combination with the deep red hair.

'Green?' he said. 'I used to be green. But I'm learning.'

LAURE-ANNE

**The story of Laure-Anne D. as told to
Nicholas Courtin**

Laure-Anne is one of the most delectable heroines to be found in Nexus books. She's French (of course), young, and utterly lovely. And she has a completely open mind when it comes to sex. I mean it wouldn't even occur to her to say no!

In the course of three books she tells her amorous autobiography. I've selected a passage from quite early in the first book, entitled simply *Laure-Anne*.

But don't expect a tale of uninterrupted fornication. *Laure-Anne* is an erotic novel rather than a book for reading one-handed in bed. Laure-Anne and her interlocutor, Nicholas Courtin, take the time to describe Paris, the French countryside, the characters that cross Laure-Anne's path – and I rather like this less intense approach to erotic writing.

Laure-Anne's story continues in *Laure-Anne Encore* and *Laure-Anne Tojours*.

Twenty is a good age for a girl, and I have never met one with this number of summers who sulked for long.

My new-found exuberance took over and I returned to the preoccupation that was uppermost in my mind. I was fascinated by my development into a mature woman. I suspected that I was filling out across the abdomen and had more flesh on my thighs and bosom. It was natural that I wanted to use my attributes, and my sensual proclivity seemed to augment day by day. I was a future Marilyn Monroe and seriously considered having my hair dyed blonde.

However, the chemistry of sex was one thing, what I wanted was the mechanics. I could have entertained a whole regiment of paratroops, such were my nubile propensities at that time. Oh, how I worked on those male guests, but to no avail! The luck of the draw was against me.

Then the insurance magnate Marcel Giraud came to my rescue, though in a surprising way. He turned up one mid-week afternoon in early September, this time as a private guest.

He suddenly appeared in one of the smaller committee rooms and found me folding some promotional material. He declared in subdued tones: 'Ah, Mademoiselle D., Laure-Anne, nice to see you again.' We shook hands. 'I've been settling in and I wanted to see you.' He pushed the door to.

'I was most satisfied,' he went on quietly, 'with our last little encounter and would like to thank you again.'

'Thank you too, sir,' I murmured, trying hard to blush and lowering my eyes. 'It was somewhat rushed, I fear, but you were most generous.'

He placed a friendly hand on my arm: 'I really hope I didn't hurt you. I was quite taken away. You've only yourself to blame for being so pretty.' I tilted my head with a tiny shake to tell him there were no hard feelings. He rushed on: 'I'm staying just tonight, and I've actually come to see *you*. Do you possibly think you could oblige me with your services once more, but in a completely different kind of way that will prove far more pleasant for you? How can I put it? I have a strong leaning towards receiving corporal punishment, if you see what I mean, and I would be extremely grateful if you would oblige.'

He paused to see the effect, and I said, 'We-e-ll, I've never done anything like that before, but I'm sure it can be arranged. How nice of you to ask me, and in such a charming way – I mean that, Monsieur Giraud, the world seems so full of mean pigs these days – and in any case you've come all this way, I couldn't possibly say no. But – er – it's rather crowded and doesn't this sort of thing make a good deal of noise? There might be trouble, I feel.'

He smiled broadly: 'And you're so well-behaved, if I may return the compliment. You've no cause to worry, I've thought of everything, even brought you a nice little outfit. All you need are some boots, because I didn't know your size.'

'Oh dear, I haven't got any, just some ankle boots.'

'What colour are they?'

'Dark brown.'

'They'll have to do, it's a detail. Now listen, we can go to some woods I have located a few miles away and we'll be safe from prying eyes and ears. Say you agree, please. I promise you that if this works out a great future beckons you.'

We continued for a while to discuss details, and I arranged to sneak out just after he left by car the next morning, and meet him a short distance from the estate.

So it was that we turned off into a cart track that forenoon, and parked the car discreetly. We stood in our ordinary clothes listening for a while to a tractor far in the distance, and then he lugged a travel bag out of the back and we sought out a small clearing in the thick wood that could hardly have felt a human foot for years. I wondered if I was crazy to have come with this virtual stranger, but told myself he was known to the hotel, and was too important a personality to dare or need to turn rough. Men in his position simply do not murder women, and nobody with his obvious interest in the call of the flesh and the money to satisfy it can be dangerous. And if he did turn the plot round and decide to give me a whipping against my will, one word from me and he would be finished; Uncle Xavier would see to that. Thus I told myself I was safe.

'This is perfect,' he stated. He wore a dark blue business suit with thin stripes, I remember. I had on a simple wine-coloured skirt and cream jumper. 'You remember your lines, how it goes?'

'I think so, you can count on me.' We smiled our connivance, and then he gave me a look that would blow-dry your hair from 50 yards. 'Right, take the bag and get changed out of sight.'

189

I emerged from hiding a few minutes later in black shiny tights, my brown bootees(!), mid-thigh leather skirt and thin leather jerkin both in glistening black. Underneath, I wore a red G-string but no bra. My hair was pulled back and tied with a red ribbon, no easy task as it was really too short for this. I carried a leather whip a foot or so in length.

'Undo a couple of buttons,' he said. 'Right, now start.'

I gulped and stood with my legs slightly apart, the whip dangled down, and swayed a little. A last look round at the sun beaming down through the trees, a deep breath of the crip earthy smell, and I began.

'Giraud Marcel,' I said in a clear voice. 'Stand to attention when I am speaking and look at me. I am given to understand that you were engaged in harassing women at your office, exposing yourself before them on more than one occasion, and generally behaving in a disgusting manner. A person in your position ought to be ashamed of himself, and I am afraid I have no alternative but to administer the necessary punishment. You have been found guilty on four counts of molesting a particular typist, whom you threatened to dismiss unless she yielded to your lecherous advances.'

I went about this way and that and swished around to show the G-string. 'How would *you* like to be fondled and pestered by an ugly woman twice your age? Be quiet! There is nothing you can say that will spare you now.'

Acting the ugly woman, I advanced upon him and groped him as he stood to attention: his member was already hard. I undid his zip.

'Remove his trousers, girls.'

I played the role of the other girls.

'Tie him up.'

The girls tied him up, facing away, to a horizontal branch, an action simulated by his placing his hands on the branch.

'Huh, I'm going to enjoy this, you don't know how cruel we can be when roused. Bend over further, your body at right angles to your legs. And don't whimper before you're touched. You'll get 12 strokes, and every time you clench up, you'll get two extra. Where's the whip?'

I approached the victim, running my hands under his shirt, then ran my hands over his rump. 'Your organ is hard even in these lamentable circumstances, I see, how disgusting, can't you control yourself? Know that you are completely in my power, nothing can save you now, you must take your punishment.'

I slowly slid down his mustard coloured underpants, to reveal his snow-white buttocks. I saw the marks of a previous flagellation, but made no comment.

Then at last I stood back, and he rasped: 'Oh no, please no!'

I snarled: 'Come on, take it like a man, you coward. The first stroke is coming, look girls, see him flinch.'

I took careful aim and as luck would have it the thong hit him dead centre. He did not move and I delivered another, harder. The whip, some two centimetres thick, went 'wheep-slap' as I delivered four more.

'Oh girls,' I said, 'you don't know how this is exciting me.'

Giraud removed his right hand from the branch and began masturbating. After four more strokes, I saw his middle heaving rhythmically. I broke off to feel his wounds.

'Go on,' he ordered (this being outside the game), and I continued more slowly. I think I got two more strokes in before he jerked forward and I left him to it, for there was no point in going on.

He recovered slowly, and I watched. I was quite unaroused myself, but made noises pretending I was. His bottom was streaked with pink weals, and I wondered how long it would be before they turned purple, before they disappeared eventually. I hoped I had whipped him hard enough, though not too hard.

After a minute or so he stood wincing and faced me. He said: 'Thank you, *chérie*, it was marvellous.' We became our normal selves and he took me in his arms and hugged me, bestowing a brief kiss on my forehead.

At that instant we heard a shout. The vague shape of a man, no doubt a farmer or a gamekeeper of some kind, was heading for us 50 yards off.

'Shit,' Giraud snapped. 'Decoy him, I'll fetch you later, decoy him!'

His underpants were up in a flash, he grabbed his trousers and went flying for the car, leaping madly over the undergrowth with his yellow-clad rear aglow.

I spun round, somehow found the bag and ran off in the other direction. I threw myself into some brambles, ripping the tights for sure. The intruder was now shouting, but I was outdistancing him. I ran frantically for a while, then halted and listened. All was quiet, and I went cautiously back to the clearing. There was no trace of the farmer, and I prudently went to find my ordinary clothes. They were all there, except the panties! I changed and put the black gear into the bag. Still no noises, and it was creepy. The erstwhile golden sun now seemed sickly, the good earth damp and chilly. The tractor was still whining away. I thought it best to quit the scene of the crime and found the stump of a felled tree not far away. And there I sat, feeling cold without my vital garment, now utterly vulnerable with the farmer or whatever lurking around.

I reasoned Marcel Giraud would leave the car on the road and walk back eventually along the cart track to fetch me. So I shifted my position so that I could see him. It was now half past ten, it would take at least an hour to get back to the Club des Ducs, but the big question was: when should I stop waiting and set out?

My partner was true to his word, and 15 minutes later I heard the car stop.

In the car, with the leather upholstery warming me, he enquired as to my fortunes and then turned to me: 'Laure-Anne, you were terrific, what an actress you'd make! We must do it again some time. Now listen, Laure-Anne, I want to be really serious. I can't discuss it now, but could you possibly come into Evian tomorrow at nine? I have a proposition to put to you.'

'Why not?'

We fixed the venue.

'Can you tell me what this is all about?'

'It's a job offer, but I really prefer to discuss it properly tomorrow.'

And discuss it we did, at a table in a bistro. He was waiting for me with an expression that told me he had eaten broken bottles for breakfast.

'Right,' he declared, 'this is strictly business, take this pad and here's a ballpoint pen. You may care to make some notes, I'm a believer in taking notes. In fact my only regret about yesterday is that I did not ask you to wear glasses like my secretary; a real beauty but I daren't try anything because she loves her husband who's a school teacher and she's a stuckup bitch. Still, never mind that. Why I asked you to render that little service yesterday, apart from the pleasure it afforded me, was this: I wanted to test you, to test your amenability. You will understand in a minute. Now this is a copy of *Pariscope* and you'll see from these pages here that Paris is full of clubs and bars where people go to meet people, and there are live porn shows and the rest. Well, I am a committee member of the most elite of these clubs, the Rolls Royce of private clubs. We don't advertise. Would you be interested in being a hostess at our club? I am authorized by the committee to make you an offer.'

'Me?' I said gaping at him.

'We really need girls like you. But before you say anything I would like to ask you some rather personal questions. Could you please give me a quick summary of your life so far, not the intimate side, but the main lines?'

He was sticking his neck out, so I had no hestitation in responding to his open request. It took about two minutes.

'Good, excellent. It does seem to me that club work would suit you very well. I need not stress that you have all the attributes: class, pleasant personality, a good body, willingness to try anything, feminine appeal, discretion, compliance and so on. Tell me, Laure-Anne, about your plans for the future, what you want to do with your life?'

I let out a short laugh and said: 'You've caught me out there, I'm just trying to enjoy life after a sheltered start, I have no special plans. I like it at the Club des Ducs, and was intending to stay there a bit, to get some experience, find my bearings. I am only just beginning to feel alive.'

'Good. I do envy you your youth. Our club is patronized by the cream of France, and there are a few foreign guests from time to time. We have ministers, army people, church people – remember that bishop who dropped dead in the Rue Saint Denis? He was one of ours – and diplomats and those sort of people. We are a kind of freemasonry of the good life, of pleasure, if I can put it that way. Epicureans, hedonists and to hell with the rest. I must stress that we look after our girls, they earn good money, and in return they keep their mouths shut for the rest of their lives.' He paused to let the information sink in. 'We are fond of our girls, hold them in high esteem, as equals. You may be interested to know that one of our ladies met her future husband there, a permanent secretary at one of the ministries; poor fellow, his wife went off with some Vietnamese refugee. Anyhow, are you interested, that's the point? It's not hard work, but the one thing we must have is total loyalty, adherence to the spirit of the thing, and silence. Personally, if I were a young lady like you I'd jump at the chance, you never know what it can lead to.'

I put a fingernail in the gap in my teeth and began snapping it, a habit I have when under great anguish. I said: 'Thank you for considering me, and for being so frank. It seems to me that you are running a kind of upper crust call-girl business.'

'Not at all. Any professional activity outside the premises is strictly forbidden. That may sound harsh, but I can only repeat that we look after you as if you were our own daughters.'

I said: 'All right, I'm interested. I think you've got a deal. Why not? I'm telling myself, but I want some more details.'

We conversed in subdued tones for a while longer, and then he handed me an envelope, fees for the whipping.

A week later I took a few days off to see the family, which was tricky, because I had to conceal so much about the recent past and my plans for the future.

I also spent part of a day and part of a night at the club in question.

I officially started my new job on November 1, 1976. A vote for hedonism if ever there was one.

The Top Club was not listed anywhere, and its two phone numbers were ex-directory.

It had a dull grey door easy to overlook, a street number, a bell and a small brass plate stating simply *Top*. It was in a busy street lined with shops and bars some 300 yards from the Arc de Triomphe.

Nobody noticed the door. Inside was the real entrance, a sort of conservatory with French windows, and it was guarded by a doorman while another man was presiding over a vestibule where the guests' coats were collected. You went through the French windows into a quiet lounge with a bar and a dozen tables. This room looked like a good hotel foyer. Immediately to the left on entering was a notice board, a letter rack and a shield reading: *Dignitas – Pietas – Fidelitas*. In due course I was given to understand that the cloak room usher had an automatic pistol under the counter, but also that it had never been used.

On any day shortly after noon you could expect to see a few of France's top people call in for a drink and a chat with the three or four girls present. But sometimes they simply got their drinks from the bar and took them to a table. Hot and cold snacks were served at the bar but no meals could be had. These refreshments were available at normal going prices as a safeguard against abuse, and members paid for them. The girls were strictly forbidden to drink alcohol, and no licentious behaviour of any kind was permitted in the lounge. Thus the tone was set. If a member desired the company of a girl or more than one, he took her or them into the other part of the establishment through a revolving door adjacent to the bar. No money was allowed to pass between the member and any of the personnel. Thus all pecuniary embarrassment was avoided. We were at the service of members, with whom no familiarity was allowed in the usual sense of the term. We employed the formal '*vous*'.

The atmosphere at this time of the day bordered on the austere, and this was deliberate. There was no music. After all, some people simply dropped in for a drink and a sit-down. Those who required sexual relief had four soundproof rooms in the recreational area at their disposal each containing two easy chairs, reproductions of paintings, a bed draped with a single sheet and an extra half-sheet that was changed after each member had finished his business. There was also a small washbasin.

The club closed at 2 p.m. and reopened at 6 p.m. The pace was far swifter after that, and at least six girls were on duty, while canned music was played. From 6 p.m. until 2 a.m. members had the use of a heated swimming pool, a room for group sex furnished with sofas and a huge round playbed, a large elliptical sunken bath with all necessary accessories, and a cellar equipped with instruments of torture – not forgetting the four cubicles. The other rooms consisted of the office, the retiring room for the girls including cupboards for clothes, and a store.

I have used the term 'top people' for a very simple reason. There were women as well as men among the members. Membership totalled roughly 500, taking one year with another. Ours was a non-profit-making establishment whose officers were elected once every two years. The resulting committee was in complete charge, and it appointed the manager and assistant manager who attended to staff and other administrative matters. The committee vetted every application for membership, the annual subscription being roughly six times the minimum guaranteed monthly wage in France.

As to the members, Marcel Giraud's description was about right. Several ministers were members, along with business magnates and others from influential walks of life. There was little we girls did not learn about sooner or later concerning their characters, but no word was breathed off the premises, and the comment within was negligible. One cabinet minister was strongly rumoured in the press to be a paedophile, but he personally swore to me that this was untrue, and his conduct at the club certainly indicated he was highly girlophile. The wife of one minister was said to have had a child by another minister and to have later teamed up with yet another minister; all I know is that she behaved like a maniac among us girls. A highly placed lady in the State was said to extract money from her husband when he wanted her to accompany him abroad on official functions; she was keener on a night out at the club, and had a penchant for our feminine company. A noted catholic priest of the traditionalist branch used to dress up in our clothes and have himself flagellated with a coat-hanger, but he was eventually asked to leave the club on the grounds that he was a disturbing influence.

It would be completely wrong to suppose that we were ravaged by the 500 members day in, day out. It was not like that at all. I estimate that on average I hosted about two or three men a day, no more, although once a week I was roped in for group activities on the playbed. We were universally known as *les girls* and were often asked to play with each other and perform in the torture room. In this connection I must amend a previous statement about free services; a bonus scale was applicable to any girl who allowed herself to be physically whipped or caned.

Having explained all this, I should like to backtrack to the day I first entered the Top Club, to sample the atmosphere and discuss contract terms.

Marcel Giraud took me in that evening round 8 p.m. and introduced me to the manager, whose name was Gérard. More about him later. We had just walked around and emerged from Gérard's office when I came face to face with none other than an old acquaintance!

'Is it really you, Blandine?' I cried. 'What are you doing here? You're the last person I expected to see in this place. What have you done to your hair?'

'*Mon chou*, what are *you* doing here?'

Neither of us answered, we simply embraced and the two men left us. We sat at one of the tables staring at each other and breathing in the leather smell.

Mademoiselle Groult, whom I later called Blandine at her request, was (or rather had been) a mathematics teacher at our school, and she gave private tuition during the run-up to the *Bac* at her nearby studio flat. She was also assistant captain of our girl guide section. A week after the *Bac* about two dozen of us went by coach to the Ardeche region of Central France, where a lorry had taken our tents and equipment. Mademoiselle Groult shared a tent with the number two girl. I was allotted a tent with a girl called Delphine, who seemed just as withdrawn in character as myself. Both of us were late starters. Mademoiselle Groult requisitioned Delphine and I for stores duty. This consisted mainly of going to the nearest village and to a farm for things like bread, milk, eggs and poultry, trundling a two-wheeled cart behind us.

One afternoon after lunch, Mademoiselle Groult asked me to go with her to the village where she had to make a phone call. We looked smart in our uniforms as we strode out on the two kilometre journey. We had dark blue knee-length skirts and matching socks, dove grey shirts and red and white scarves with a woggle, plus berets. About 200 metres from the camp, my superior took my hand and we walked along gaily in step, telling ourselves how lovely the countryside was looking, pointing out birds and wild flowers. I decided I really quite liked 'La Groult' as she was tagged by the guides. She obviously sought friendship because, after I had been calling her mademoiselle for a while, she said: 'Do call me Blandine.' I smiled and repeated 'Blandine'. She asked me to say it again as I had 'a charming low-pitched voice, with clear diction'. I said it again twice to please her, more than flattered by her comment.

The village was having its siesta in that early part of the afternoon, and we were able to admire the old houses and shops at our leisure and without noise and fumes, many of the buildings dating from centuries back. Even the post office was ancient, for it was merely a counter in the grocer shop that looked out onto the village green. I sat on a bench there while my companion made her phone call.

On the way back we decided to take a short rest on a tree trunk that lay back from the path in the shade of a small beech tree. We tarried, breathing deeply and saying, 'Ah, fresh air' once or twice.

Then suddenly Mademoiselle Groult, who was on my right, took both my hands in hers, and said: 'Laure-Anne, what a romantic name!' To which I naturally replied: 'Blandine's enchanting.'

She said: 'I'd like to kiss you, Laure-Anne.' And she

acted on this wish without delay, placing one arm round my waist, turning me towards her and slipping the other arm round my neck. Her mouth was on mine and I was completely flabbergasted. I felt her lips opening, trying to force mine apart, and I was so unprepared that they yielded. She increased the pressure and kneaded my neck. I gawped at her and she stared into my eyes with a sort of frightened look, then kissed me on the lips again and this time my mouth was already receptive and the kiss spread. I felt her tongue enter my mouth and touch my own. She moved her head about so that her lips took mine with hers. She drew apart. The daringness of what we had done left me with a scampering heartbeat. There was no doubt as to her inclinations now, but the implications for me were tremendous.

'Oh Laure-Anne, how sweet you are, I am quite overcome. You don't mind do you? Kiss me back, please, at once!' I did so and found that I was quaking.

In the depths of the next night, my feet were gently shaken.

'It's only me – Blandine,' I heard as I struggled to my senses. She was unzipping my sleeping bag and taking my arm. I followed her out of my tent in a daze.

She led me into her tent, where I found her companion, a girl of about 18 called Christine who was setting out three beakers. We sat down, and the light of a torch shed a dull gleam on us from one corner. I told myself I was safe from La Groult's attentions with another person present.

'We're just having a little drink, and we thought you'd like to join us,' said La Groult. They both smiled at me, and produced a bottle of Johnny Walker, along with a packet of cheese biscuits.

Leaning back on the sleeping bags, we shifted from one elbow to the other and felt pleased with ourselves.

201

All three of us were in pyjamas of course: mine were white with small flowers, Christine's pale blue and La Groult's wine-coloured and edged with white piping.

At length Blandine, as I was calling her now, drew nearer to me and placed an arm round my shoulders, ostensibly to give me support. I stiffened, knowing in a flash that I was the victim of a conspiracy, that Christine and she were both lesbians! Before I could arrange my thoughts, Blandine was playing with my hair and saying: 'She's lovely, isn't she Chris!' Christine was stroking my legs, and I saw she was pressing her nipples with the other hand. I was 'so warm and cuddly like a kitten,' La Groult observed, moving to my own bosom. I knew I ought to get up and rush away, but the whisky and the intimate radiance of the torch, the very secrecy of the gathering and the congenital nature of my conspirators, all had their effect. An appealing animal fragrance was issuing from Blandine, and this made me more susceptible. Her soft kneading of my breasts was breathtaking, and I could feel my nipples projecting under my pyjama top. Christine had ample breasts and I wanted now to feel what they were like. In a gesture of commitment, I put out a hand and touched them, lifting them and pinching them, as Blandine was doing to me. Christine shuffled forward and kissed me on the mouth and I kissed her back. She had generous lips like my own.

Blandine withdrew, leaving us to play with each other. We sucked each others' orbs, and I looked round for Blandine, wanting to bring her into the game, and saw that she had a hand inside her trousers and was caressing herself with her legs apart. I found Christine's moist aperture, and did it for her, faster and faster until she suddenly opened her mouth and her eyes grew enormous. She stuffed a bit of a sleeping bag into her mouth and squeaked, her hair flaying around. I was absolutely fascinated and kept going. Then we were all on our knees and Christine heaved and heaved before falling back. Blandine clamped her lips to mine, her tongue slipping back and forth like a jelly, her fingers on my clitoris. She withdrew them to stroke my tummy and then returned to my orifice. A wave of heat poured into my lower body and I forced her hand against me, squeezing my legs together as the pleasure unfurled. A tidal wave engulfed me and I completely lost control, blowing into her mouth and biting at her cheek and neck.

We ended all three enfolding one another in a flurry of joy.

And now in the Top Club she was telling me: 'This isn't my hair, dear, it's a wig. Are you a member here, Laure-Anne? It can't be true.'

'It isn't. I've been offered a job and I'm taking a peek at the place. How wonderful to meet up with you again. To tell you the truth I'm lost, you can fill me in on the details here. But tell me about yourself first.'

She said: 'Well, after they threw me out of that school, I did various jobs connected with accountancy, but they never lasted. Except one at the offices of an art dealer next to the Rue Drouot auction rooms. And to cut a long story short I married the boss. But save your breath, this is a *mariage de convenance*. You see, he's a pederast and it wasn't doing him any good in the business, being so old a bachelor, so, as I don't go with men, he married me as a cover. We go our own ways, and I nominally act as his wife, in return for which I am handsomely provided for. He's tremendously rich and I get the spin-off. It means attending dinners and whatnot with him, and we sometimes entertain. It works out very well.'

I was blinking, and she went on: 'Now, as to this outfit, they call me in occasionally when they have a woman who wants to go with another woman. I'll name no names of course, you'll find out. I'm over age of course but I still count as a girl, especially with this wig. Rather nice, all these blonde curls, don't you think? Get's damned hot though sometimes. They also like me to come in for the Thursday passion parade.'

'Huh?'

'Yes, passion parade. Once a week we all take part in a kind of orgy on the playbed, and sometimes members like to watch girls having it off together, which believe me or not is pretty hard to simulate, so they ask me in to give it the authentic touch. Some members like to watch two of us in action privately too. Gaston got me the job, he's my husband.'

I whistled low in astonishment, and she told me she was at that moment waiting for a lady member to arrive from the *Assemblée Nationale*. We had gone on for a few minutes discussing the *mores* of the club and what the female staff were expected to do, when her client arrived. The lady knocked back a quick drink at the bar and came straight over. She was plump and fiftyish, and of course I did not know her as I took no direct interest in politics. She wore a wedding ring.

There was no time for introductions, as she said: 'Sorry I'm late, Blandine *chérie*, and I haven't got much time. My man's due back home at eleven. Let's go, shall we?' And they went through the revolving door.

DIPLOMATIC PLEASURES

Antoine Lelouche

More French fun and frivolity! Antoine Lelouche (what a delicious name!) serves up a tropical feast of sun, sweat, sex, more sex, and a little bit of espionage in the first of his three Diplomatic books.

I must admit I can't remember the plot at all – some nonsense about spying – but the international cast of love-hungry diplomats, the paradise island of Santa Sabina with its ever-willing natives, and the variety of the sexual encounters are all memorable. And that's because M. Lelouche knows how to write: *Diplomatic Pleasures* is deft, witty, and gently erotic throughout. The following extract is a fine example of the style.

Marcel's unflagging career can be followed in *Diplomatic Secrets* and *Diplomatic Diversions*.

By the undemanding standards of Santa Sabina the Gran'Caffe Camille was regarded as fashionable. It was to be found on the ground floor of a once flamboyant but now crumbling baroque building across the square from the church of the Four Crowned Martyrs. Because of the oppressive heat, no one except the owner ever sat inside the café, even though there was a large wooden-bladed fan turning slowly on the ceiling to keep the air moving about. Camille's customers – the cream of Santa Sabinan society – sat at the little round tables outside in the square to drink mint tea or iced coffee or the vivid orange or violet drinks that were thought to be chic.

Two days after Francesco's party, Marcel was gossiping over a drink at Camille's with the Dutchman Pieter van Buuren. The long siesta hours were over but neither had any intention of returning to their Embassies that day – the damp heat was appalling, even for Santa Sabina. The good and great of the island capital evidently thought so too, for every table was occupied and the waiters were plying their loaded trays back and forth with whatever last shreds of energy they could muster.

Pieter van Buuren was a fair-haired, pink-skinned

and short-necked man of Marcel's own age, with the muscular build of an amateur boxer. They had struck up a friendship from the day they met, based to some extent on the shared joke of the cul-de-sac nature of their present posting. But apart from professional interests, both had a hearty appetite for the delights offered by pretty women. They were talking about Eunice Carpenter, with whom Pieter had spent the night recently.

'What a woman!' he said. 'She kept me at it all night. I can't remember how many times I had her.'

'You mean how many times she had you,' said Marcel.

'Maybe you're right. Every time I dozed off she woke me up by playing with me to make me hard again. The last couple of times I was too far gone and she climbed on top of me.'

'Yes, Eunice has learned the ways of Santa Sabina,' said Marcel. 'Can you imagine her doing that to a man in Britain?'

'This country is good for women,' said Pieter. 'Something in the air brings out the best in them. Do you know what time I woke up the next day? Two in the afternoon – alone in her bed. I was so exhausted I could hardly stand upright, and she's got up to go to her office at nine that morning!'

'I've had invitations but I've never been to her apartment,' said Marcel. 'All the times that I have made love to her have been what she calls *hit-and-run*, and I do not want any more involvement than that.'

'You're afraid she'd be too much for you!' Pieter exclaimed with a grin. 'I never thought I'd hear you admit you'd met your match! But it's no surprise really – the French have a reputation for fire and flash and no staying-power.'

Before Marcel could refute this disgraceful and insulting suggestion, Pieter tapped his arm and said *look over there!* He half-turned in his seat and saw Errol Hochheimer in uniform striding away from the terrace, his face set in a scowl. He was leaving a table set back unobtrusively against the front of the Gran'Caffe, and he had got up from it so forcefully that he had knocked his chair over backwards. A white-coated waiter bent to pick it up and Marcel saw that Madame Kristensen sat alone at the table, her pretty face pale with suppressed fury.

'A lovers' quarrel, do you think?' Pieter asked, grinning.

'Yes – the night you had Eunice in the Embassy cloakroom he took her out into the garden and had her against a tree.'

'You followed and watched them do it?' Pieter enquired. 'That's real degeneracy! But the French were always voyeurs – they invented the word!'

'At some other time I shall teach you not to defame your betters,' Marcel retorted with mock severity, rising to his feet, 'but at this moment I have important business with Madame Kristensen. *Au revoir*, Pieter.'

The waiter was setting the overturned chair upright again, when Marcel said *bonsoir, Madame* to Inge Kristensen. She stared at him as if she had never seen him in her life before, her hand raised to wave him and the waiter away. At once Marcel took it and kissed it respectfully, then sat down and ordered the waiter to bring another of the pink liqueurs that Madame was drinking and a tiny glass of cognac for himself.

Deserted by her lover, Inge Kristensen was upset, angry, hurt and insecure. Marcel had the ability to be very charming. He fixed his gaze on Inge's dark brown eyes and narrow face and exerted his inborn talent to

209

the limit. Her suspicions were soon dispersed when she was reminded that he was with the French Embassy and she recalled that he had been introduced to her. In a quarter of an hour Marcel had dispelled her anger and coaxed a smile to her face, and they had almost become old friends.

A single drop of rain fell on his hand. He looked up and saw that the thick white cloud layer which so often covered Santa Sabina had turned a dirty grey and was darkening by the minute.

'There will be a storm soon, I think,' he said, reluctant to interrupt promising developments.

'I hope not!' Inge exclaimed sharply. 'I hate thunder – I must go home at once.'

Marcel put money on the table for the drinks and led Inge by the arm across the square to where two or three carriages stood for hire outside the Martyrs' church. They were the open four-wheelers that the locals called a *barossa*. Elsewhere in the world they would have had horses between their shafts, but in Santa Sabina horses cost too much and the carriages were pulled by mules. Marcel felt several drops of rain on his face and noted that the coachmen were putting up the collapsible hoods that were supposed to keep the passengers dry.

He handed Inge up into the leading *barossa* and asked her where she lived. It proved to be a villa outside the town, on the coast road, but before he could instruct the coachman, it began to rain heavily. Marcel got in beside her and suggested that she should drop him off at his hotel. Up on the box, the coachman pulled his straw hat down hard on his head and wrapped a cracked old waterproof sheet round his shoulders to keep the rain off. He seemed to be having a long, though one-sided, conversation with his ambling mule.

Marcel raised his voice a little over the steady drum of

the rain on the carriage hood, but Inge was staring nervously about her and not listening to him. The *barossa* had turned out of the square and was rolling slowly along the broad and tree-lined Avenue of the Constitution, for the wet heat had disinclined the mule to go faster than a walk. Without warning there was a split-second of blazing light in the sky, followed by a deafening crack of thunder. The mule whinnied and jerked its head up in either fright or protest, its long ears laid back and its yellow teeth bared. The effect on Inge was equally dramatic – she shrieked and grabbed Marcel's hand in both her own.

'Don't be alarmed,' he said, 'it's only thunder.'

'I'm terrified of it,' she stammered, her pretty face pale, 'I can't help it!'

'There, there,' he soothed her, slipping an arm round her waist to comfort her.

She cowered against him, gripping his hand so tightly on her lap that her nails were digging into him. As if the thunder had been a signal, the steady rain changed into a rushing torrent of water falling vertically from the sky. The mule whinnied in displeasure yet again and broke into a trot when it felt the cascade on its back, while the driver disappeared under his waterproof sheet. The rain hammered noisily on the black hood of the *barossa* and splashed up so hard from the road that it came in the open sides of the carriage, soaking Marcel and Inge from the knees down.

The sky was illuminated from horizon to horizon with blazing white light and the simultaneous roar of thunder was ear-splitting in its intensity. The mule squealed and broke into a gallop that its driver did nothing to check.

'Too much storm,' he shouted over his shoulder through the noise of the rain. 'We must wait for it to end!'

There was no point in trying to compel him to take them to the Kristensen villa outside town. Even if the coachman had been willing, his mule evidently was not. It had already turned off the Avenue of the Constitution without instruction from him and was making at breakneck speed towards a goal of its own choosing.

'Get us under shelter,' Marcel shouted back.

Inge was trembling like a leaf as she pressed herself close against him. *Well, why not?* Marcel asked himself and slid his comforting arm up from her waist until his hand was cupping a soft breast through her cream silk blouse. She huddled against him even harder and he could hear her terrified gasping.

The carriage lurched and almost tipped over sideways as the determined mule turned sharply right through an open gateway into a yard. Marcel was thrown on top of Inge, his face against hers, her nose in his mouth and his tongue in her ear. Her legs were flung wide as she fell half out of the crazily tilting carriage, her skirt up her legs and Marcel's hand so far up between her thighs that his thumb was in her hot groin. The grip of his other hand dragged her blouse open, but neither of them had time or opportunity to notice.

With a jarring crash the *barossa* rocked back upright on four wheels and came to a halt at last. The mule had made its way to the lean-to which served as its stable and it stood steaming and snorting, safely out of the rain, while the carriage and passengers were still out in the yard.

'Damn clever mule,' said the coachman, in all the pride of ownership.

The rain was thumping on the *barossa*'s leaky hood with unbelievable violence. The instant Marcel stepped out he was under a deluge. In the few seconds it took to help Inge down and hurry her under the lean-to roof alongside the mule, his thin suit was soaked right through. The lightning flared again, the thunder roared like an avalanche sliding down a mountain. Inge flung herself bodily into his arms and clung wetly to him with all her strength.

'Where are we?' he asked over her bedraggled head.

'This is my house, Monsieur,' the elderly coachman answered. 'You can stay here until the storm is over, then I will drive you and your lady to where you want to go. It is dry here and you will be private.'

His light-brown face wrinkled in a grin as he winked at Marcel and jerked his chin slightly at the open front of Inge's blouse.

'Put this round you and come with me,' he added, taking the old waterproof sheet from round his shoulders and handing it over.

His living-quarters were reached by a rickety wooden staircase up the outside of the white-washed building. Marcel put the waterproof over Inge's head and his own and draped it round them as best he could. She stared at him wild-eyed as, with an arm round her waist, he helped her up the steep climb behind the thoroughly saturated coachman. The room they entered contained the coachman's facilities for sleeping, washing, cooking and eating – all under a low roof of palm-leaf thatch placed over exposed wooden poles. The noise the rain made as it fell like a waterfall on the thatch was unnerving at first, but soon became a background roar.

'Tell me your name,' Marcel suggested, looking at the bed under the eaves by the back wall.

'It is Mateus, Monsieur. Is my house to your satisfaction? There is half a bottle of araq on the table if the lady needs it for her nervousness.'

Inge shrieked as the thunder rolled with terrifying loudness right overhead and wound her bare arms so

213

tightly round Marcel's neck that he was afraid she would choke him. He took hold of her wrists and eased her grip a little.

'I can shut the lightning out for your lady,' said Mateus, and he closed a wooden-slat blind over the one small window.

'Thank you,' said Marcel, 'your house will satisfy our needs very well until the storm finishes.'

He took his sodden money from his back-pocket and peeled off five 50-tikkoo notes, bringing a warm glow to the coachman's eyes.

'Thank you, Monsieur. My house is yours for as long as you and your lady want it. When you are ready to leave, I shall be below with the mule to take you anywhere, but please do not hurry yourselves.'

With a deep bow and a flourish of his disintegrating straw hat he was gone, closing the ramshackle door leading to the stairs carefully behind him. Marcel unwound Inge's arms from his neck and led her gently across the room to sit on the end of the low bed. The only mattress was loose straw spread thickly over wooden slats, but the red and blue country-weave blanket over the straw looked clean. He took off his soaked white jacket, hung it over the back of a chair and spread out his paper money to dry on the square dining-table.

'I fear your clothes are soaked,' he said, sitting on the bed beside Inge, 'we must dry you before you catch a chill.'

It was true that the furious tropical storm had cooled the temperature, but the prospect of catching cold was remote in the extreme. Inge looked at him vaguely for a moment and seemed grateful for his care. Certainly she did not resist when he unbuckled the patent leather belt round her waist, tugged her blouse free and eased her arms out of it. The skirt unclipped and came off with no difficulty, leaving her sitting in a semi-transparent slip. Marcel could see through the wet and clinging garment that she wore no brassière over her small and pointed breasts.

Inge's slip was interestingly short – its hem descended no lower than the top of her thighs – revealing the scarlet triangle of her tiny briefs. Like all the European women in Santa Sabina, she went bare-legged in the daytime because of the heat. Hardly able to believe the good fortune that had fallen to him, Marcel stroked from her knees up to her bare thighs, savouring the satin-smooth touch of her skin. He prised her legs gently apart and sighed in delight at what he saw.

In his dream on the night of the Embassy reception, Inge had pulled down pale blue knickers to show off a neat little tuft of chestnut curls between her legs. No doubt his dreaming mind had envisaged it like that because that was the colour of her hair. And indeed, the unconscious assumption had been correct – the fleece between Inge's legs *was* a rich chestnut. But it was far from being a neat tuft. It grew so thickly that the curls bushed out from both sides of her tiny briefs.

'But how charming,' Marcel could not prevent himself from saying, and Inge looked at him with a puzzled expression.

'What are you doing, Monsieur?' she asked, a frown creasing her forehead.

'Your clothes are soaked right through,' he told her again, 'I shall hang them up to dry while I rub you with a towel.'

Before she had time to consider the proposition, thunder exploded overhead. She screamed and grabbed for him, her arms round his waist and her face pressed to his wet shirt.

'It's all right,' he said, trying to soothe her panic by rubbing her back, 'the storm will end soon and I will take you home. But in the meantime I must get you dry.'

She was still trembling with fright when he removed her wet slip. She put her arms round his neck again and held on to him while he got her scarlet briefs under her bottom and down her long legs. Then he stood up and lifted her in his arms easily, feasting his eyes on her body, naked except for the bright red coral necklace round her neck.

'Promise you won't leave me alone!' she whimpered as he carried her round the side of the bed and laid her on the red and blue blanket.

Mateus' rough towel was hanging on a nail in the wall by a bamboo wash-stand. Marcel stripped himself to his striped underpants, thinking that a cautious approach was sensible in Inge's unnerved condition. She offered neither protest nor comment when he rolled her over face-down on the blanket and rubbed her back briskly with the towel. She had an interesting back, long and narrow, with a circular brown mole under her right shoulder-blade. He rubbed with both palms through the towel, dipping into the small of her back and up over the round cheeks of her bottom and down her slender thighs.

Her legs were modestly together and as he massaged down to her knees he pressed them slowly outwards and away from each other. Soon he was able to see the chestnut curls, thick and strong enough to conceal her *kuft* from his inquisitive eyes. *So beautiful*, he thought, hardly able to restrain himself from dropping the towel and feeling between her thighs with his bare hand. His *zimbriq* stood fiercely to attention in his underpants, but he forced himself to remain calm while he pretended to dry her thighs.

When his tension was too great to contain any longer, he turned Inge on to her back and applied the towel gently to her pointed little breasts. Perspiration had trickled down between them and her polished coral necklace was shiny from it. But her fear was not the only reason for that – the temperature was such that Marcel felt the drops running down his own dark-haired chest. He dried Inge's flat belly and saw that her legs were together again, which he found dis-appointing.

'But you are so hot, my dear Inge!' he said, trying to keep his voice level and not betray his state of excitement. 'You must be feverish – we must cool you before some harm is done.'

He had seen that there was a white enamel bowl on the washstand, filled with clean water. He brought it to the bed, dipped his handkerchief in it and wiped round Inge's breasts. That seemed to bring her a little relief and he got her to put her hands under her head so that he could dabble the wet handkerchief in the smooth hollows of her armpits.

'That feels good,' she said tremulously – her first rational words since the storm began. 'Where are we?'

'In a safe place,' he answered. 'We are waiting for the rain to stop.'

He dipped his handkerchief in the cool water again and spread it over her hot belly.

'Have we been here long?' Inge asked. 'What is the time? My husband will wonder where I am. And my children.'

Marcel glanced at his wrist-watch and told her that it was almost half past five and there was no need for anxiety. The downpour had assuredly brought the whole of Santa Sabina to a total standstill and her husband could no more get home than she could.

His little attentions to her with the towel and the water had lulled her fears to a large extent. The constant rattle of the rain on the palm-leaf roof had become almost comforting and the dimness of the room seemed positively restful. When he squeezed out the handkerchief again in the bowl and touched her thigh to indicate his intention, she opened her legs for him to bathe her hot groin.

'Does that make you feel a little better?' he asked, dipping his handkerchief in the water once more.

'Much better,' she answered, opening her long legs wider.

From her chestnut-curled groin he progressed slowly to her *kuft*, parting the thick curls with his fingers to press the wet cloth to it. She gave a little cry of surprise at the touch and her legs jerked nervously. Marcel smiled at her reassuringly till her body relaxed, her bare feet turning outwards, while he dipped his handkerchief in the bowl and laid it between her thighs again. This time he did more than just hold the wet cloth against her. He used it to caress the fleshy folds between her legs, combing her thick curls out of the way with gentle fingertips.

For two brief heartbeats Inge's pale cheeks flushed a delicate pink, then she gave herself up to the sensations of the moment. She was breathing quickly and her eyes were closed, but she did not need her vision to tell her that the wet handkerchief lay on the blanket and that Marcel had separated the lips of her *kuft* to caress her little bud. Nevertheless, for reasons of female logic she thought it appropriate to ask about his intentions.

'What are you doing?' she murmured.

'Calming you, dear Inge,' he replied, 'the storm was making you hysterical.'

'You won't make me calm by touching me there,' she

218

said, opening her beautiful hazel eyes to stare at him.

'Do you want me to stop?' he asked, feeling her legs tremble to the sensations he was stirring.

'You ask me that – your victim?' she exclaimed. 'After you've kidnapped me in broad daylight and dragged me to your hide-out to ravish me? Now you seek my opinion on whether you should continue or not – what kind of rapist are you?'

'The tender-hearted type,' he answered, his fingers deep in her warm and wet *kuft*.

'What lies!' she said. 'How can you claim to be kind and gentle when you are threatening me with that enormous thing bulging out of your underpants!'

Her hand darted through the slit of his shorts and extracted the long and swollen part she meant. It was with some justice that she called it enormous, for the excitement of his ministrations to her had aroused him to a high pitch and he was at an impressive full-stretch.

'Oh!' said Inge. 'It's monstrous – you cannot possibly stick *that* in me! You'll split me wide open!'

In spite of her protest, she did not appear to find the idea utterly out of the question, to judge by the way she flipped her hand up and down the hard shaft she had exposed.

'Resign yourself,' Marcel said firmly, 'there is no escape now that you are in my secret hide-out. After I have violated you to the point of unconsciousness I am going to tie you naked to the bed by your wrists and ankles.'

'No, I beg you not to use me for your depravity!' she gasped. 'Let me go and my husband will pay the ransom!'

'I shall keep you here for as long as I wish,' he insisted.

His body was shaking to the thrills caused by her

219

busy hand stroking him, just as she was squirming under his stimulation of her *kuft*.

'Will you make me wear a black silk mask?' she asked breathlessly. 'I beg you not to – please don't tie me to the bed, naked, with a black silk mask to hide my face!'

'But of course you must be made to wear a black silk mask,' Marcel said at once, amused by her fantasy. 'I shall leave you here on your back with your legs wrenched wide apart by cruel bonds. And when you least expect it, I shall come back and ravage your helpless body, time after time.'

'Get it over with and let me go, please!' she begged.

'I shall keep you prisoner for weeks,' he replied, his fingertips skimming over her slippery bud, 'and violate you hundreds of times, and even when you have fallen into an exhausted sleep you will wake to feel me in your belly.'

Inge made a gasping sound, perhaps of terror at the fate which he was describing, but her manipulation of his shaft did not stop or even slow down.

'No, not again,' she pleaded, 'I'm not strong enough, it is too much! You will *zeqq* me to death!'

Her eyes were rolling up in her head to show the whites and Marcel could see she was on the threshold of a climax. But at that very moment the forgotten thunder crashed out above them in a mind-splitting explosion. Her mouth gaped open in an unheard scream and her body jerked up into a sitting position, her hands pressed flat over her ears to shut out the noise.

'No!' Marcel howled in frustration.

Unable to restrain himself, he slammed her down on her back and hurled himself on top of her while the thunder roared out again, throwing her into an instant

220

hysterical seizure. Her head was hard back pushing her round little chin up sharply, and there was a trickle of saliva from one corner of her wide open mouth. She was uttering a continuous high-pitched shriek, her hands pressed over her ears to shut the storm out. Her body rolled from side to side, and her long legs were kicking out wildly. All this violent activity continued as Marcel slid into her wet slit.

He was so far gone that he hardly heard the thunder boom out once more, but it had its effect on Inge. Her heels thumped up and down on his legs with bruising force and her perspiration-wet body squirmed in convulsions so frantic that Marcel had to pin her to the bed with all his strength to keep from being dismounted. Naturally, in his advanced state of arousal the writhing of her body under him brought on his crisis at once. With savage thrust he fountained his essence into her belly and cried out in the exaltation of release.

When he came to himself again, Inge was still making her shrill noises and heaving beneath him. He thought it best to stay on top of her and restrain her movements as much as he could, so that she did not accidentally hurt herself. Very gradually she slowed down, until at last she stopped shrieking and her hands fell away from her ears. He felt the fading tremors of her belly and prayed that the thunder would not start her off again. Slowly her hazel eyes opened and she looked up into his face. She took two or three deep breaths, licked her lips and gave him an exhausted smile.

'You're too much for any woman,' she whispered, hardly able to get the words out. 'I've never felt anything like that in my life before.'

Marcel kissed her cheek and climbed off her to fetch a glass of araq from the bottle on the table to revive her. It was evident to him that Inge was confused. The strong sexual sensations she had been experiencing from his manipulation of her mind and body had somehow become integrated and fused into the hysterical seizure brought on by the thunderstorm. As a result, she believed that she had experienced the world's most stupendous climax.

It would have been cruel to disillusion her. And besides, it might even be true – there was no way of knowing what she had felt. He put an arm round her shoulders to help her sit up while he held a cup to her mouth and persuaded her to take a few sips of araq. A rumble in the sky made her start and spill some of the spirit down between her breasts, but the thunder had moved a long way off and she was soon calm again. He eased her down on the bed again and heard her contented little sigh as he licked the spilled araq from her belly.

'The storm is going away,' he said, stretching out beside her. 'The *barossa* is waiting below to take you home when the rain stops. But first you must rest a little.'

'Yes,' Inge agreed. 'I must rest after what you've done to me. You are incredible, Marcel, truly incredible.'

A little before seven o'clock the rain stopped falling with a dramatic abruptness. At one moment it was tumbling out of the sky like a waterfall, then it became a gentle drizzle and, only a moment later, it had stopped completely. Marcel assisted Inge to dress in clothes that were not yet dry – like his own they were clammy to the skin. He kissed her and took her down to the stable, where Mateus were asleep on the straw beside his mule.

'I shall remember this afternoon all my life,' she said, leaning out of the *barossa* to kiss him once more.

She drove off and Marcel strolled towards the town centre. Santa Sabina's antiquated drainage system was inadequate to cope with the quantity of rain that had descended on it in so short a time and the streets were ankle deep, even the Avenue of the Constitution. Marcel did as he saw others doing – he took off his shoes and wet socks and put them in his jacket pockets, rolled his trousers up to his knees and waded on through the warm water.

The bolting mule had carried his passengers a long way down the Avenue of the Constitution before turning off into the poor quarter where it was stabled. And as Marcel strolled back, he saw that neither the cloud-burst nor the steamy heat had done anything to depress the natural cheerfulness of the Santa Sabinans. Little groups of men sat on the public benches under the palm trees, swishing bare feet in the flood water while they chattered away. The irrepressible women were on the look-out for virile young men and Marcel declined more than one offer with a charming smile of regret.

Since leaving the stable, he had been trudging through dirty rain-water for twenty minutes, and he decided it was enough. He was in no hurry to get anywhere and it would be better to wait for the drains to empty the streets before continuing to his hotel. Apart from the discomfort of paddling along the pavement, another reason for his decision was that the woman on the balcony had reminded him of the pleasures of love and he was not far from the building where Eunice Carpenter lived.

Her apartment was on the fourth floor and, needless to say, the electricity had failed and the lift had stopped working when the storm broke. He climbed the stone stairs and knocked at Eunice's door. There was a long pause that made him think that she was out, and he was turning away when he heard a bolt rattle. Eunice opened the door and looked both surprised and pleased to see him. She was bare-foot and in a light satin négligé of an unflattering electric blue shade.

'You invited me to drop in at any time,' Marcel reminded her, 'but I fear that I have arrived at an inconvenient time.'

'No, I'm all alone,' she said with a smile of welcome. 'Come in and dry your feet.'

Her apartment was in one of the older buildings and had a hardwood floor. Marcel felt pangs of guilt as he left wet marks the length of the passage from the entrance to the small bathroom. He washed the mud-streaks from his feet and joined Eunice in the sitting-room, not bothering to put on his shoes and socks. The french windows to her small balcony were wide open, but there was no breeze at all and she looked distinctly hot and uncomfortable, sitting on a wicker-work settee. Marcel poured himself a glass of whisky from a bottle on the sideboard, filled the glass to the rim with ice-cubes and sat down beside her.

For relief from the heat, or perhaps for another reason, she had taken off her obtrusively-coloured négligé and was displaying herself in shiny satin pyjamas of a lavender tint. Marcel was constitutionally incapable of being alone with any woman under sixty, without making at least some preliminary advance. He laid his hand against her chubby belly. He found it to be very hot under the thin pyjamas and when Eunice turned her head to smile at him he saw drops of perspiration on her forehead.

'My poor Eunice,' he said, his success with Inge vivid in his thoughts, 'I must cool you down a little.'

He picked a couple of ice-cubes from his glass, put

224

his hand down the waist of her pyjama trousers and rubbed the ice gently over her belly.

'Marcel!' she exclaimed. 'That's lovely!'

She raised her bottom from the settee to push her pyjamas down her thighs and opened the buttons of her jacket. Marcel rubbed her belly with a circular motion, enjoying the view he had of Eunice's brown-haired *kuft*. The fleshy lips were pouting slackly and gradually he let his hand circle lower until he touched the fast-melting fragment of ice to them. She gave a little shriek and giggled.

'Has someone been here already?' he asked with a grin. 'Am I following Pieter van Buuren yet again?'

The final speck of ice turned to water and she sighed to feel Marcel's fingers press inside and caress her in a short and rhythmic motion.

'I was so hot and sticky when I got home that I stripped off and stood under the shower for ages,' she said, 'but it didn't help much. I was sitting here in a day-dream fingering myself.'

'My apologies for interrupting you,' he said. 'It shall be my pleasure to make restitution at once.'

'The pleasure will be more mine than yours,' she murmured.

She slid her legs further apart on the settee cushion and her round face flushed slowly red from the sensations aroused by his busy fingers. She put an arm round his shoulders, to pull him tightly against her body.

'What entertaining little day-dream was in your mind when you sat here with your hand between your legs?' he asked.

'I was thinking how nice it would be if a lovely man like you pushed me on my back and ripped my knickers off,' she murmured.

'I am flattered!'

225

'You should be!' she answered. 'If you knew how many times you've had me on my back over a table at the Gran'Caffe with hundreds of people looking on!'

'What a beast I am!' he said. 'What else have I done?'

'You've had me naked across your lap in an open *barossa* dozens of times. You say you'll *zeqq* me all the way down the Avenue, but we never get past the Convent before I climax.'

Marcel pushed his free hand up inside her unbuttoned satin pyjama jacket to bare her big soft *gublas* and fondle them.

'I like this *barossa* ride of yours – it sounds amusing,' he said. 'I know a coachman who would drive us – late at night when there's nobody about? Dare you ride with me naked?'

'Oh yes, yes! Tonight if you like!' she gasped, her chubby belly quaking in a sudden passionate climax.

Marcel continued to play with her until she exhaled a long sighing breath and stopped shaking. He gave her time to recover by fetching her another drink from the sideboard.

'You haven't cooled me down at all, but you've made me feel a lot better,' she told him with a broad grin.

'It was my pleasure . . .' he started to say, then changed it to *our* pleasure.

Eunice felt his long hard *zimbriq* through his trousers and said it was certainly going to be his pleasure in a minute.

'I'm glad I decided to drop in,' he said. 'I was passing your building and I thought how nice it would be to see you. And to find that you were caressing yourself and thinking of me is a most agreeable coincidence.'

Eunice put his hands on her fat breasts to keep them out of the way while she unzipped his trousers.

'Don't get upset,' she said, stroking his *zimbriq*, 'but

226

for once you weren't the star of my day-dream.'

'You are unfaithful to me!' he exclaimed, trembling with pleasure as her clasped hand slid up and down. 'What was this other person doing to you?'

'We were in a changing-hut on the beach. He was making me bend over for him.'

'You were thinking of Piet,' Marcel gasped, 'he's on the beach nearly every day.'

'You're wrong,' she chuckled. 'And what difference does it make to you who I invite to *zeqq* me in my imagination?'

He had a soft *gubla* in each hand and tugged at them to pull her sideways along the settee so that he could mount her but she shook her head.

'It's far too hot to have you lying on top of me,' she said.

She handled his swollen *zimbriq* so expertly that he could feel that only seconds were left. He pulled her open pyjama jacket down from her shoulders and grasped at her *gublas* with feverish fingers.

'That's how I like to see it!' she murmured, 'hard as iron and with a head purple and swollen as a plum. You're going to *zboca* for me!'

He gave a long gasp and gushed his sticky excitement up the front of his white shirt.

'Nice!' Eunice exclaimed. 'Very nice, my dear.'

While he was getting his breath back she went to the sideboard for more cold drinks. Marcel took a long swallow of Scotch whisky and water and grinned at her.

'I know who you bent over for in your day-dream,' he said, 'it was Errol Hochheimer.'

'How did you guess that!' she asked in amazement.

'Remember the night he passed us in the Embassy garden? There was something in the way you spoke of

227

him that suggested you would be happy to open your legs for him.'

'Him and a dozen others,' she said, 'I found out who was with him that night. Inge Kristensen – do you know her?'

'I've met her,' Marcel answered in a neutral tone, thinking it unwise to let Eunice know he had come straight to her from *seqqing* Inge.

'You'd better take your shirt off and let me put it to soak for you,' said Eunice, 'I can iron it dry before you go – if you stay the night, that is.'

Marcel stripped off his stained shirt.

'I was planning to take you out to dinner,' he said. 'How can I do that without a shirt?'

'It's too hot tonight to go out,' she answered. 'I'll make a light meal here. We've had the hors-d'oeuvres already.'

He half-turned on the settee to watch her walk across the room away from him and smiled to see the bare and heavy cheeks of her bottom roll below the lavender pyjama jacket. There was something enchanting for him in the way the two halves of a woman's rump slid up and down alternately in walking. More than one girlfriend in Paris had thought it an odd request but had pleased him by walking naked round the room while he sat and stared at her swaying cheeks. Even more enchanting was a pair of breasts bouncing up and down when a woman ran naked, but in a city this was not easy to arrange.

He sipped his drink while he amused himself with these thoughts and then went after Eunice into the bathroom. She was putting his shirt to soak in the hand-basin and he stood behind her, his arms round her so that he could dandle her breasts.

'You have the most shameless *gublas*,' he said, looking over her shoulder at her breasts reflected in the mirror. 'They are too big, too round, too soft, too plump – I swear it would *aboca* immediately if I put my *zimbriq* between them!'

'I'd love to see you,' she said, 'if it would only cool down a bit! The first time I have you all night and it has to be so hot that even I'm wilting!'

He peeled her pyjama jacket off, slid his trousers down his sweating legs, turned on the shower and pulled Eunice under the cold water with him. In reality the water was not cold at all, merely tepid, but it brought some refreshment on hot flesh and Eunice was content to lean her back against the tiled wall while he soaped her body. When he let the water wash the creamy lather from her breasts, their red-brown buds were standing up very prominently. He put his head down and sucked them in turn.

'You think my *gublas* are too big and fat, do you?' she breathed, her eyes closed in pleasure.

'Big and round and soft and shameless,' he corrected her, one hand circling on her belly until she moved her feet apart for him to feel between her thighs.

'What is it about Errol Hochheimer that makes you eager to get him into bed?' he asked, his fingers tititlating warm folds of flesh. 'Is it the uniform? You'll have to hurry up, because they say he may be recalled very soon.'

'I know,' she breathed, her hand clasped round his *zimbriq*. 'He's made a mess of his job and he's in trouble.'

There was no opportunity to question her further just then. Eunice tugged him towards her by his stiff handle and with a dip and a long slow push he slid up into her and heard her little moan of pleasure. Tepid water cascaded down between them, washing over her *gublas* and down between their bellies. It served to cool their skin a little while he see-sawed back and forth in a motion that conserved energy while producing delightful sensations.

On a night as hot and clammy as this it was going to be all too easy to *zeqq* Eunice to a standstill, he reflected. He had accepted Piet's challenge, but it would be no victory at all to see her collapse from the effects of the climate rather than his ability as a lover. Even moving as steadily as he was, her breasts were heaving and falling as she laboured to breathe. Her fingernails sank sharply into his bottom and she rammed her bulging belly against him in ecstatic convulsions, moaning and panting her mouth wide open. The sight of a woman's climax never failed in its effect on Marcel – he stabbed into her with short quick strokes that brought on his crisis at once.

When they were calm again, they stayed where they were, under the shower, letting the water stream down over them. Marcel's *zimbriq* softened until it slid out of its warm hiding-place, to hang between his legs and be cooled by the water running down his body. He pushed Eunice's wet hair back from her face, and kissed her cheek.

'Since you're so interested in Errol Hochheimer, do you know about his agreement with Ysambard D'Cruz?' he asked casually.

Eunice gave him a sideways look. Her hands were still on his bottom and she massaged the cheeks thoughtfully.

'Tell me something,' she said, 'and tell me the truth – were you ordered to come here and interrogate me?'

'Good God!' he exclaimed. 'Is that what you think? I swear to you that I had no other reason for coming here than the desire to make love to you.'

'You did that very well,' she said, glaring down at him over her bare breasts. 'You softened me up for your questions in record time. I suppose you think I'm a fat old fool.'

'No, no, no,' he said anxiously, 'I like you a lot.'

He reached out to put a hand on her knee but she pushed it away and stood up.

'I'm going to bed,' she said angrily. 'You can get your clothes on and clear out. I never want to see you again, you rotten Frog.'

She pushed past him and his last view of her was her rolling bare bottom as she walked out of the room, leaving him dumbfounded.

COCKTAILS

Stanley Carten

After all that Gallic charm, it's time for some no-nononsense Americana. So we'll cross the Atlantic and head for the sunshine state: California. And Stanley Carten's *Cocktails*.

The title (and the brazen waitress on the book's cover) tell you all you need to know about the style of this book. Subtle it isn't. There's even a Korean character named Phuc Yu.

And the sex scenes are just as up front, if you'll pardon the expression. The book tells the various stories of the staff and customers of a cocktail bar in Silicone Valley. As the waitresses don't wear very much, the manager has access to closed-circuit video that films every part of the premises, the customers tend to be looking for a good time, and everyone is sex-mad, every story turns rapidly into a detailed description of orgiastic behaviour.

Here's most of Chapter Eight, as a sample. It's called Screwdriver, and like every chapter it includes the relevant cocktail recipe. Bottoms up!

Stanley Carten's later Nexus books are *The City of One-Night Stands* and *Hard Drive*.

Screwdriver

Mix

1½ oz. Vodka
5 oz. Orange Juice (preferably fresh)

Pour into highball glass over ice cubes
and stir well.

Kerry was a little worried that she was dressed too casually for her debut at a high-tech-high-flyer party. She hadn't intended to go out this evening so she'd gone to work in her old sweater, leggings and cowboy boots. In the lift on the way up to the penthouse suite she'd taken the time to add a little make-up to accent her naturally pretty features. With a quick brush of her auburn hair she peered into the lift's shiny doors and gave herself a quick boost of confidence.

'You'll have to do, Kerry Farnum.'

She wasn't quite sure what to expect of this party, but she kept telling herself that she'd stay no more than half an hour, an hour, tops. Bob would be waiting for her. She paused at the door. It didn't sound too noisy, but she could hear a little laughter and what sounded like opera. She knocked on the door and waited. No one came – the laughter continued – an aria was reaching its climax. Again she knocked. Muffled through the sound of a very solid door she heard Mr Yu's unmistakable tones.

'Coming,' he said, his words followed by quite a bit of giggling.

Mr Yu opened the door, startling Kerry. She just

wasn't prepared to see her host and prospective employer open the door with a glass of champagne in one hand, a towel in the other, dressed only in the shortest of Japanese silk robes.

'Ah, welcome Kerry. So glad you could join us. Have some champagne.'

He handed Kerry the glass which she took hesitantly. As he shut the door behind her and chained it shut she felt obliged to offer her apologies for disturbing him. It appeared as if he were ready for bed.

'I'm sorry if I'm late, or if I'm disturbing you, but . . .'

'Not at all. We were just taking a jacuzzi and admiring the view of my prospective kingdom. Won't you join us?'

'Oh – I don't have a bathing suit with me.'

'Not to worry. We can accommodate you.'

What that exactly meant caused Kerry no small concern as she followed the Korean into the suite. Her concern was amplified by a brief flutter of Mr Yu's light silk robe as he turned to lead her to the jacuzzi. She hoped it was his leg that she caught a glimpse of. It had to be his leg. No one has a willy that big, she kept telling herself as she followed Yu into the splendour of the suite.

'Wow!' Immediately that she had uttered the superfluous superlative, Kerry felt slightly stupid. In her defence, even the most experienced of commentators or jaded of travellers would have been at a loss for words when confronted with the sight of the Regency penthouse suite.

The room was mostly dark except for the ambient lights of the Valley and a few well-placed candles. Some tragic Italian opera reverberated around the room. Floor-to-ceiling windows over twenty feet tall arched almost a full three hundred and sixty degrees around the suite revealing a twinkling wonderland of lights that was the high-tech playground of Silicon Valley. Far in the distance lay San Francisco, with all of its diversity and perversity, shimmering like a far-off jewel. Kerry, like a small child peering hopefully in a toy store window at Christmas-time, walked to the centre window and pressed her hands and face to the glass. Mesmerised, she stared at everything, not really seeing anything but a blur of sensory overload.

It was a loud splash heard somewhere between a lull in the soprano's agonising and the rising of the heart-stretching strings of the orchestra that disturbed Kerry's silent musing. Quickly she turned around to see that the centre of the room was occupied by a huge circular sunken jacuzzi barely illuminated by hanging candelabras. The impression was one of Roman decadence. From her vantage point at the windows she could barely make out three smiling faces staring at her.

'It is rather breathtaking isn't it?' The voice was Janet's.

'I've lived here all my life – I never really realised how beautiful . . .'

'Yes – it is, isn't it?' This time it was Phuc Yu.

'Come on in, Kerry – the water's fine.' Hazel was ebullient.

Kerry advanced the jacuzzi sipping her champagne as she went. Her cowboy boots clicked sensually on the marble floor.

'Where shall I get changed?' Kerry felt bold about her presence in the room and the prospect of entering the jacuzzi. Somewhere in the back of her mind she wondered where the other guests were, but the sights and sounds surrounding her made all concerns pale in comparison.

'My dear, we have no bathing suits. We are naked under the water, but have no fear – in the cloak of darkness your modesty will be protected.'

'Oh, I'm not worried . . .'

Kerry couldn't believe her mouth. She didn't really want to take off her clothes in front of Phuc Yu, let alone Hazel and her wandering hands and her friend Janet, but her inhibitions seemed so childish, so meaningless in these surroundings. A part of her brain kept yelling that Bob was nowhere near to protect her, so be careful. Bob – Bob – oh yes – she was supposed to see him this evening, but all thoughts of her commitment to him seemed to fall away with her panties as they dropped to the cool marble floor like a falling leaf commemorating the end of summer. Without further ceremony she stepped naked into the hot bubbling water.

'Indeed, quite beautiful.' Yu was deliberately ambiguous.

'Yes – the view is overwhelming.' Kerry sat opposite Yu and adjacent to Janet and Hazel. She shrank down in the water to cover her breasts from anyone's gaze. Kerry couldn't help but notice that Hazel's tits floated on the surface and were bounded around by the hot water jets. The sight of the milky white globes dancing like some drunken deep sea creatures was repulsively hypnotic to Kerry. It was Janet who broke the spell.

'More champagne, Kerry?'

'Oh – certainly.' Janet was standing intimately close to Kerry as she poured the champagne. Their legs brushed. Kerry pretended not to notice the feeling of flesh on flesh, skin on skin.

Phuc Yu began to pontificate.

'Kerry my dear, I must propose a toast. A toast to Silicon Valley and its beauty. The beauty of the money

240

to be made here, and the beauty of its women.'

The clink of champagne glasses could hardly be heard over the bubbling water and the opera.

'Mr Yu is too modest to brag, Kerry, but as of today he owns a vast portion of those lights. Although not yet public knowledge, Mr Yu has purchased Integrated Machines, Levity Software, All Purpose Electronics and Floppy Devices with options on four other companies. I think we should toast the new King of Silicon Valley – Phuc Yu.'

Janet and Hazel stood up to toast the Korean entrepreneur, so without thinking Kerry followed suit. What a sight greeted the Oriental. Three women of varying degrees of beauty, completely naked, standing before him holding champagne glasses erect in his honour. This is what I work so hard for, he told himself. Before him he could see the boyish small tits of his European assistant, the mammoth jugs (no other word would come to mind) of the plentiful American waitress and the pertness of the young Berkeley student's full breasts. And tantalisingly revealed by the varying level of the bubbling water he could see the silhouettes of their public mounds and their furry bushes outlined by the lights of his Valley and the flickering of the candles overhead.

Deep down below the water his huge cock stirred at the sight of these three eminently fuckable women toasting his achievements. As he stood to clink glasses with them his hardness broke forth from the water like some huge torpedo homing in on a defenceless ship. Kerry gasped at the sight of the monster not realising that she had taken the behemoth once inside her. The champagne dulled her sense of shock and heightened her curiosity. It was the largest cock she had even seen. She began to wonder . . .

Little did she know that she already knew the answer.

And for his part, Phuc Yu had no idea that it was the delectable young student that he now desired so that he had pinioned behind the Pump's dumpster just a few days ago. He had slept heavily that night, waking late in the afternoon, the previous evening somewhat of a mystery. Even a cold and clammy used condom in his pocket didn't jog his alcohol and sex-bashed memory into remembering the intimate details of the night before. And his Oriental reserve prevented him from asking the crude Mr Wize for the full story that the 'Ugly American' would not doubt readily convey, replete with grins, winks and nudges.

He had put the Sunday's escapades completely out of his mind and successfully closed the deals. And this – these three women – were his reward. It was time, Yu reasoned, for the special part of his celebration to begin. By now it should be ready.

'Please sit down, my lovelies. I have something special for you. Make yourselves comfortable amongst the bubbles. Let the hot water ooze over you.'

Down amongst the hot water, her body once more hidden by the bubbling foam, Kerry glanced at Hazel who looked at Janet who looked at both of them with an air of expectancy. Mr Yu reached behind the taps of the jacuzzi to a small cabinet and retrieved an urn from which a pale smoke gradually escaped.

'I have for you a special gift from the Far East. It is very expensive and available only to the most privileged. In my hour of triumph here, I wish to share it with you. Please accept this delicacy with my compliments.'

From the urn he retrieved four long-stemmed pipes and handed them to the three ladies, retaining one for himself.

242

'Please be careful not to get the pipe wet. We do not want the burning embers to be dampened. At your convenience please suck deeply on the pipe. Hold in the vapors. Let them permeate your very being. As the warmth flows through you, breathe out. The pipe will last about thirty minutes, by which time we shall all be in a sensual heaven.'

Janet began inhaling right away. Hazel looked at Kerry, shrugged her shoulders and did likewise. Kerry looked up from the pipe to see Phuc staring at her as he consumed the pipe's contents. For a series of moments he did not break eye contact with her until he began to exhale. As he did so he closed his eyes and spoke as if residing in a far-off place.

'You have nothing to fear, my dear. Neither the pipe nor its contents will harm you. You will find a true peace – ectasy that you can never know through any other means. Please join me there.'

'What is it?'

'It is an extremely rare form of opium. It is quite mild and certainly not addictive at this dosage. It is farmed only in a remote area of Thailand known to my family and controlled by a small religious sect to which we belong. It's used on rare occasions to commemorate events of great importance. As I said before, do not worry – it is not addictive in small quantities, but I do warn you that you will experience pleasures that even your most personal of moments must pale in comparison to.'

Yu's warning served to excite and entice Kerry. She glanced around the jacuzzi. Both Janet and Hazel looked completely out of it. They had their arms around each other, gently stroking each other's skin and hair as the pipe's smoke permeated their brains. Their eyes were closed, yet they appeared to be looking

243

at each other with a deeper vision.

Opium – the word bounced around Kerry's mind and rolled around her mouth, drooling out of her lips, forming an ideal receptacle for the pipe she held in her hand. Apprehensively, Kerry touched the pipe to her lips but did not inhale. The vapours rose through the pipe without her assistance, titillating her throat. In reaction she breathed deep, taking a gulp of acrid smoke. It was not distasteful, but it was not truly pleasurable. Kerry had never been much of a dope smoker – only twice during high-school parties had she ever joined in. It had done nothing for her then, but this was not like that. The smoke stayed with her, bringing a peace that only the dead should have the pleasure of knowing. Time stood still. She never even remembered taking another drag of the pipe. Instead of inhaling air she felt as if she was breathing constantly the smoke – as if the air in the room had been replaced by the penetrating vapours.

The bubbles in the jacuzzi seemed to engulf her, encapsulating parts of her body, floating her above the jacuzzi and around the room. Her eyes perceived movement, like shadows in a darkened room that disappeared once looked at carefully. Her senses deceived her. She could not tell reality from the cotton-wool that seemed to surround her swimming brain.

She was sure that she stepped out of the jacuzzi at Yu's invitation, taking his outstretched hand, but she could not swear to it. She was sure that Janet and Hazel swamped her in extremely soft towels drying her sodden skin, but she could have been mistaken. She was sure that she enjoyed the feeling of their muffled hands rubbing dry her pert breasts, and she was sure she even parted her legs ever so slightly so that Janet could stroke her pussy to dry it from the waters of the jacuzzi just so her cunt would get wet again, this time from her own juice. But it could have been wishful thinking.

But it wasn't. The opium smoke, the champagne, the earlier cocktails and wine all mixed together in the bubbling cauldron of the jacuzzi, warmed by the lights of the Valley and stirred with four sexually charged bodies to create a potion guaranteed to conjure up an orgy of lustful excess.

After a festival of drying each other with large, soft and warm towels, Yu led the three women to a huge semi-circular bed that looked out over the sprawling lights below. With his outstretched hand he invited the women to lie down on the bed. Janet guided Kerry into the middle of the bed and motioned for Hazel to take up a position flanking Kerry. Surrounded by female flesh that had already begun to explore the intimate details of her throbbing sex, Kerry felt completely submissive, as if she was watching this orgy unfold from a distance. The swirling tones of the opera added to the illusion telling her hazy brain that this wasn't reality.

In unison both Hazel and Janet each took one of Kerry's breasts and began to lick the nipples with soft languorous strokes. It was as if Janet and Hazel divided Kerry's body down the middle like some gourmet delicacy and feasted on their respective portions. Hazel's and Janet's hands met on Kerry's pussy, providing the placid girl with ten rhythmically massaging fingers. Together, their fingers would pressure and squeeze Kerry's clit while occasionally a lone finger would slide softly inside her quim, teasing and coaxing her juices deep from within.

To Kerry this felt like an extremely randy and nasty dream. It was as if she was floating above the Valley on a passing cloud, being fucked by naughty angels who just happened to be Janet and Hazel. At the very edge of the cloud, right above what she thought was the Pumping Station, floated a huge and angry dick belonging to the leering Mr Yu. Phuc stroked his cock in eager anticipation. As if speaking in slow motion, like a tape recorder with failing batteries, Phuc Yu moved his lips and Kerry thought she heard him ask, 'Is she ready for my tool?'

Janet took her finger from Kerry's quivering pussy and licked the full length of her cunt juice coated finger. 'Hmmmm – she is ripe for the fucking.' Janet and Hazel reached and took the club like cock of Mr Yu and guided it to Kerry's opening. For the second time in just a few days, the massive cockhead forced its way into Kerry's tight cunt. This time, Kerry did not struggle but gladly accepted the dick within her, sliding her body down its mammoth length and gently squirming as her juices melted around the dick's throbbing shaft. Yu rocked backwards and forwards while Hazel and Janet squeezed each one of his pendulous hanging balls, actually providing the thrusts that fucked Kerry into obliviousness.

Something inside Kerry told her not to be completely submissive. Her mouth sought Yu's lips but he resisted, preferring to see the three women kiss each other beneath him as he fucked the young cocktail waitress. Still, Hazel and Janet continued to fondle Kerry's breasts, pinching the tight little nipples into points for Yu to bite and snap at. In Kerry's mouth she could feel her own tongue being massaged by the enfolding tongues of Janet and Hazel. Lips encircled lips in an orgy of kissing, as Yu's gigantic cock threatened to burst through Kerry's ecstasy-racked body and join the entwined tongues to be sucked as well as fucked.

As Yu's massive cock cycled through its pendulous journey in and out of Kerry's come-drenched opening, her body was forced to and fro on the silky sheets of the huge bed. Janet and Hazel, surrounding the younger woman with their bodies, gripped Kerry's hips with their pubic mounds. As Yu fucked Kerry and she slid around, her hips rubbed the other women's cunts as she became an extension of Yu's gigantic dick. The effect he was having on the three women did not escape his all-seeing eyes. The high it gave him to feel the power of fucking three women at once – actually to be fucking them – using one as a giant dildo attached to his already massive dong – was a feeling of power even better than the charge he got from closing a deal.

In Yu's mind the two – business and sex – were almost identical. As he fucked Kerry, Janet and Hazel he glanced over his shoulder to see what he regarded as his domain, and he smiled a wicked grin. He had fucked the American companies with his ruthless competition, and now he fucked their women. Just as he had done some years ago in Europe in which Janet had become his personal assistant in charge of European operations, he wondered at what the future offered for the young engineering student in which his dick was readying to unleash its load of come. As he came Yu was thinking of all these things. Of the tight cunt in which he was squirting and his desire to possess the body and brain of its owner, just as he had taken control of the Valley's major companies.

Such complicated power trips were far from the minds of the women surrounding Yu's cock. As he arched his back in orgasm, Janet reached around and stroked the back of his balls with her finger, just below the anus. Yu emitted a small moan in perfect key with the rising opera music that was the orgy's unwitting soundtrack.

The throws of Yu's orgasm provided the catalyst that

initiated Kerry's release. It began not in her pussy but in her breasts under the ministrations of Janet and Hazel's lips. Her nipples felt as if they were melting under the heat of the other women's breath. As the hot saliva of the two tit-suckers dripped down Kerry's boobs, she began to come. She was convinced her tits were showering out come like ornamental fountains into the faces of Janet and Hazel. As Janet stroked Yu's balls, Hazel slipped her hand between Kerry's pussy and Yu's thrusting pelvis. Adding her own pressure to that of Yu's body, Hazel inserted the final critical energy into Kerry's near-boiling cunt. In waves of rolling intensity Kerry was shocked by a feeling of total and unequivocal release. It was as if she had popped like a balloon with all her juices flowing out of every exploded opening.

Kerry's come-induced writhings sympathetically ignited first Hazel and then Janet. Kerry could feel their cunts oozing over her hips as they too joined in the communal climax. Together they bit hard on her tits as they released their pent-up tensions over Kerry's hips. In wanton lust, Hazel had begun to hump Kerry's hip, slowly at first and then violently, threatening to destroy the intimate coupling of the four bodies with her thrashing motions. Gasping for breath, lying on her side, Hazel's large tits slumped onto Kerry's and covered the smaller woman's body. The sight of such large breasts moving beneath him gave Yu further desires. He had barely finished coming inside Kerry as he withdrew his dick and began to direct the next phase of his celebratory fuck.

Yu gave the women little time to rest. In their drugged state they really didn't need much of anything other than direction. To the come-drenched Kerry, Janet and Hazel life seemed to be moving at half speed. The opera music slurred about the room – their words stumbled into incoherence – and their bodies felt like no effort was required to do anything. They were willing puppets of Yu's imagination and desires. He, being that much more used to the effects of the mild opium smoke, was definitely in control. There was no resistance or reluctance whatsoever from the women as Yu motioned for Hazel to take Kerry's position in the middle, and for Kerry to take Hazel's place.

Phuc Yu was already hard from looking at the awaiting sight of Hazel's huge tits falling to the side of her chest. Now there were a pair of tits worthy of his dick. On none of his travels, and certainly not in his homeland of Korea had he ever had a really delicious tit-fuck. Women had tried. He had tried. He'd even come a few times on several womens' tits, but it had never been as good as he'd imagined. Then he'd seen Hazel's breasts – he'd stared at them thinking how good it would be to wrap them around his meat and jack off into her face. And now he had the opportunity to do just that.

From the bedside table he retrieved a bottle of hand cream courtesy of the Regency Hotel. The women paid him little attention, satisfied enough to touch each other's bodies lazily in a slow dance of sexual patience. As Janet and Kerry made random finger motions on Hazel's boobs, Yu emptied the hand cream on to the tits. Quickly Kerry and Janet coated the expansive flesh with the slippery liquid. As if mounting one of his polo ponies, Yu leapt onto Hazel and straddled her waist with his legs. His throbbing boner slapped right between Hazel's tits and was caught between the globes as Kerry and Janet entrapped it between each tit by pushing the boob over and around Yu's dick, forming a cunt-like tunnel for him to fuck.

Yu let out his trademark moan. 'Hmmmm-mmmmm-mmmmm . . .'

Somewhere deep in Kerry's opium-laced brain that sound registered as having been heard before – some-where – but there were more pressing matters to attend to. The brain said, 'later'. Kerry complied with her brain's request and concentrated on forcing Hazel's pliant flesh around Yu's hardness. Hazel's tit was doing its best to escape from Kerry's grasp, so she found it best to use two hands to ensure that the full length of Yu's cock was immersed in the soft warm tightness of milky white tit-flesh. Janet was doing the same, having the time of her life squeezing the adorably huge tit of Hazel's around her darling Mr Yu's dick. This fucking was a cornucopia of minor sensations cascading into a massive overdose of sexual feelings. Every so often Janet's hand would graze Hazel's hardened nipple as she brushed against the delectable Kerry. Beneath the oozing breasts Janet and Kerry could feel the hard ridges of Yu's cock sliding back and forth, and Hazel's hips – somewhat larger than Kerry's, bumped into the pubic mounds after each thrust of Yu's dick with a firm and exciting slap.

Hazel could see the purple swollen head of Yu's dick forcing its way with each stroke through the compress of her tits. As it burst through the supple barrier of Hazel's tits, the dick's skin was pulled back causing its slit to open the slimy liquid to ooze out and trickle down to join the lubricating mess of sweat and hand cream. If Yu thrust as hard as he could Hazel was able to flick the sensitive purple head with her fat tongue driving Phuc Yu into convulsions. On a few thrusts Hazel was able to get her lips attached to Yu's dick head sucking on him like a vampire desperate for blood. To Phuc it was like being fucked and sucked at the same time.

This was everything that Yu imagined fucking the big tits of the American cocktail waitress would be. He decided very early on in this tit-fucking session that it was better than fucking cunts, for these tits were bigger than any cunt could ever be and just as tight as the tightest pussy he'd ever had. Under the urgent control of his helpmates Janet and Kerry, Hazel's tits gripped his full length like no cunt ever could. And it wasn't only his cock that was getting the full treatment. Under the pressure of his weight, Yu's balls were being squeezed against Hazel's stomach and subsequently between her tits, giving the bucking Korean the sensation that his gonads were being held in the tightest of grips. As he stroked his cock in and out of Hazel's tit-trench, his balls slid up and down her rib cage to smear cream all over her stomach. His soggy pubic hairs left slimy little trails all over her belly that gradually worked their way down to Hazel's dark furry bush to mingle with her own rapidly approaching wetness.

Hazel was approaching oblivion. She moaned from deep within as if she was experiencing an extremely lewd dream, 'I want a good tit-fucking. Feed my tits with your come, Phuc Yu. Grease me up like a stuck pig with that big dick of yours. Squirt on my titties – please. I've never been tit-fucked like this before. Such a big, big dick . . .'

Such filthy talk was too much for Yu to take, given the sensations he was feeling. Half of him wishing it wouldn't happen just yet, and the rest of him screaming for release, he felt an eruption of come beginning to travel upward from the throbbing base of his cock. He stopped thrusting and forced Janet and Kerry to encapsulate completely his dick with Hazel's tits. To bring him off he motioned for the two women to squeeze his dick through Hazel's tits. He didn't last long as he came into the tight breast cavern, squirting copious amounts of semen into every nook and cranny. The pressure was too much to bear – come squirted between Kerry's and Janet's hands and all over the room, splattering even on the floor to ceiling windows.

To Yu it felt as if his dick had exploded, such was the force with which his orgasm had burst the fleshy seals of Hazel's tits. He collapsed off her and on to the floor, writhing in exquisite agony. Janet and Kerry paid him little attention, content to feed each other with sticky little drops of his come that had stuck to their fingers. Hazel was sound asleep, snoring ever so slightly. Looking into each other's eyes, Janet and Kerry continued to feed each other Yu's juices off of the slumbering Hazel's tits. It was an extremely decadent thing to do – but it fitted right in with the mood of the night. At that moment, under those circumstances, it was, in both their minds, the perfect thing to do.

As Hazel slept, Kerry and Janet fed on her tits like ravenous savages until every last drop of Yu's come had been eaten. They finished their feeding nose to nose, eye to eye, with their lips fastened on one of Hazel's nipples. They paused, staring at each other's wild-eyed gaze. Finally, Janet broke the silence of their heavy breathing.

'I want to fuck you.'

She spoke the words in her very proper English accent. No one could have refused her. Kerry didn't want to. Having sex with this petite and prim young Englishwoman seemed the wickedly erotic thing to do. With her boyish good looks and long blonde pony tail she carried an androgynous air about her that intrigued Kerry so. The opera was reaching a climax – far above the hills the first rays of the morning's sun were peeking like a crazed voyeur into the room – she wanted to feel this woman's mouth on her cunt, and she wanted to do likewise to her. It amazed her that before this night she had never done such a thing – and now it seemed so natural. Perhaps Hazel had been right that first night at the Pumping Station . . .'

'And I want to fuck you.'

'Please, be my guest.'

Janet climbed over Hazel's slumbering form and pivoted completely around so that her head was facing the foot of the bed and Kerry's feet. She gripped Kerry's ankles and buried her face deep into the American girl's sodden bush. It tasted salty with sweat and spunk. Janet thrust her bottom into Kerry's face. Her odour was intense as Kerry stuck her tongue forward for Janet to fuck madly. Kerry reached around and held Janet tightly around the waist, pressing each of their bodies together. They rolled around bumping into Hazel, but not waking her. Their bodies became as one – a blur of sex consuming sex with an intensity of passion rarely found. Neither woman remembered distinctly coming at any particular moment so much as always feeling like they were melting over each other's faces.

They dared not separate from each other lest the sensation stop. Long after they had finished actively tonguing each other they still remained locked in the classic position, sleeping soundly, their bodies racked from too much pleasure. Kerry was briefly disturbed – as least she thought she was, she might have been dreaming – by the bed creaking under the weight of Phuc Yu pounding his dick into the sleeping Hazel's cunt. Kerry smiled and began to drift off back into a deep slumber scented by the aroma of Janet's still dripping cunt. Before she was completely asleep her eyes focused on Phuc Yu's hands gripping the sleeping

Hazel's shoulders to steady himself as he pounded away.

There was something very familiar about those pudgy fingers and those rings. Where had she seen those rings before? It was recently she was sure . . .

Her brain was tired of all this effort. It had exhausted itself this evening with too many new sensations. It didn't need a puzzle right now.

'Later,' said her slumbering consciousness. 'Much later.'

MS DEEDES
AT HOME

Carole Andrews

Take one English rose. Transplant her to the United States. Feed her with the best education that money can buy. Omit to train her; allow her to grow wild and free. Watch as she blooms into a blonde bombshell. Return her to England.

That's the background of Ms Ella Deedes, Nexus's sexual secret agent, licensed to seduce and sexualise everyone she meets. *Ms Deedes at Home* is, at first, about the clash between frank, fearless, ever-ready Ella and the quaint, reticent customs of village England; later the villagers' reluctance to frolic (at least without Ella's promptings) is revealed to be the work of a Texan villain – and Ella gets into serious trouble before saving the day.

I've chosen a chapter from the early part of the novel, to avoid the later plot complications. Ella's methods are amply demonstrated here, as is her innocent enjoyment in sheer lechery.

Ella's adventures continue in *Ms Deedes on Paradise Island*, which is about to be published, and in the later *A Mission for Ms Deedes*.

Ella slept soundly in her new home. She was woken by a long sequence of reverberating dongs from the church clock and she struggled to the windows in her black satin camisole to close them. An hour later the clock sounded again with an even longer fanfare, as if to congratulate her on putting together an excellent brunch for herself and shedding the slinky camisole at last for a cotton sun-dress with a bold floral print and thin shoulder straps.

Goode knocked courteously at the open kitchen door and stuck his head in.

'Watch that pickle!' he warned cheerfully. 'They say the devil never comes near Pod Parva for fear of being chopped up and put in Mrs Pringle's pickle.'

Ella deliberately scooped the last of the spicy, piquant pickle on to a finger of bread and slid it enticingly between her hungry, pouting lips.

It was enough to stall any impulse Goode may have felt to step inside. He fidgeted in the doorway while she completed her performance and then said hurriedly: 'The well-dressing committee starts work this afternoon in the village hall. Lots of colour and tradition: a good photo opportunity as they say. And it runs all week. I'll let you have the words once you're hooked.'

And with a half-wave of his camouflaged bird-survey board he was gone.

As radiant as a bird of paradise in her colourful dress, Ella dragged her chair over to the open doorway and perched in the full sun while she finished her meal. An enormous spray of rambling rose drooped below the lintel of the door, the feminine fragrance of its coppery pink flowers a luxury of reassurance and excitement. She lingered over her first glass of the local tipple, reflecting that if Mrs Pringle packed the devil's flesh into her pickle, she surely kept a little of his spirit for her perry. Then she reached for her Roman sandals, slipping her nicely tanned feet into the white leather and leisurely criss-crossing the thongs round her ankles and calves before tying them just below the knee. She stood for a long enriching draught of scent before stepping through the arch and sauntering forth in search of the village hall.

There she found a small group of mostly elderly people with an air of sombre purpose as if they had gathered to debate the choice of next Sunday's hymns. One of them tried to shoo her away: 'The erection ceremony isn't for three days.'

'Maybe I can help you get it up a little quicker,' Ella answered glibly.

A stony-faced woman tried to bar the entrance with her formidable frame, but the expert at inspiring quick erections slid past. She shot a few pictures and as though now in possession of incriminating evidence, knew that she would not be expelled.

Precisely what the evidence amounted to, Ella wasn't sure. It didn't look very exciting. The men were fiddling about with carpentry tools and bits of wood. Wood could be extremely erotic. Ella loved to slide her hand along a piece of newly planed and sanded pine. But these men were hammering grey planks together with no grace or sensibility, arguing about which piece went where. The women, all in plastic aprons, were clustered round a long table. They were each kneading a lump of something on a flat board. Bread-making was extremely sexy. All that pummelling and pounding on warm rising dough, while the germ within was making babies by the million. But these women were poking at it nervously, as though it might bite them. They seemed frightened of getting dirty.

'She was taking pictures at the cricket,' one of the women said.

'I'm researching English customs. For an American paper.'

'More Americans,' the woman grumbled, making room for Ella to nudge in the circle. 'It's useless trying to keep them out.'

It was clay they were working, Ella saw, but they were kneading it like dough. And opposite her, she noticed at once, there was a younger woman, about her own age. She had a beautiful face, strikingly clear and very soft, almost too soft, with a touch of sadness. Ella fought back an impulse to reach over and stroke it.

'We puddle the clay the men have dug,' the woman on Ella's right explained. 'And then tomorrow we'll smooth it into the frame they're making, about an inch deep, and start mapping out the design. The day after that we'll start petalling, and you can come and work with us.'

But Ella was working with them already. She was shooting film, trying to capture the earthiness of the scene, working round to the other side of the table. Someone spoke to the younger woman, calling her Susan. Ella felt herself weaken momentarily at the knees.

Susan.

She could see her from behind now.

Susan was wearing tight blue jeans, size eight at the most, tucked into little white pixie boots. Here was a genuine English village maiden, soft and shy, and Ella wanted to touch more than her face. She wanted to run her hand down the perfect arch of her back and over that sweet petite bottom, and then up underneath her prim striped blouse to cup those cute tiny breasts and frisk their pretty nipples. She worked with her camera. But she didn't want to screw Susan through the lens, the way so many male cameramen worked. She wanted to search out the sexuality, draw on it, colour it and celebrate it.

Susan was not co-operating, however. She seemed oblivious of the effect she was having on Ella. She seemed to inhabit her body like a schoolgirl might a Wendy house. She poked at the clay prudishly, just like the others.

When the frame was finished, the men left. One of the women filled a metal pail from a tap in the corner and walked round flicking water to wet the wood all over. Then she dragged out an old tin bath tub and they all in turn carefully lowered in their lumps of clay. Susan dribbled water on top to keep it moist overnight while the others cleaned up and Ella feigned a problem with her camera to keep her posing. She asked if she would mind standing just so, as an excuse to put a hand on her hip and guide her into position. It was a deliciously tender body and this first slight contact made her hungry for more.

The other women were leaving.

'Do you call that puddled?' Ella asked Susan, in a desperate ploy to hang on to her.

Susan looked at the clay, not the questioner. She had

medium-length black hair parted down the middle, and two thick swathes of it fell across her narrow face when she looked down. 'Not really,' she answered meekly. 'We'll have another go at it tomorrow, I suppose.'

'You and I could have it done in half an hour, if we did it properly.'

Susan made no response except to flick her hair out of her eyes and stare in astonishment as Ella unfastened her sandals and stepped out of them and then pulled up the skirt of her frock and tucked it in the elastic of her knickers. They were the only two left and Ella grabbed Susan's arm for support as she stepped onto the slippery clay inside the tub.

'This is the way to puddle clay where I come from.'

Susan tried to pull her arm away but Ella kept a firm hold of it as she worked her feet up and down and flattened the individual lumps into one squelchy mess.

'What did she mean, about *more* Americans?' Ella asked. 'You get a lot of tourists?'

'Oh no,' Susan answered, with a false tone of relief which to the more experienced woman shrieked of a desperate need for a fling with a colourful stranger. 'We don't get any tourists here. She meant the Americans who bought Pod Manor.'

'And who are they?'

'I've never seen them. I don't really know.'

No, she wouldn't, Ella thought. And soon she would be rushing home to help Mummy with the tea. But what a gorgeously tender, untrammelled body!

'I ought to be going,' Susan said.

'But I need you!' Ella insisted. 'And look how well it's coming along.' Together they looked at the thick globules of red clay oozing up between Ella's toes. 'I need some more water . . .'

Susan reached for the pail and flicked water on to

261

Ella's feet, and then moistened the entire surface of clay. Now she was an accomplice. And she could obviously appreciate the effectiveness of the method.

'Why don't you join me?'

Susan shook her lovely slinky hair in the negative and said she had to go soon to help with tea.

'We could have it done in ten minutes, if you joined me.' Ella sensed that an appeal to daring, or mischief, would be counter-productive, but simple efficiency might do the trick, and she was right. Susan silently lifted one foot and slid the pixie boot off by the heel, revealing a delicate white naked foot. Then the other one. Erotic shivers tickled Ella's crotch. Then Susan pulled up the legs of her jeans as far as they would go, which was only to mid-calf.

'You could take them off,' Ella suggested as nonchalantly as possible. But Susan had already stepped into the tub, flexing her fragile tendons and arching her foot into a heavenly curve of nervous expectation as her toes came down on the cold wet clay, and she pretended not to hear.

They squelched together. Ella felt she was having sex already. The raw earth working its way up between her toes and around her ankles . . . her long legs glorying in their nakedness . . . and the angelic physical presence beside her . . . all conspired to bring her to a delicious pitch of sexual alertness. She was enjoying herself and felt no need to rush towards orgasm. And she knew now instinctively that Susan was a virgin. The woman was her own age, with a tremendous capacity to give and enjoy sexual pleasure, but she was not as yet thoroughly inhabiting her body. Perhaps it was simply inexperience, or ignorance. Or maybe she was hung up in some adolescent mind-frame. She had an air of someone with a little knot somewhere from the past, waiting to be exorcised. Ella launched blindly into an impoverished schoolgirl fantasy, playing for time and hoping for a lead.

'This reminds me of once at school when the biology teacher took us pond-dipping. He was a real tartar, the sort of biologist who's all books and microscopes and never gets his hands dirty. When he wanted some fresh material for making slides he made us girls take off our socks and shoes and tuck our skirts in our knickers, just like this, and wade into the pond to get it. The edge was bare clay and when I'd collected my algae I'd squelch around in it just for fun. I wasn't the mischievous kind at all; in fact I was a bit of a teacher's pet.'

Ella smiled to herself and deliberately brushed her knee against the thigh of the real teacher's pet beside her.

'I was mortified once when he called us in and I slipped in my puddle and landed fair and square on my backside. My knickers clung to my cheeks with brown wet mud. No way would he have me back in his classroom! He told me to stand exactly where I was, with my hands on my head, until he came back and told me to move. And so I did.'

She demonstrated with her hands clasped together on top of her head, her legs apart, her bosom thrusting at the bewildered Susan.

'And then he forgot all about me. It seemed like hours. My arms went stiff and my knickers dried out, stuck to my skin. But worst of all, I needed a pee. I needed to pee so badly I couldn't move a muscle, not even if he came and told me I could go. It was agony standing still: it would be *impossible* to move. I couldn't imagine a way out. I wanted to die.

'Then the art mistress came by, on her way home after classes. She was my favourite teacher; gentle and

263

understanding. But that made it worse! It was too utterly humiliating! And still I couldn't move!' Ella picked up the bucket and sprinkled more water around her feet. '"What on earth are you doing?" she asked me, shocked. So I told her. Then her eyes melted with pity and she made as if to put an arm round me. But I flinched away. And that nearly made me burst!

'"Don't!" I begged her. "It hurts!"

'"Where?" she asked.

'Something in my eyes must have told her. She put her hand out and touched me very gently, right there.' Ella reached forward and placed the flat of her hand against Susan's jeans over her crotch. 'And she smiled understandingly as my pee seeped out against all my efforts at control and soaked my knickers and dribbled and then poured hot and endless over her loving fingers and down my thighs to splash on my feet in the clay.'

Ella had wanted to splash water over Susan's crotch, to bring wet and dirt together with sex to mimic the release and the sense of freedom, but Susan took the bucket from her and stepped away.

'I was crying by then, pee still pouring out of me unstoppably, and I started shaking with what I thought ought to be shame but was really relief . . . heavenly, wonderful, pleasurable relief.'

Susan washed her feet in the bucket and patted them dry on a towel. 'What happened then?'

'The teacher took me to her apartment,' Ella answered, much encouraged. 'She stripped me and put me in the shower. Then she undressed and came in with me. It was just what I needed. I felt so helpless. She lathered my entire body. She cleaned the caked-on mud from my bottom. She soaped her hands and slid them between my legs. Then she rinsed me clean. I think she even kissed away my tears. She wrapped me in a huge bath towel and cuddled me. Me, in tenth grade, cuddling with my teacher! I think I'd always had a crush on her. It was blissful.'

Susan pulled on her boots. 'I think we're all done now,' she said matter-of-factly, looking at the smooth sloppy clay.

Ella smiled from the frontiers of her fantasy, knowing very well that she and Susan were far from being all done now.

When Goode next put his head round her kitchen door, Ella asked him what this well-dressing was all about.

'Pacifying the water gods,' he said.

'How appropriate.'

'A pagan business but harmless enough.'

'I couldn't agree more.'

He found her passive smile disconcerting. 'They stick flower petals in clay to make a picture,' he added. 'And put it up near where the pond used to be, to appease old Neptune.'

'I think it's a lovely idea. I'm going to help.'

'They make pictures of birds and trees and so on,' Goode said, as he walked with her along The Row. 'Nothing very cosmopolitan.

She turned on him with delight. 'Not even a mermaid?'

Susan was wearing purple jogging pants and a baggy sweatshirt for the next stage of the operation. Ella found them very fetching. The clay had been trowelled into the ten-foot square frame and smoothed flat, and sheets of tracing paper with the design drawn on them laid on top. Two older women worked at the foot and Susan at the top, pricking through the paper into the clay with a cocktail stick to mark the outline of the picture.

'You like sports?' Ella asked as she sat next to Susan and started pricking.

Susan shook her head.

'Jogging? Aerobics?'

More shakes. The shiny black hair fell forward and Ella wanted to kiss the soft spot at the back of her neck.

'Ever had a massage . . . you know, in the gym?'

A single, very definite shake. Ella decided that if she was going to carry the entire conversation she might as well do it her way.

'I had my first massage a long time ago . . . the day after the shower I was telling you about, with my art teacher. I went back to her place the next day to say thank you and she asked me if my arms were still feeling sore. They weren't really, but I had a feeling she wanted me to say yes. So she stood behind me and started to rub my shoulders. It was lovely. She worked down each arm in turn, gently squeezing, stretching and then stroking me smooth. It was wonderful. I didn't want it to stop. I said the trouble with biology classes was that you didn't learn anything about human bodies; not anything useful anyway. So she asked me if I'd like a massage all over, to learn something lovely about the human body.'

Susan edged away towards the top corner. If she really wanted to avoid what was coming, Ella thought, she should have moved towards the two women who were nattering to each other down the other end, not further from them.

'She told me to strip off and lie face down, and then she undressed too, so we should be equal, she said, and more equally in touch. Then she started on the soles of my feet and gradually worked up my calves, the backs of my knees, my thighs, buttocks, back . . . with plenty of oil in her warm hands . . . cobbling, hacking,

266

kneading and then draining away. Ah! You know what it's like, the luxury of total caress!' It was a rhetorical question. Susan was pricking away with her methodical efficiency.

'But when I turned over on to my back and she reached my genitals it was something else! "We have special techniques for this area," she said. She pushed my thighs apart and knelt between them. And then she took hold of a single pubic hair, in the top corner of the triangle, and pulled on it slowly and gently, and then let go. She searched out the next between her thumb and forefinger and pulled again, long and slow. She worked her way right along, pulling every hair it seemed to me. And then back again lower down, pulling every hair right down to the bottom tip of my bush. It was an ecstatic tease, almost a torture . . . not because she pulled too hard, but because of the tantalising attention to detail. Pricking out these holes brought it all back to me. It was like a thousand little pin pricks in reverse, building up into something really special.'

The something special had to wait. The tissue paper was lifted off, now the outline was pricked into the clay, and they had to go over it with black hemlock seeds, Ella kept the story of her genital massage going in parallel.

'Then she traced the lines of my flesh with a single finger dripping with oil . . . down the crease between my abdomen and thigh, right from the hip down the sides of my bush, along the edge of my vulva to my anus. Then back up the other side. Again and again, infinitely slowly. Then gradually she focused in on the vulva, circling the outer lips, around the top of my clitoris, never touching it, down to my bottom . . . round and round . . .'

The more she stretched out the movement, keeping

267

her voice slow and sensuous, the more Ella was drawn into her fantasy herself. She nudged closer to Susan than ever, not with much hope of a physical break-through with her, but desperate to rub her crotch against a table leg as she reached forward with her seeds.

And then it was lunchtime.

After lunch came the petalling. A second squad of worthy ladies had been scouring the meadows and hedgerows, gathering flowers. Now they started filling in the spaces between the lines of seeds by pressing individual petals into the clay. Susan was plucking tiny pieces off the head of a yellow marigold, and pressing them into the round space in the sky which was to be the sun.

'It's a bit painting-by-numbers isn't it?' Ella said. 'My art teacher would never have approved. She'd have encouraged some spontaneous, individual creativity.' She picked a red rose from a tray and held it next to Susan's sun. Then she bent down and ran her nose around the edge of it, spiralling inwards to the conical, unwrapped centre and breathing deeply with delight.

'That's what my art teacher did to me next.' Ella whispered. 'First with the tip of her nose and then with the tip of her tongue. My love's like a red, red rose . . . Round my outer lips, and then the inner, swollen and red by now just like this rose. Then on to my bud, the heart of my display, tingling with the raw freshness and joy of it all.'

Susan plodded on with her work, pulling off petals and jabbing them in the clay.

'And when my teacher sucked at my bud, I felt my nectar rushing out of me. She plunged her tongue deep inside me and swept it round, lapping up my juices. My rosebud quivered, my petals trembled; stem, branch, root . . . the whole plant of me shook like fury, as though a storm had come up out of nowhere.'

All this poetry was making Ella's knickers soggy, but was having no effect at all on Susan.

'And I've been coming happily ever after,' Ella said forlornly to end her story. She reached for the tray of roses.

'Just look at all these different cunts,' she said loud enough for all to hear but quickly enough for none but Susan to be sure. 'Some saying, "Aren't I lovely, come and pick me." Some spread open fit to pleasure the whole world. Some too puffed up with self-importance and some too tight for their own good.'

She took a few pictures but she knew there was no vital presence to them. Then she tried a bit of petalling herself, filling in the sky with blue hydrangea. Susan soon corrected her.

'You must overlap them properly, like roofing tiles,' she said. 'So they throw off the water if it rains.'

Not like roofing tiles, Ella thought to herself. Like chain mail, my little English maiden with your stiff upper lip and your stiff lower lips, locked inside your suit of armour.

That night Ella dreamed of Susan in her chain mail. She was transformed into a Joan of Arc figure, small and soft in her suit of armour. She imagined her naked inside the metal. Her white delicate-boned feet were hot and sweaty inside their rigid casing with long pointed toes. The nipples on her tiny breasts brushed erect against her breastplate. And her virgin labia rubbed as she walked against the hard crotch of her corselet.

Then she turned into a mermaid, with no crotch at all. Just silver scales from the tip of her tail to her abdomen. But what enchanting breasts!

When Ella woke she determined she would get her revenge. The well-dressing was erected late that evening. She would steal out in the night and bring the boring landscape to life.

She spent the morning scouring village gardens in search of silvery leaves and petals, and stealing them. She made sketches. And she practised petalling until she could perfect the seductive mermaid and the erotic knight errant.

After supper Ella went out with her camera round her neck and her shoulder bag full of petals. From the front of the pub she watched the committee trying to get their tableau vertical on the green without all the clay falling out. She took a few shots but the only life was in the sky. There the water gods, in the form of puffed-up rain clouds, struggled against the dying sun which seemed to bleed on the woods silhouetted at the far side of the green.

A fine drizzle started. The committee finished their task and quickly dispersed. Ella pressed back against the wall of the pub and quickly stowed her camera in its waterproof bag, stuffing the petals down the front of her blouse. Then she called out to the last of the retreating women, 'Susan!' and dashed over the road.

Susan zipped her track-suit top right up to the collar and hurried back across the road.

'What's the matter?' She stopped dead as soon as she reached the green. 'Oh, it's you!'

Ella crouched low to the ground in front of the dressing, pulled her blouse up out of her skirt at the front and shook her breasts. Silvery leaves and petals fluttered to the ground like confetti. Susan watched as though transfixed. It was quite dark now, a single street light fifty yards away barely penetrating the curtain of drizzle across the open green. But Ella could tell that for the first time Susan was really looking at her.

'Don't worry. I won't bite.'

'No, I suppose not,' Susan said, with a giggle covering a tone of voice which almost said she wished Ella would.

'Do you want to help?'

Ella had called out to Susan on impulse. A prank like this was more exciting if there was a witness. She never imagined she'd make her an accomplice. But Susan eagerly bent down and picked up a handful of the silver petals.

'I'm going to add a mermaid,' Ella said.

Susan giggled again, like a cheeky schoolgirl.

Something is happening here, Ella thought. She smiled to herself as she cleared a space by the river on the picture and blocked out the shape of her mermaid with her fingernail.

'I'll do the bottom half,' Susan volunteered. 'That's easy.'

They worked alongside each other but Ella couldn't concentrate. She kept glancing sideways. Susan's face glistened in the wet, only inches away. Droplets of water gathered on the end of her angelic nose, backlit against the distant streetlight, and either dropped unnoticed, or were shaken sideways with a laugh. Occasionally her tongue shot out and teased the drop into her mouth, as if she was thirsty.

This was a new Susan. Her every movement breathed desire.

'I can't get the breasts right,' she muttered.

'You need a model to work from,' Susan said. She stepped back half a pace and her eyes came up to fix on Ella's in a deep, compelling gaze. Slowly she unzipped her top and took it off; pulled her T-shirt up over her

271

head and tossed it to the ground beside her; unhooked her bra and cast it away. Then she broke the chill, lustful stare and leaned back, her neck exposed in a long convex arch, her small high breasts stretched and staring at the sky. She shook her hair and came back to the vertical smiling. Now her creamy white chest was glistening with the fine warm rain, with larger droplets forming on the ends of the brown nipples. Ella reached forward with one hand to touch them lightly, to release the rain, and she lingered there with the gentlest of caresses.

'They are exquisite,' she said.

Susan's lips parted and moved silently. She was going to say something about being too small, or too unknowing, Ella guessed. She sensed a slight tremor of pent-up desire not yet clear of its former wrapping in layers of shyness and fear of the forbidden. She responded by meeting the quivering, uncertain lips with the rich assurance of her own.

The soft thin lips did not withdraw from Ella. They became still. But they did not move to meet her. So Ella pressed against them gingerly, and at the same time probed with the moist tip of her tongue. She ran it around the line of her own lips, and then made contact with Susan's. At the same time she brought her chest up against the naked breasts and let them touch. She could feel the other heart pounding in its pearly ribcage.

Then she slid her tongue forward into the other mouth. It opened like a magic door, as sweet with gifts as Aladdin's cave, and Ella's tongue swept on its sensual search until it met and rejoiced with Susan's. The girl kissed her back with a freshness and vigour which made Ella gasp and grip her body tighter. The passion of their sudden meeting took both by surprise.

Susan started to fall backwards. Ella put a hand behind her and leaned over to pull her forwards, but she was too late. Susan fell, with Ella on top of her.

For a moment they lay there on the wet grass in each others' arms, kissing deeply. Ella rolled on to her back, pulling Susan on top of her. The scent of the drenched earth was divine, and as she lunged into Susan's mouth she reached round to grab her bottom and press it down against her. The jeans were sodden and Susan struggled away and stood up, pulling the material away from the cleft to which it was stuck.

'Ugh!' she said. 'I'm caked with mud.'

Ella wanted to pull her back down and cake her breasts as well, to roll naked with her in the patch without grass where the cricket crease had been. She started to unbutton her own sopping blouse and her breasts burst out, engorged and erect with arousal. They seemed enormous to Susan, flooding her again with a sense of her own girlishness, for all their similarity of age.

'Oh dear,' she said shamefaced. 'Oh dear!'

Ella put a hand up to Susan's crotch and could feel the pressure of the pee coming out. She was like a little nervous, excited kitten.

Ella rose to her feet, reading correctly the girl's doubts and daring. 'Don't worry,' she said, taking her hand in a matronly way. 'Your whole body is an invitation to sex. I'll show you how.'

The headlights of a solitary car swept away over the far end of the green as it turned on to the road beside them.

'Quick!' Ella said, pulling Susan by the hand and running away from the village into the pitch blackness at the centre of the green. The car sped on its route and the sound of its engine faded from hearing, leaving

273

them only with the racing of their two hearts. Susan collapsed on to the grass, panting. The rain had stopped and the wet ground seemed to steam as the heat of the previous day lapped up the liquid refreshment of the night.

Ella crouched at Susan's feet and pulled off her pixie boots. She rolled the thin cotton socks down over her ankles, tugged them off by the toes, and stuffed them into the boots. Then she loosened her belt and unfastened the waist button. She knelt at the girl's side and pushed one hand down the front of her jeans into the panties she felt there, to nestle in the small patch of dank hair. At the same time she lowered her mouth on the nearest nipple and kissed it.

As the breasts rose up to meet her, Ella ran her tongue in circles round the nipple and then flicked it from side to side. She sucked hard, then very gently caught it between her teeth and pretended to bite it. Susan began to whimper with a passion and Ella responded by sucking hard, taking almost all of the tit in her mouth. She held it up from the chest with her spare hand and sucked deeply and rhythmically, as though she were milking her.

Susan began to gasp with tormented pleasure as Ella abandoned the first breast and leaned over to minister to the second. Susan thrust her chest up to meet the mouth, at the same time raising her hips against the hand in her crotch.

'Easy, easy,' Ella said soothingly. 'Take your time . . .'

'But I want it! I want it!'

'And you shall have it, sweetheart . . .'

Ella took a firm hold of the jeans at the waist and tugged them forcibly over hips and abdomen, crotch, thighs, knees, calves . . . and off her lovely little feet.

One naked thigh half crossed the other in a spontaneous gesture of modesty. Ella could just see the tiny triangle of black hair. She paused to slide out of her own skirt and Susan rolled over and over in the rough wet grass, as if to get away from her.

Then Ella pounced. She grabbed hold of the two legs, drenched again now as if with dew, and held them stationary. She wrenched the thighs apart, kneeling between them, went down on the cunt, and thrust her tongue straight up inside it.

Then she came out, as she recalled the fantasy she had shared with Susan.

The girl gave a little cry of surprise, more at the coming out than the going in, Ella thought. She briefly kissed the hidden button at the top of the vaginal opening and began to mimic the art teacher's genital massage. In the dark it was all by feel, and she condensed the strokes. She took a tiny clump of pubic hair in her teeth, stretched it out, tugged, and let go. Then another clump. At the same time her index finger traced the line of the outer labia. She could feel them engorged with the stimulation. Then round the inner lips. They swelled too, and separated. She dipped inside with her finger to feel the juiciness. And with her finger now lubricated she swept around the hood of the clitoris, gradually pushing it back until the very bud of her rose was exposed, thrusting and tight and indescribably intent.

Susan groaned desperately.

Ella let go of the hair and slid her tongue down to the clitoris, licking it from side to side as it grew tighter, harder, greedier. She swung one of her own legs over one of Susan's, sliding her own cunt up and down the arch of the tiny foot as she licked at Susan's cunt. She fell into a rhythm: a deep thrust into the vagina then up to swirl around the clitoris, then deep inside again, as her own cunt rubbed up against the ankle then slipped down to the toes.

Susan's hips began to move up and down, locked in the same rhythm. The knee which was pressed against Ella's abdomen rose and fell. The foot which was unknowingly fucking Ella's clitoris arched, pressed, and slid away incessantly.

'Oh! . . . I can't stop . . . I can't stop it . . .'

'Ride it! Ride it!' Ella whispered firmly. And as Susan's hips forced her cunt even harder against Ella's tongue, the experienced woman moved her hands under the firm little bottom, grabbed its cheeks, squeezed them, rolled them, forced them apart . . . pushing ever upwards as her tongue forced down.

'It's coming . . .'

Ella placed one finger against the tiny rose hole of Susan's bottom and pressed the very tip of it inside. She felt the muscle grip her for dear life. Then she pursed her lips around the clitoris and sucked strongly as her tongue kept on stroking it from side to side. Two fingers of her other hand plunged into the vagina.

'Oh! Oh! Oh!'

The crotch jerked a foot higher off the ground then wrenched to one side. It shuddered quickly and twisted back. Three or four times it writhed from side to side, pinioned by fingers in both holes and a mouth at the pinnacle.

As the panicky noise subsided into controlled gentle groans, Ella gradually let the centre of the body lower itself to the ground. Barely touching, she stroked the outer thighs. She planted soft kisses randomly in soft places. Every now and then Susan would kick out with an electric spasm, or shake her arms involuntarily and gasp with relief. And her bosom heaved.

Ella was patient, loving.

At last Susan stirred herself back into consciousness.

'What about you?' she said with gratitude but also some effort.

'You could simply do for me whatever felt good to you,' Ella answered, wanting to empower the girl. 'But your lovely little body has given me so much pleasure already, I can come very quickly without you instigating anything. Just lie back and let me ravish myself on you.'

She knelt up, lifted Susan's foot by the heel and pressed the ball of it against her vulva. Susan wriggled her toes obligingly as Ella rubbed herself against them. Then Ella moved up, straddling Susan's middle, mingling thatch with thatch and swaddling Susan's tender clitoris in her own lower lips. Susan flinched at first and Ella drowned the rawness of the contract by opening her labia with her fingers and rubbing her own lubricating juices over both of their cunts. Then up again, creeping forward with a knee on each side until she could bring her cunt down on each pert breast. She fucked them both in turn. Then on again. She heard Susan inhale deeply with joyful surprise at the scent of her as at last she straddled her face.

'Your tongue,' Ella whispered, asking.

She felt it enter her, small and tentative. She dropped down on it and fucked. It grew bolder and longer as it searched inside her. Ella leaned forward and rubbed her clitoris against Susan's nose. She was going to blow in seconds.

But there was another surprise for her. Susan reached up and swiftly fondled her breasts. Her hands moved quickly down Ella's waist, perhaps sensing the galloping speed of events. They swept round to Ella's bottom, grabbed the cheeks, and sank their nails into the flesh as Ella spent her force. She had to lift herself, or she would have smothered the girl in the enthusiasm of her orgasm. But in doing so she felt a magnificent communion with the greater world, the grass, the wetness, the village, the night . . .

Soon they would get cold and have to move, Ella knew. But there was time first to marvel at the experience. There was the fantasy, just as there had been with the cricket. There was frustration at the sexual apathy. And then, in both instances, there was the village green, where her frustration exploded in the most incredible, urgent, uninhibited sex. What on earth was going on?

ONE WEEK
IN THE
PRIVATE
HOUSE

Esme Ombreux

I suddenly find myself at a loss for words. It's very difficult to write a puff for one's own novel!

The publisher tells me that I should point out that *One Week in the Private House* was one of the best-selling Nexus titles in 1991 – the first one to go into a second reprint. I'm not being big-headed, you see: he made me say it.

I enjoyed writing it, anyway. It seems like such a long time ago. And I hope you like this extract. The plot isn't awfully complicated, but it is bound up with the activities of three heroines, so I won't try to unravel it for you here.

Julia is married to a stuffy financier and is overjoyed, if nervous, about being summoned back to the Private House. Lucy is an ambitious valkyrie of a policewoman who is determined to investigate the place. Jem is half American, half pixie, she finds she has a natural aptitude for getting her own way in a secret establishment that's based on sex and power.

Authors put themselves into their characters, they say. So which one is me? Yes, of course: it's Jem. She's so feisty!

In this extract Lucy, incognito, is being initiated into the ways of the Private House with a little help from Jem; and then Jem, at an uncharacteristic loose end as her carefully-laid plans begin to come to fruition, amuses herself with Julia's infatuated maid.

One Week
in the Private House
Esme Ombreux

280

Bathtime had been a surprisingly pleasant experience. Melanie and Patrick had discarded their uniforms and their severe demeanour, and had joined Lucy in the huge pool of scented bubbles. They had washed her thoroughly but gently, and when she had found herself sitting between them with Patrick, behind her, massaging suds into her breasts and Melanie, kneeling between her legs, carefully inserting her submerged fingers into all of her most intimate crevices, Lucy had started to think that perhaps she would enjoy her self-imposed undercover operation after all.

Patrick had blow-dried her hair into a cloud of spun gold. Melanie had made up her face with subtle shades of highlighter and blusher, and a touch of scintillating green above her eyes. Lucy had not protested even when Melanie methodically rubbed red-brown rouge into her lips and nipples. Patrick had dressed her in a thin black suspender belt, black stockings, and black shoes with impossibly high heels. The costume, he had told her, was the basic uniform for guests in the Private House.

Now, tottering as she practised walking in her heels, Lucy towered above her jailers. She caught sight of herself in the mirror that took up one wall of the enormous dressing room. I look quite something, she thought: tall, slim, fit, glowing with health, and definitely very sexy. In these shoes it's impossible not to wiggle my bum when I walk. And my legs seem to go on for ever.

She saw that Melanie and Patrick were encasing themselves in their sinister uniforms, and she sensed a change in the atmosphere.

'Time to start your initiation now, Lucy,' Melanie said with a twisted smile. She folded back a set of double doors to reveal a dark room beyond. 'Everyone's enjoyed watching you get ready. Now they'd like to meet you in person. Come along into the Equipment Room.'

Lucy scanned the room. There – in the corners of the ceiling – are those the lenses of closed-circuit cameras? Or are they just trying to put the frighteners on me?

Trying to project more confidence than she felt, she stepped into the darkness. Melanie and Patrick guided her past bizarre and unidentifiable shapes, and abandoned her in an empty area. She was about to set off to explore her surroundings when lights suddenly flashed on, pinning her in a crossfire of spotlight beams. The darkness around her was now impenetrable, but she could hear voices murmuring indistinctly.

More lights began to glow. Some, like cinema lights set high above her, cast a dim illumination that allowed her to see the full extent of the chamber she was in; others were spotlights, trained on the chrome and leather contraptions that surrounded her. She could make out, hanging among the spotlights, video cameras that shifted automatically to track her slightest movement.

The place was like a modern gymnasium, she

282

thought, although she had never seen exercise machines quite like these, with chains and manacles, and none of the gyms she'd used had had seating for spectators. About twenty people, vague but colourful shapes in the semi-darkness, were sitting restlessly in the nearest two tiers of the seats that sloped up one side of the room.

'Ladies and gentlemen!' a voice boomed. 'This is Lucy, a new guest.'

The audience murmured. A spotlight threw a beam and picked out the announcer, standing only a few metres from Lucy. He was a tall, thick-set, giant of a man, wearing only chains, a collar, and a bulging pouch of black gauze. Lucy felt imprisoned within her circle of light, and could only watch him as he advanced towards her, dragging with him his own spotlight beam.

'Lucy,' he said, his voice still loud enough to be heard throughout the room, 'welcome to the Private House. The first thing you must understand is that you are one of us now, and you can never leave. You are inside, and it is impossible to return to the outside. Do you understand?'

Lucy tried to think. Had it started like this for everyone in the Private House, she wondered. Those indistinct watchers in the seats? Melanie and Patrick? The big bruiser bearing down on her? Julia, if Julia really was an insider? The mysterious redhead with the cloak and the whip-marks? And her darling Asmita? Had they all been through this ritual?

'Well, Lucy? Do you understand?'

She nodded, taking care to make a mental note that confessions made under duress are not admissible as evidence. The big man was standing next to her now; their pools of light had merged. He was taller even than she was in her heels, and she tried to stop herself being intimidated by his physical presence.

'The rules of the Private House can be summed up in two words,' he said, 'obedience and sexuality. Once you have learnt unquestioning obedience, your life will be devoted to sex. That is all you need to know.'

Lucy felt her shoulders stiffen. She'd never bothered to attend the Force's psychological warfare courses, but she had an instinctive determination not to succumb to brainwashing.

'I am your Mentor during your initiation,' the man said. 'The first lesson you must learn is respect for authority. Don't speak unless you're spoken to, and always address me as "Sir" Do you understand?'

Despite the cold tightness in her stomach, Lucy almost smiled. If only he knew how familiar she was with regimentation and the use of formal titles. 'Yes, sir!' she responded.

'Good.' He stepped back into the darkness, leaving Lucy alone in the converging beams of light. 'Now turn your back to the audience and bend over.'

Lucy's mind raced. What exactly did he want? Was this some sort of medical inspection? She turned slowly, and leant forward.

There was laughter from the audience. 'Lucy's not a natural, is she?' shouted the Mentor from the darkness. 'Legs apart, Lucy, and bend right over. Touch your toes.'

Not medical, Lucy thought. It's a sex thing. I can't do it! I won't do it! Not in front of all these people!

She straightened, and stepped out of the pool of light. The beams followed her, trapping her again just as she was met by two young women in uniforms that were the same as Melanie's. They grabbed her; she tensed, about to throw one to the floor and break the other's arm. Just in time, she rememberd that she had to avoid showing her hand too early, and she allowed herself to be led back to the Mentor.

'Don't worry, Lucy,' he said with sinister cheerfulness, 'very few novices show complete aptitude at first. You will be trained to obey.'

I won't! Lucy told herself as she was dragged towards one of the gleaming, spotlit machines. I'll never do what they want!

'This is a simple device,' she heard the Mentor saying for the benefit of the audience. 'We call it the Basic Stimulator.'

Lucy struggled, but a small army of black-garbed guards converged on her, removed her shoes, and positioned her on the polished wooden platform. Chains were looped around each of her ankles and were used to separate her legs and secure them to metal hoops at the bottom of metal uprights at the sides of the platform. Her arms were lifted above her head and chained to a metal bar than ran between the two uprights; the bar was then cranked upwards until her body was stretched taut. A second, padded bar was then inserted between the uprights, across the small of her back. Now she could move only her head, and despite her frantic movements, she could not prevent a blindfold being secured across her eyes.

She sensed that the guards had dispersed. Thankful, in a way, that she could no longer see the audience, Lucy forced herself to remain calm and await developments. They can tie me up, she thought, and they can inflict whatever diabolical tortures they can think up; but they'll never make me do anything I don't want to.

She heard movements all around her, and suddenly a cold object nudged her between the legs: the merest brief touch of something hard against her exposed crotch. She jumped to her toes, and felt the tips of her breasts bump into soft material. She lowered herself again, slowly, and as her heels touched the floor the hard object was there again, just touching her private parts. She felt it move slightly, as if someone were adjusting it, making sure that it was positioned exactly beneath her centre, resting against the line that divided the outer lips of her sex. She breathed deeply, and concentrated on preparing herself for excruciating pain.

'The Stimulator is ready, ladies and gentlemen.' The Mentor was speaking again. 'It is a fully automatic device, with electronic sensors and cybernetic feedback mechanisms, all housed with this charming mock-Victorian machinery. I'll switch it on in a moment, and I'll turn it of again – just as soon as Lucy asks for permission to dance for your entertainment. Do you understand, Lucy? Whenever you're ready to dance for us – with some decoration, of course – just ask me nicely, and the machine will stop.'

He's off his rocker, Lucy thought. Ask his permission to dance naked, in public? I'd rather die. 'What do you mean – decoration?' she asked.

'A bum plug with a tail of horsehair,' the Mentor said offhandedly. 'It will look very fetching when you swivel your arse. We'll be expecting a dance with lots of bumps and grinds, of course.'

You kinky bastard, Lucy said to herself. You'll never get me to do that. Do your worst!

'No comment?' the Mentor said. 'In that case, I'll switch on the Stimulator.'

There was a quiet click. For a moment Lucy, muscles rigid and teeth clenched, thought nothing had happened. And then she felt it: the thing between her legs was moving, vibrating very slightly, a persistent buzz that began to tickle the curls of her pubic hair. She raised herself onto her toes, and the tickling stopped, but her nipples had again come into contact with the soft stuff, and now it, too, was moving – rotating in tiny circles, brushing against the very tips with gossamer lightness, a velvety, soft and yet tickly feeling that Lucy decided she could put up with while she tried to collect her wits.

They're not hurting me! was the thought that went round and round in her head. The sense of relief was so overwhelming that she could think of nothing else, until she realised that her nipples were hardening and her breasts swelling as the Stimulator relentlessly buffed her roughed tips. She allowed herself a smile of relief, and pushed her breasts forward, revelling for a moment in the innocuous mechanical caress.

They're not hurting me – yet. What if this is a trick, she thought, a ruse to lull me into a false sense of security? What is that thing between my legs? And as she thought of her legs, she became aware that the straining muscles in her calves were crying out for a rest. Cautiously she lowered herself from her tiptoes; and, just as her nipples dropped out of the range of the ticklish velvet caresser, she felt the vibrating object touch her lower lips and push between them.

Whatever it was, it had grown. A little bit of it was inside her now, just inside the mouth of her sex. It's vibrating, she thought; therefore, it's probably a vibrator. Perhaps they think it'll turn me on. If so, they must be really stupid. But then again, it is bloody insistent. Hard to ignore. I think I prefer the soft thing rubbing against my tits.

She stood on tiptoe again, and couldn't restrain a shiver as her sensitised nipples touched the velvet pads. She knew the were separate pads because they moved independently. They were no longer rotating; instead they were flicking up and down, the left one brushing downwards as the right moved up. She shivered again. Her nipples felt as big and hard as peach stones.

When the pain in her calf muscles obliged her to rest on her heels again, the vibrator impaled her. It was unmistakeably embedded in her slit, and now it was moving a little, up and down, forward and backward, from side to side, as well as vibrating. Lucy shook her head, refusing to admit that the machine's buzzing was beginning to set off an answering tingle in her loins. She felt hot, she knew she was blushing, she wanted to move her limbs but all she could do was to wiggle her hips, and that only increased the sweet tension building inside her. She sagged, trying to envelop more of the vibrator; and she felt something else as well.

It was in front of her; there was something just in front of her pubic mound, something brushing against the golden curls that clustered round the top of her slit. She moved her hips forward, and it touched her skin: something cool, thin and hard, moving very slowly downwards as it crept towards her. It was heading straight for her clitoris. She stood on tiptoe again, and offered her breasts to the machine.

The pads were moving faster now, catching against the bottom and then the top of her rock-hard nipples as they flicked up and down. Lucy bit her lip and told herself that the strokes were too brisk, that she wasn't enjoying the sensation.

The Mentor's voice intruded. 'How's it going, Lucy?' he said in a loud and extravagant voice, as if she were a contestant on a television game show. 'Are you ready to dance for us yet?'

Lucy had forgotten all about dancing. She had forgotten the cameras and the audience watching her every movement. Behind the blindfold, she had started to forget everything except her aching muscles, her titillated nipples, her vibrating insides. The Mentor's voice induced a sudden pang of fear.

She was no longer afraid of pain. She would even welcome it. This was going to be far worse. They would leave her tied to this machine, watching her writhe and wriggle, listening to every breath, until . . . No. It was unthinkable. Surely she couldn't, not like this, with a machine? She would die of shame. But if she didn't agree to the Mentor's despicable demands . . . How long would they leave her here? How many times could she . . ?

She set her jaw. No: she would not give in. She'd stay on the machine until it blew a fuse, if necessary.

She lowered herself on to the vibrator, guiltily aware that the device's easy passage revealed her state of excitement. She couldn't help rotating her hips as the buzzing, roving cylinder slid into her. She felt the second object probing the front of her slit, rubbing against the hood of her clitoris, each touch triggering a tremor in her entrails. And then she felt the third object, and froze.

There it was again. She hadn't imagined it: the tip of another vibrator, nuzzling the cleft between her buttocks whenever she moved her hips backwards. She clenched her arse-cheeks together, and was mortified to hear laughter as the Mentor pointed out her reaction.

She shook her head. 'No, no, *no!*' she protested; and then realised that the vibrator was still and the room was suddenly silent.

'Master!' said the Mentor. 'We're glad to see you. I was beginning to think you wouldn't make an appearance. As you can see, we've started without you.'

'That's alright, Mentor,' said a deep, powerful

voice. 'I was – unavoidably detained.'

'He means it was my fault,' said another voice. 'I guess I'm just an unreliable kind of a girl.'

Lucy inclined her head. She knew that woman's voice. That was it: the redhead, the cloaked woman she had met in the tennis pavilion. She heard footsteps approaching, and sensed people gathering around her.

'A good-looking guest,' said the Master's voice, from just in front of her. 'Will she require a long training, Mentor?'

'Difficult to tell with this one,' the Mentor said. 'She's not exactly taking to it like a duck to water, if you know what I mean, but as you can see she's got loads of sexual potential. The Stimulator's working well. She's been totally resistant so far, but it's very hard to know how long we'll have to work on her before she sees reason.'

'There are no marks. Has she been flogged yet?'

Something in the Master's tone made Lucy's blood run cold.

'No, Master. Of course not. I was waiting for you to arrive.'

'Very good. Proceed with the Stimulator a little longer. I rather hope she remains obstinate.'

Lucy shuddered as a large, warm hand stroked the lower curve of her left buttock.

'May I tease her, Master?' said the redhead, giggling. 'Can I tell her what you'd like to do to her?'

'By all means,' the Master said, as his footsteps receded.

The next thing Lucy heard was an urgent whisper. 'Are you crazy?' the redhead hissed. 'What kind of game do you think you're playing? You're still stuck in the first stage. Just do what they tell you, or this initiation routine'll go on for days.'

Lucy was taken aback. 'But – but you don't know what they want me to do.'

'I can guess the kind of thing. And you're going to have to do it. Now, while you're still in one piece, or later, after they've put you through the grinder. But you'll do it. You'll do whatever they tell you. These guys have had a lot of practice. They're experts.'

'What about the cameras? They're getting this on film. If I give in . . . Well, I've got to think about my job . . .'

'You're worrying about your promotion prospects at a time like this? If you crack this place wide open, you're made. Anyhow, I can fix the cameras, if they worry you. I have a thing going with the guy who created the filing system. I can delete anything that gets recorded, OK?'

The redhead's voice seemed persuasively reasonable to Lucy. 'So – you think I should just give in and do it?'

'Yes! Goddammit, that's the only way you'll get on the inside of this operation. You're no use to me stuck in here chained to these machines for a week. Do what they want.'

'Well – alright.'

'But not right now. That way you'll blow my cover and yours with it. So make it look good. OK? Another fifteen minutes of saying no, stiff upper lip. Dunkirk spirit of defiance, and all that stuff. Then the sudden collapse, abject surrender. Can you do that?'

'If I have to.'

'You have to. Hell, you might even get to like it. Good luck!'

She was gone. Lucy heard her voice again, as her heels tapped across the floor. 'Hey, Master! This one's real pig-headed. We're going to have a whole bunch of fun initiating her, I can tell you!'

Lucy swallowed. Her mouth was dry. Another quarter of an hour of stimulation, she thought, and then I have to beg to be allowed to perform a sexy dance with a tail hanging out of my arse. All in the line of duty, I suppose. A policeperson's lot is not always a dignified one. At least I know I won't be recorded on video tape for posterity.

There was a click; the vibrator inside her recommenced its exploration of her vagina.

Jem lay on the bed in her chamber in the Round Tower. It had been one hell of a busy day, she reflected, but a successful one.

Maxine must have freed herself and then tidied the room: there was no trace of the black ribbon Jem had used to bind her, and not a speck of dust anywhere. Sebastian was a lovely man, and the information he'd provided was even lovelier. And Lucy had, in the end, succumbed very realistically to the Mentor's training methods: after two noisy and, Jem thought, genuine orgasms while on the Stimulator, Lucy had performed an arse-waggling dance of unbridled sensuality. Headman had been disappointed, but Jem had diverted his wrath and his riding-crop towards one of his slaves – the one who had tormented Jem while tying her to the chandelier in Headman's bedchamber the previous evening.

Everything is going just fine, Jem thought; so why do I have this nasty feeling that the situation is slipping out of my hands? And where the hell is Julia?

Jem was surprised by the intensity of her sudden yearning for her pretty bodyguard. She wanted to feel Julia's face between her thighs and Julia's tongue inside her; she wanted to see those dark, long-lashed eyes looking up at her.

She wasn't used to feeling indecisive. Why hadn't Headman asked for her this evening? She was glad to be away from him, as his temper was becoming increasingly unpredictable. But she didn't like not knowing what he was up to.

Should she go upstairs and find out whether he was in his chambers? Or perhaps she could spend the evening with Sebastian? That would be a pleasanter option, but a trifle self-indulgent. Or should she try to find Julia? That might be the easiest to achieve. She picked up the telephone and dialled the servants' quarters.

'Hi, it's Jem. Yeah, yeah, cut all that stuff out. Can you find Maxine, Julia's maid, for me? Thanks, honey. Ask her to come up to my room, would you?'

Jem jumped from the bed, crossed the room to the vast, dark wardrobe, and shrugged off her silk peignoir. She looked over her shoulder and considered the reflection of her naked body. The marks made by Headman's crop were still just visible as dull red lines. No permanent damage, Jem thought; that's a relief. Just a little pink shading to make my pretty little butt even prettier!

She dabbed perfume into her pubic hair and under her breasts, and watched her nipples harden as she ran her fingernails lightly around them. Aware of the effect of the sight of her naked body on Julia's adoring maid, she decided to wear nothing but a thin leather belt buckled about her hips.

There was a knock on the door.

'Come in!' Jem called, and turned. Maxine stood in the doorway, wearing her maid's uniform.

'Close the door, Maxine, and strip. Everything off!'

The maid smiled happily, turned to shut the door, and came to stand in front of Jem. Her eyes came to rest on the gleaming band of leather slung round Jem's hips; Jem parted her legs and ran her fingertips along the belt, and as if startled into action, Maxine started to undress.

Her breasts strained against the thin material of her blouse as she put her hands behind her to untie the little white apron. She held the scrap of cotton uncertainly for a moment, and then dropped it on the floor. Jem enjoyed the blush that appeared on the maid's round cheeks as her hands went to her throat and she tried not to hurry and fumble as she undid the buttons of her black voile blouse. She left the garment hanging open as she tugged it from the waistband of her skirt and then unbuttoned the cuffs. Then, with a quick glance at Jem, she pulled the blouse from her shoulders and let it fall from her body.

She stood for a moment, the white mounds of her breasts rising and falling in the half-cups of her corset, then with one deft movement, she unfastened her short black skirt and let it fall round her ankle-boots. She smiled shyly, her eyes darting to Jem's face and away again. Jem waited, enjoying the lascivious thrills that were spreading gradually through her insides.

'Should I take off my stays, Miss?' Maxine said.

'Your what, child?'

'My corsets, Miss.'

'Of course, Maxine. I want you completely naked.'

The maid bent forward to unlace her boots, and her breasts swung free of their supports, sliding against each other and against her bare arms as her fingers tugged at the boots.

In her stockinged feet Maxine was no taller than Jem, and Jem found herself gripping the black leather belt to contain her impatience. The temptation to handle the maid's heavy breasts was almost beyond endurance, but Jem made herself watch and wait while Maxine unfastened her stockings and rolled them down her legs.

Maxine took a step towards Jem, as if to offer her magnificent bosom, while her hands were busy behind her back unfastening the hooks and eyes of the corset. She pulled the black lace and whalebone away from her front and tossed it aside. She stood, eyes lowered, waiting for instructions.

Jem studied Maxine's body. The maid had a perfect and well-padded shape. No part of her could be described as thin, but the lushness of her breasts, the flaring of her hips, and even the rotundity of her belly only served to emphasise the incurving at her waist. There were dimples where her plump thighs joined her pelvis, and where her breasts jostled against her upper arms. Her chubby mount of Venus was covered with a glossy forest of dark curls that disappeared into the deep valley between the rounded hills of her belly and thighs.

'Loosen your hair,' Jem said, and bit her lip with delight as the girl put her hands behind her head and her breasts rose up her ribcage. A curtain of long, wavy dark hair fell round the maid's face. Her eyes peeked out at Jem like those of a rabbit peering from a thicket of long grass.

'Come closer,' Jem said, her voice a little husky. 'Ask permission to kiss my right breast.'

The maid took small steps forward until she was only centimetres from Jem's body. Jem could feel Maxine's warm breath on her neck; their nipples were almost touching.

'Please, Miss,' Maxine said almost inaudibly, 'please may I kiss your right breast?'

'Oh yes,' Jem breathed, 'lots and lots.'

Jem closed her eyes and put her head back as the

maid's soft lips touched the upper slope of her breast. The first kiss was just a brush of the lips, the second a lingering touch. And then Jem thrust her fingers into the maid's thick hair, and held her face against her body, and Maxine's kisses became a barrage of sense-explosions.

'Lick me,' Jem ordered. 'Underneath, yes, just there. Harder than that! And now the nipple, Maxine. Not so fast! Little kisses first. Very good, that's very nice. Now use your tongue . . . Yes, like that, but let me see you doing it. Good, good. Now you can suck, Maxine, and keep on sucking until I say stop . . .'

Jem's legs were trembling. She pulled back Maxine's head.

'Please may I kiss the other one now, Miss?' the maid said, her lips glistening and her eyes sparkling.

Jem shook her head. 'Not right now,' she said. 'We have things to discuss first. Tell me: what did I promise you this morning?'

'Well, Miss, you said that if the Master punished me, Miss, you'd count the lines on my bottom and give me twice as many on my tits.' Maxine grinned and cupped her hands under her breasts, lifting them towards Jem.

'Let me see,' Jem said. 'Turn round.'

Maxine turned on her heels, parted her legs, and bent forward to clasp her hands round her ankles.

Could I ever be as obedient as this girl? Jem wondered. Would I be like this, if I spent long enough being trained by those thugs in Security?'

The sight of Maxine's arse drove the speculations from her mind. The beautifully smooth, white, dimpled curves, framing the deep, dark furrow and the plump sex-lips, were an enchanting sight; and the sight of pink blotches and haphazard red lines covering the pale skin sent a jolt through Jem that made her catch her breath. She had only to extend her hand to touch the inflamed flesh, and as she made contact she and Maxine gasped in unison.

'How many?' Jem asked.

'I'm not sure I know, Miss. I wasn't counting. Perhaps you'd better count them.'

Jem smiled: Maxine seemed to be able to find an infinite number of excuses for Jem to touch her. Jem's fingertip traced a faded red line from the centre of Maxine's right buttock to the satin-soft hollow at the top of the inside of her thigh. 'One,' she said, and Maxine whimpered.

Jem forced herself to count slowly and carefully, following each stripe with the lightest, most lingering of touches. 'Twenty,' she announced at last, moulding her palm to the curve of Maxine's buttock as an indication that she had finished counting.

'Is that all, Miss?' Maxine's voice sounded distinctly disappointed.

'I guess maybe some of them have faded away,' Jem said, inspecting the maid's delectable bottom more closely as a suspicion formed in her mind.

'Anyway, Miss,' Maxine said, 'that means I get forty on my tits, is that right?'

'Yes, Maxine,' Jem replied absently, her hands straying across the pink orbs.

'Is that forty on each one, Miss?' Maxine went on, almost falling over in her eagerness to look back at Jem.

'No,' Jem said briskly, removing her hands and walking away. 'I'll have to think up something a whole lot more unpleasant than that. You haven't been straight with me, Maxine.'

The maid stood upright, and whirled to face Jem; then, suddenly remembering that she had not been given permission to move, she stood indecisively, her mouth open, her protest unvoiced.

Jem, chortling inwardly, contrived to look severe. 'You've been lying to me, Maxine. The Master didn't give you that rosy backside, did he?'

Maxine's eyes filled with tears. 'No, Miss,' she said in a dejected whisper. 'But how did you know?'

'For one thing, the Master likes things regular, and those stripes are all over your arse, going every which way. For another, he'd have given you more than twenty – and at least some of them would look a bit more serious than any of those. But the clincher is that if the Master had whipped you this morning, your butt wouldn't still be glowing like a brazier. Elementary, my dear Maxine. Who did it, by the way?'

'I asked Cook to do it, just before I came up here. I'm ever so sorry, Miss, really I am. It's just that – well, you know . . .'

'What, Maxine?'

The maid took a deep breath. 'I thought you'd send me away, Miss, if you weren't going to punish me.' Her cheeks were blazing, her moist eyes were wide, her lustrous hair was wild about her face, and her magnificent chest was heaving with emotion. Jem pitied her, despised her, desired her, suffered with her, and above all felt delirious in the knowledge of her power over the girl.

'Come here,' Jem said. 'Kneel in front of me.'

A glimmer of hope appeared in Maxine's eyes. She knelt in front of Jem with her knees apart, her hands behind her back, her breasts pushed forward and her head lowered.

'Look at me,' Jem said, and thrilled as Maxine's wide eyes lifted to stare up at her face. 'What would you do for me, Maxine?'

'Anything, Miss,' the maid replied, as if the answer was obvious.

'If I told you to go to the Master, right now, and ask him to flog you all night –'

'I'd do it, Miss.'

'If I told yu to jump from the window – this window half-way up the Tower?'

'I'd do that, too.'

'You'd die, Maxine. You couldn't survive a fall like that.'

'I know, Miss.' Two tears trickled down Maxine's face. 'But I'd do it, all the same, if you told me to. But please don't, Miss, not yet, please.'

Jem stroked the girl's hair. 'It's all right, Maxine, it's all right. I'd never tell you to do that. But never try to trick me again, you understand?'

'Yes, Miss. I promise, Miss. I only did it because I love you so much.'

'I know, I know. And I ought to spend all evening punishing you.'

'Please do, Miss,' Maxine said, burying her face between Jem's thighs.

'Maxine, you're incorrigible,' Jem laughed. 'I don't have time tonight. I have other things to do.'

Maxine moaned, and collapsed to the floor, raining kisses on Jem's feet.

'OK!' Jem giggled. 'OK, you win. I'll whip your lovely big titties. Just a little bit. Now kneel properly.'

In an instant Maxine resumed her kneeling position.

'Unbuckle my belt,' Jem said. As the maid's fingers tugged at the buckle, thrills of sexual expectation coursed through Jem's body with renewed force. 'Fold it in half, Maxine. That's right. Kiss it, Maxine; it's about to kiss your breasts. How many would you like?'

Maxine, trembling with emotion, was unable to speak for a moment. She tore her lips from the loop of leather. 'Forty,' she said, thrusting the belt up towards Jem.

'Twenty will be enough for now,' Jem said, taking the belt and swinging it experimentally. 'There's always tomorrow, and the next day. Stand up!'

Maxine jumped up and spread her legs as far apart as she could without falling. She crossed her arms behind her back, pushed out her chest, and gazed steadily at Jem. Her eyes dared Jem to be merciless; only her quivering lower lip betrayed apprehension.

Jen smiled wryly. 'Never thought I'd find myself doing this kind of thing,' she said, half to herself. 'Leastways, I never thought I'd get to enjoy it. You've got the most beautiful pair I've ever seen, Maxine.' Thoughtfully, she stroked the looped leather in a W beneath the maid's breasts.

Maxine's nipples crinkled and stood out stiffly from her large pink aureoles. 'Oh no, Miss,' she gasped, 'yours are much prettier. Mine are so big and fat.'

'False modesty,' Jem laughed, and swung the belt gently against the side of Maxine's left breast. The maid bit her lip, but made no other movement. Jem watched closely as the heavy bulb of flesh swung from side to side and then came to rest. A stripe of fiery pink appeared where the belt had made contact, but it faded even as Jem watched. 'One,' she said, and raised her arm again.

Apart from rocking back and forth slightly, as if pushing her breasts forward to meet the belt lessened the unexpectedness of the blows, Maxine remained still and silent as Jem whipped her. Her breasts moved, though, independently of her body, as the band of leather struck them. At first Jem's blows alternated between the two pendulous orbs. She would strike at one of them three times in quick succession, from the right, from the left, and then upwards; and then she would pause to watch the trembling flesh come to rest and blush redly, before she started on the other breast.

She continued in this way until Maxine's breasts were as quivering and thoroughly pink as raspberry blancmanges, and her arm was beginning to feel tired, and Maxine was at last beginning to utter an *oh*! of pain or of pleasure at each blow. Then she stopped, flexed her wrist, and moved to stand beside the maid.

'Keep very still, Maxine,' she said, although she could hardly control the tremors that shook her own body. She aimed a succession of swift, sharp strokes that landed across the front of both breasts, striking the proudly jutting nipples until Maxine's gasps merged into a continuous sobbing cry and the girl began to topple forwards.

Jem dropped the belt, grasped Maxine's shoulders, and turned the girl towards her. 'How many was that, Maxine?' she said softly.

Maxine's breathing slowed. 'I – I don't know, Miss,' the maid said. 'I lost count. About ten, I think.'

Jem laughed, shaking her head in amazement at the girl's gluttonous craving and at her own bewildering lust. 'You've had enough,' she said, raising her hands to sink her fingers into Maxine's hot tormented mounds.

The maid stiffened, threw back her head, and released a long, raucous gasp of pain. Then she fell against Jem, who caught her in her arms. Maxine's burning globes smothered Jem's tight buds and their lips met; as the kiss developed into a mutual caress of hungry tongues, their hands moved downwards to paddled in the lakes of wetness beneath each other's arses.

Some time later, Jem remembered why she had ordered Maxine up to her chamber.

'Stop, Maxine,' she said. 'No, stop for a minute. I

have to ask you something. Do you know where Julia is this evening? I can't find her.'

'Sorry, Miss,' the maid said, looking almost sullen. 'She popped in for a bite to eat at the end of the afternoon, and I haven't seen her since. I supose you'll be wanting her tonight?'

'Not for what you think,' Jem chided her, mentally crossing her fingers. 'A maid in the hand is worth two of her mistress not immediately to hand, or something like that. Let's get comfortable on the bed. Looks like you need to rub a little lotion into these poor nipples of yours.'

'Shall I fetch some cream, Miss?'

'Don't bother, Maxine. I've got some creamy ointment right there where your hand is. Come to bed and rub your nipples into me, girl.'

Letter from Esme

Dear Reader

This is something of a novelty isn't it?

Let me explain what I'm doing here.

I've lost count of the number of times the editor has telephoned me to beg me to write a sequel to *One Week in the Private House*. The poor man had tried everything. But I'm much too busy, you see.

He was so relentlessly charming that I had to promise to do something. The result is that I agreed to write a monthly letter. This is the first.

It is appearing in all three of the Nexus titles published in February 1993: the two brand new books, *Hard Drive* and *New Erotica 1*, and the new edition of *Man With a Maid 2*.

And next month, I'll write another letter for all the March titles! But let me tell you about this month's books.

New Erotica 1 is mine of course. Well, I edited it. Oh, all right then: I read the books and chose the extracts. And wrote the introductions. As I said, the Nexus publisher was *so* relentlessly charming . . . How could I refuse?

Anyway, it's a sort of sampler: spicy extracts from thirteen Nexus titles, chosen to illustrate the range of styles and subjects that Nexus books contain. I'll leave you to imagine how much I enjoyed doing the research! I've done my best to select extracts that are both typical of the various different books and very exciting. I hope you like them.

Hard Drive is a very strange book. Virtual reality and cybersex! It's written by Stanley Carten who wrote *Cocktails* and *City of One-Night Stands* for Nexus, so it's not anything like as confusing as it sounds. Because, you see, Stanley just likes writing books about sex. *Hard Drive* is full of it. But the most fascinating thing about the book is that you, the reader, are in the story. You can make decisions about the plot. It's quite amazing.

And *Man With a Maid 2* – do I need to tell you that it's the sequel to *Man With a Maid 1*, republished in a new edition last month? This series is a must for collectors of Victoriana – and for anyone who relishes tales of proud beauties and innocent maidens succumbing to a combination of male sexual power and rigorous chastisements. Haven't we all dreamed of owning our own private 'snuggery' complete with soundproofing and padded furniture with convenient leather straps? I know I have.

Next month, watch out for – guess what? – *Man With a Maid 3*, of course, in which our hero is joined by the imperious Helen Hotspur. She conjures up games that he hasn't yet thought of, to play with his disobedient captives.

One of the two brand new books will be *Stephanie's Revenge*, the third in the series. Having discovered her sexuality and then a penchant for the wilder side of discipline and leisurewear, Stephanie falls into the hands of a ruthless Italian – and suffers further mishaps as she strives for revenge.

The other new book is *Castle Amor*: a Ruritanian romp, *The Prisoner of Zenda* with knobs on. And not only knobs, I can assure you. The young ladies of the Conservatoire in the Principality of Friedenbourg are coached in the arts of Perfect Pleasure. But when a competition is announced to find a bride for the Crown Prince, their life of endless bliss is threatened. It's a story full of swashing and buckling. (I can never make up my mind which one I prefer!)

That's all for now. I'll be back in next month's Nexus titles to tell you about more books for you to enjoy. If I get into my stride, I might branch out — I might deviate from the norm, take a few risks . . . What I mean is, I would talk about some of the things the editor chappie takes so seriously: where he finds authors for his books, the results of his readers' questionnaire, the naughty subjects that he hasn't put into print.

Let me know what you'd like to know about. You can write to me — the address is in the front of the book. I won't reply of course — I'm much, much too busy, as you can imagine. But I'd like to know your ideas. No, not that sort of ideas — I mean what you think about Nexus books. I'll make sure the editor receives your views (suitably censored, of course: he has such genteel sensibilities. I'm always shocking him!).

Bye Bye! And see you again soon!

Esme

THE BEST IN EROTIC READING – BY POST

The Nexus Library of Erotica – almost one hundred and fifty volumes – is available from many booksellers and newsagents. If you have any difficulty obtaining the books you require, you can order them by post. Photocopy the list below, or tear the list out of the book; then tick the titles you want and fill in the form at the end of the list. Titles marked 1993 are not yet available: please do not try to order them – just look out for them in the shops!

CONTEMPORARY EROTICA

AMAZONS	Erin Caine	£3.99	
COCKTAILS	Stanley Carten	£3.99	
CITY OF ONE-NIGHT STANDS	Stanley Carten	£4.50	
CONTOURS OF DARKNESS	Marco Vassi	£4.99	
THE GENTLE DEGENERATES	Marco Vassi	£4.99	
MIND BLOWER	Marco Vassi	£4.99	
THE SALINE SOLUTION	Marco Vassi	£4.99	
DARK FANTASIES	Nigel Anthony	£4.99	
THE DAYS AND NIGHTS OF MIGUMI	P.M.	£4.50	
THE LATIN LOVER	P.M.	£3.99	
THE DEVIL'S ADVOCATE	Anonymous	£4.50	
DIPLOMATIC SECRETS	Antoine Lelouche	£3.50	
DIPLOMATIC PLEASURES	Antoine Lelouche	£3.50	
DIPLOMATIC DIVERSIONS	Antoine Lelouche	£4.50	
ENGINE OF DESIRE	Alexis Arven	£3.99	
DIRTY WORK	Alexis Arven	£3.99	
DREAMS OF FAIR WOMEN	Celeste Arden	£2.99	
THE FANTASY HUNTERS	Celeste Arden	£3.99	
A GALLERY OF NUDES	Anthony Grey	£3.99	
THE GIRL FROM PAGE 3	Mike Angelo	£3.99	
HELEN – A MODERN ODALISQUE	James Stern	£4.99	1993
HOT HOLLYWOOD NIGHTS	Nigel Anthony	£4.50	
THE INSTITUTE	Maria del Ray	£4.99	

LAURE-ANNE	Laure-Anne	£4.50	
LAURE-ANNE ENCORE	Laure-Anne	£4.99	
LAURE-ANNE TOUJOURS	Laure-Anne	£4.99	
A MISSION FOR Ms DEEDS	Carole Andrews	£4.99	1993
Ms DEEDES AT HOME	Carole Andrews	£4.50	
Ms DEEDES ON PARADISE ISLAND	Carole Andrews	£4.99	1993
MY SEX MY SOUL	Amelia Greene	£2.99	
OBSESSION	Maria del Rey	£4.99	1993
ONE WEEK IN THE PRIVATE HOUSE	Esme Ombreux	£4.50	
PALACE OF FANTASIES	Delver Maddingley	£4.99	
PALACE OF SWEETHEARTS	Delver Maddingley	£4.99	1993
PARADISE BAY	Maria del Rey	£4.50	
QUEENIE AND CO	Francesca Jones	£4.99	1993
QUEENIE AND CO IN JAPAN	Francesca Jones	£4.99	1993
QUEENIE AND CO IN ARGENTINA	Francesca Jones	£4.99	1993
THE SECRET WEB	Jane-Anne Roberts	£3.99	
SECRETS LIE ON PILLOWS	James Arbroath	£4.50	
SECRETS IN SUMATRA	James Arbroath	£4.99	1993
STEPHANIE	Susanna Hughes	£4.50	
STEPHANIE'S CASTLE	Susanna Hughes	£4.50	
STEPHENIE'S DOMAIN	Susanna Hughes	£4.99	1993
STEPHANIE'S REVENGE	Susanna Hughes	£4.99	1993
THE DOMINO TATTOO	Cyrian Amberlake	£4.50	
THE DOMINO ENIGMA	Cyrian Amberlake	£3.99	
THE DOMINO QUEEN	Cyrian Amberlake	£4.99	

EROTIC SCIENCE FICTION

ADVENTURES IN THE PLEASURE ZONE	Delaney Silver	£4.99	
EROGINA	Christopher Denham	£4.50	
HARD DRIVE	Stanley Carten	£4.99	
PLEASUREHOUSE 13	Agnetha Anders	£3.99	
LAST DAYS OF THE PLEASUREHOUSE	Agnetha Anders	£4.50	
TO PARADISE AND BACK	D.H.Master	£4.50	
WICKED	Andrea Arven	£3.99	
WILD	Andrea Arven	£4.50	

ANCIENT & FANTASY SETTINGS

CHAMPIONS OF LOVE	Anonymous	£3.99	
CHAMPIONS OF DESIRE	Anonymous	£3.99	

CHAMPIONS OF PLEASURE	Anonymous	£3.50	
THE SLAVE OF LIDIR	Aran Ashe	£4.50	
THE FOREST OF BONDAGE	Aran Ashe	£4.50	
KNIGHTS OF PLEASURE	Erin Caine	£4.50	
PLEASURE ISLAND	Aran Ashe	£4.99	
ROMAN ORGY	Marcus van Heller	£4.50	

EDWARDIAN, VICTORIAN & OLDER EROTICA

ADVENTURES OF A SCHOOLBOY	Anonymous	£3.99	
THE AUTOBIOGRAPHY OF A FLEA	Anonymous	£2.99	
BEATRICE	Anonymous	£3.99	
THE BOUDOIR	Anonymous	£3.99	
CASTLE AMOR	Erin Caine	£4.99	1993
CHOOSING LOVERS FOR JUSTINE	Aran Ashe	£4.99	1993
THE DIARY OF A CHAMBERMAID	Mirabeau	£2.99	
THE LIFTED CURTAIN	Mirabeau	£4.99	
EVELINE	Anonymous	£2.99	
MORE EVELINE	Anonymous	£3.99	
FESTIVAL OF VENUS	Anonymous	£4.50	
'FRANK' & I	Anonymous	£2.99	
GARDENS OF DESIRE	Roger Rougiere	£4.50	
OH, WICKED COUNTRY	Anonymous	£2.99	
LASCIVIOUS SCENES	Anonymous	£4.50	
THE LASCIVIOUS MONK	Anonymous	£4.50	
LAURA MIDDLETON	Anonymous	£3.99	
A MAN WITH A MAID 1	Anonymous	£4.99	
A MAN WITH A MAID 2	Anonymous	£4.99	
A MAN WITH A MAID 3	Anonymous	£4.99	
MAUDIE	Anonymous	£2.99	
THE MEMOIRS OF DOLLY MORTON	Anonymous	£4.50	
A NIGHT IN A MOORISH HAREM	Anonymous	£3.99	
PARISIAN FROLICS	Anonymous	£2.99	
PLEASURE BOUND	Anonymous	£3.99	
THE PLEASURES OF LOLOTTE	Andrea de Nerciat	£3.99	
THE PRIMA DONNA	Anonymous	£3.99	
RANDIANA	Anonymous	£4.50	
REGINE	E.K.	£2.99	

THE ROMANCE OF LUST 1	Anonymous	£3.99	
THE ROMANCE OF LUST 2	Anonymous	£2.99	
ROSA FIELDING	Anonymous	£2.99	
SUBURBAN SOULS 1	Anonymous	£2.99	
SURBURBAN SOULS 2	Anonymous	£3.99	
THREE TIMES A WOMAN	Anonymous	£2.99	
THE TWO SISTERS	Anonymous	£3.99	
VIOLETTE	Anonymous	£4.99	

"THE JAZZ AGE"

ALTAR OF VENUS	Anonymous	£3.99	
THE SECRET GARDEN ROOM	Georgette de la Tour	£3.50	
BEHIND THE BEADED CURTAIN	Georgette de la Tour	£3.50	
BLANCHE	Anonymous	£3.99	
BLUE ANGEL NIGHTS	Margaret von Falkensee	£4.99	
BLUE ANGEL DAYS	Margaret von Falkensee	£4.99	
BLUE ANGEL SECRETS	Margaret von Falkensee	£4.99	
CAROUSEL	Anonymous	£4.50	
CONFESSIONS OF AN ENGLISH MAID	Anonymous	£3.99	
FLOSSIE	Anonymous	£2.50	
SABINE	Anonymous	£3.99	
PLAISIR D'AMOUR	Anne-Marie Villefranche	£4.50	
FOLIES D'AMOUR	Anne-Marie Villefranche	£2.99	
JOIE D'AMOUR	Anne-Marie Villefranche	£3.99	
MYSTERE D'AMOUR	Anne-Marie Villefranche	£3.99	
SECRETS D'AMOUR	Anne-Marie Villefranche	£3.50	
SOUVENIR D'AMOUR	Anne-Marie Villefranche	£3.99	

WORLD WAR 2

SPIES IN SILK	Piers Falconer	£4.50	
WAR IN HIGH HEELS	Piers Falconer	£4.99	1993

CONTEMPORARY FRENCH EROTICA (translated into English)

EXPLOITS OF A YOUNG DON JUAN	Anonymous	£2.99	
INDISCREET MEMOIRS	Alain Dorval	£2.99	
INSTRUMENT OF PLEASURE	Celeste Piano	£4.50	
JOY	Joy Laurey	£2.99	
JOY AND JOAN	Joy Laurey	£2.99	

JOY IN LOVE	Joy Laurey	£2.75	
LILIANE	Paul Verguin	£3.50	
MANDOLINE	Anonymous	£3.99	
LUST IN PARIS	Antoine S.	£4.99	
NYMPH IN PARIS	Galia S.	£2.99	
SCARLET NIGHTS	Juan Muntaner	£3.99	
SENSUAL LIAISONS	Anonymous	£3.50	
SENSUAL SECRETS	Anonymous	£3.99	
THE NEW STORY OF O	Anonymous	£4.50	
THE IMAGE	Jean de Berg	£3.99	
VIRGINIE	Nathalie Perreau	£4.50	
THE PAPER WOMAN	Francois Rey	£4.50	

SAMPLERS & COLLECTIONS

EROTICON 1	ed. J-P Spencer	£4.50	
EROTICON 2	ed. J-P Spencer	£4.50	
EROTICON 3	ed. J-P Spencer	£4.50	
EROTICON 4	ed. J-P Spencer	£4.99	
NEW EROTICA 1	ed. Esme Ombreux	£4.99	
THE FIESTA LETTERS	ed. Chris Lloyd	£4.50	
THE PLEASURES OF LOVING	ed. Maren Sell	£3.99	

NON-FICTION

HOW TO DRIVE YOUR MAN WILD IN BED	Graham Masterton	£4.50	
HOW TO DRIVE YOUR WOMAN WILD IN BED	Graham Masterton	£3.99	
HOW TO BE THE PERFECT LOVER	Graham Masterton	£2.99	
FEMALE SEXUAL AWARENESS	Barry & Emily McCarthy	£5.99	
LINZI DREW'S PLEASURE GUIDE	Linzi Drew	£4.99	
LETTERS TO LINZI	Linzi Drew	£4.99	1993
WHAT MEN WANT	Susan Crain Bakos	£3.99	
YOUR SEXUAL SECRETS	Marty Klein	£3.99	

Please send me the books I have ticked above.

Name   ....

Address   ....

              ....

              ....Post code ....

Send to: **Nexus Books Cash Sales, PO Box 11, Falmouth, Cornwall, TR10 9EN**

Please enclose a cheque or postal order, made payable to **Nexus Books**, to the value of the books you have ordered plus postage and packing costs as follows:

   UK and BFPO – £1.00 for the first book, 50p for the second book, and 30p for each subsequent book to a maximum of £3.00;

   Overseas (including Republic of Ireland) – £2.00 for the first book, £1.00 for the second book, and 50p for each subsequent book.

If you would prefer to pay by VISA or ACCESS/MASTERCARD, please write your card number here:

_ _ _ _   _ _ _ _   _ _ _ _   _ _ _ _

Signature: _____